READERS ARE RAVING ABOUT ALYXANDRA HARVEY!

"Witty, sly, and never disappointing. . . . Fun, funny, and a relief from Twilight wannabes."   —*Booklist* on *Hearts at Stake*

"A smart mix of darkness and humor."
                    —*Publishers Weekly* on *Hearts at Stake*

"A highly entertaining and funny book that will be sure to make you smile the entire time through."
                    —*Juciliciousss* on *Hearts at Stake*

"An action-packed story full of intrigue, suspense, and romance with a great cast of characters."
                    —*School Library Journal* on *Blood Feud*

"Will keep readers entertained from start to finish. . . . Fast-paced and engaging."   —*VOYA* on *Out for Blood*

ALSO BY ALYXANDRA HARVEY

The Drake Chronicles: *Hearts at Stake*
The Drake Chronicles: *Blood Feud*
The Drake Chronicles: *Out for Blood*

Haunting Violet
Stolen Away

Bleeding Hearts

THE DRAKE CHRONICLES

ALYXANDRA HARVEY

Walker & Company ❋ New York

First published in the United States of America in December 2011
by Walker Publishing Company, Inc., a division of Bloomsbury Publishing, Inc.
www.bloomsburyteens.com

For information about permission to reproduce selections from this book, write to
Permissions, Walker BFYR, 175 Fifth Avenue, New York, New York 10010

Library of Congress Cataloging-in-Publication Data
Harvey, Alyxandra.
Bleeding hearts / by Alyxandra Harvey. — 1st U.S. ed.
p.   cm.   — (The Drake Chronicles)
Summary: Lucy, her boyfriend Nicholas, and his brother Connor try to keep secret the undead drama of Violet Hill when Lucy's cousin Christabel comes to live there, but after Christabel is kidnapped by the ruthless Hel-Blar vampires, they must let her in on the secrets and the battle.
ISBN 978-0-8027-2284-3 (paperback) • ISBN 978-0-8027-2285-0 (hardcover)
[1. Vampires—Fiction. 2. Interpersonal relations—Fiction. 3. Cousins—Fiction. 4. Brothers and sisters—Fiction. 5. Moving, Household—Fiction.] I. Title.
PZ7.H267448Bk 2011   [Fic]—dc22   2010051081

Book design by Danielle Delaney
Typeset by Westchester Book Composition
Printed in the U.S.A. by Quad/Graphics, Fairfield, Pennsylvania
2 4 6 8 10 9 7 5 3 1 (paperback)
2 4 6 8 10 9 7 5 3 1 (hardcover)

This one's for my very creative readers and their mini-movies, collages, role-playing games, and poems!
Thank you.

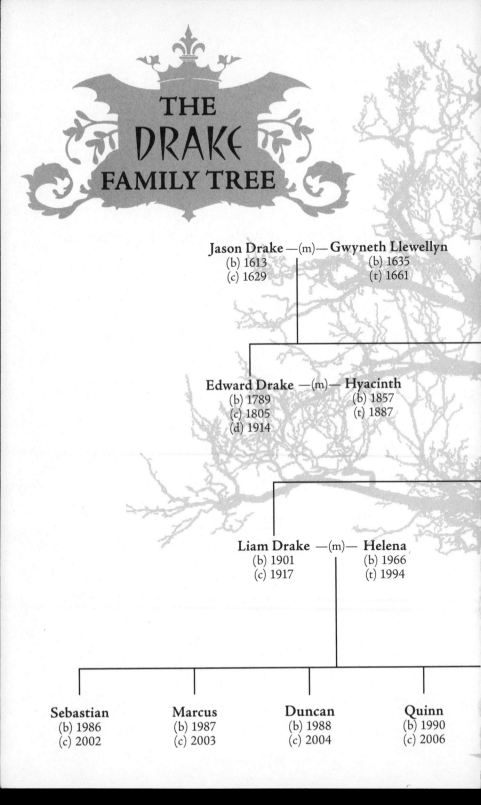

THE DRAKE FAMILY TREE

Jason Drake —(m)— **Gwyneth Llewellyn**
(b) 1613   (b) 1635
(c) 1629   (t) 1661

Edward Drake —(m)— **Hyacinth**
(b) 1789   (b) 1857
(c) 1805   (t) 1887
(d) 1914

Liam Drake —(m)— **Helena**
(b) 1901   (b) 1966
(c) 1917   (t) 1994

Sebastian   **Marcus**   **Duncan**   **Quinn**
(b) 1986   (b) 1987   (b) 1988   (b) 1990
(c) 2002   (c) 2003   (c) 2004   (c) 2006

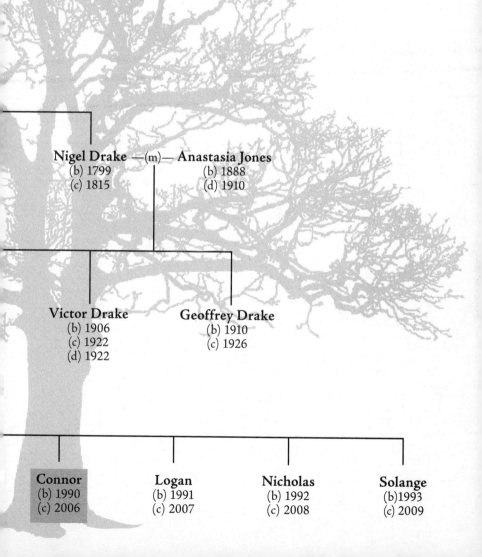

KEY

(b) ✦ Born
(d) ✦ Died
(t) ✦ Turned by another vampire
(c) ✦ Changed genetically into vampire
(m) ✦ Married

For a complete Drake family tree see
www.facebook.com/thedrakechronicles

Nigel Drake —(m)— **Anastasia Jones**
(b) 1799   (b) 1888
(c) 1815   (d) 1910

Victor Drake   **Geoffrey Drake**
(b) 1906   (b) 1910
(c) 1922   (c) 1926
(d) 1922

Connor   **Logan**   **Nicholas**   **Solange**
(b) 1990   (b) 1991   (b) 1992   (b)1993
(c) 2006   (c) 2007   (c) 2008   (c) 2009

PROLOGUE

◆

Connor

"The fact that we have to fetch our baby sister home because she's out later than we are is just sad," Quinn grumbled.

"Gives me a chance to check out these dishes though," I said from halfway up an old-growth cedar. The trunk, mossy and glittering with gold-dust lichen, was big enough to support half a dozen tree houses. I was perched comfortably on one of its many massive branches, repositioning the angle of a hidden satellite dish. "What's it say now?"

Quinn refreshed the screen on my laptop from down among the roots. They were like an old woman's gnarled fingers from this perspective. "Looks good," he called up.

I tweaked it anyway and double-checked it on my iPhone link before climbing down the branches as if they were steps. "That was the last one for this section," I said, taking the last six feet in one leap. "I'll have to disable the other ones. They might be in range of the camp." I'd have to patrol nightly as well to block any new signals, even if the encampment was right up against the mountain and it was highly unlikely.

I knew that for a fact.

I'd already tried.

A lot.

The Blood Moon was a rare vampire gathering, and no Internet or cell phones were permitted for security's sake. I wasn't looking forward to that part. I mean, I don't care about the diehards who run around in corsets or fifteenth-century plate armor to represent their lineages, but the lack of Internet access is just barbaric.

"I have a phone full of hot girls' phone numbers, Connor," Quinn remarked as I stashed my equipment in the pack on my motorcycle. "Before I delete them you should totally put the identical twin thing to good use."

I rolled my eyes. "Twin or not, no one's going to believe I'm you."

"Well, not if you show up in a Star Trek T-shirt."

Okay, yes, I have watched every episode of every *Star Trek*, *Battlestar Galactica*, and *Stargate* ever created, but I have never owned a Star Trek T-shirt.

Just saying.

"Forget it."

"What about Hunter's friend Chloe? You guys got your geek

on until the late hours of the night a few weeks ago." We'd been helping Chloe and Quinn's girlfriend, Hunter, figure out what was making students sick at the Helios-Ra Academy.

I shrugged one shoulder. "We still e-mail, but it's not like that."

He shook his head sadly. "Who will carry on my fine legacy?"

"You've got a girlfriend, not a terminal disease."

"Still, I've said it before and I'll say it again: with great hotness comes great responsibility."

Though Quinn wears his hair longer, we technically have the same face. But that's not why he's so popular with girls young and old—it's something more indefinable. And he's always been like that. He's the one who likes girls, and I'm the one who likes comic books. Still, we get each other. We always have. I might have six brothers but I only have one twin.

I grinned at him. "Try Duncan."

"Yeah, right."

I might prefer computers to people, but Duncan was downright antisocial. Mind you, that doesn't seem to stop the girls from following him around, either. Quinn likes that sort of thing, but it makes Duncan mental. Which is part of the fun.

"Guard, three o'clock," I said with a sigh.

Quinn made a face and kicked his motorcycle into gear. We grinned at each other and took off.

The motorcycles growled as we sped around thick old trees and through giant ferns. We pulled into a narrow meadow, which was really more of a strip of wild grass and late-blooming goldenrod, and left our bikes in a row with the others. Between the oak trees was a path leading to numerous tents and vampires everywhere, talking, watching, unrolling family banners, and polishing swords. No cell phone signals—but swords were okay. I grumbled to myself.

There were more guards than I even knew existed, wearing various family insignias and stationed by every tent. The Drake crest currently outnumbered the others, but vampires were arriving nightly from all over the world. There was another secret guard, the Chandramaa, rumored to be roaming around, but no one had actually seen them. *Chandramaa* was a Sanskrit word for "moon," and they were as old as the language itself.

Aware that we were probably being watched, we warily followed the path out of the woods, into the open field. It went against everything our mother had ever taught us. Luckily Solange was easy to find, loitering on the outskirts with a guy, well out of the torchlight. His back was to us, and he didn't look familiar. It wasn't Kieran—humans were allowed only when attached to a vampire family, and vampire hunters weren't allowed at all. He was tall, with black hair, and he was standing entirely too close to her.

Quinn scowled. "Who the hell is that?"

I scowled too. "No idea."

"Sol," he called out to her. "Let's go."

She looked up at us, red-veined eyes narrowing warningly. "In a minute." She clearly wanted us to stay where we were and butt out of her business.

Quinn and I exchanged a glance.

Not a chance.

We were crossing the field when it happened.

A vampire stepped out from between two sheltering dogwood trees. She looked *Hel-Blar*, except that her skin was a very light blue, not the usual mottled bruise color. Her smell was more like wet earth in spring than mushrooms, but it was close. Too close. She held a bow, nocked with an arrow.

"Solange, down!" I yelled, even as the vampire she was talking to knocked her back, covering her with his body. Quinn rushed at them. I grabbed a stake to try to throw the arrow off its trajectory.

There were assassins somewhere on the planet *not* currently gunning for my mother or my baby sister, but they were probably very lonely.

The arrow thunked into a tree. The paper wrapped around the shaft unraveled, fluttering like moth wings.

It wasn't meant for Solange, after all.

It didn't matter.

The woman was dust and ash, with only a thin dress and a yew-wood bow left lying in the grass to show she'd ever existed. Even the odd smell of rich soil was gone, taken by the cold mountain wind. A crossbow bolt, painted the red of all Chandramaa weapons, had pierced her heart even as her messenger's arrow bit through tree bark. She never had a chance.

There was a moment of silence, followed by the eerie sound of vampires moving too fast, like bat wings. Fangs and swords and even a katana flashed. Solange was pulled to her feet by the black-haired stranger. His hand passed over her shoulder with a familiarity I didn't like. There was a crowd gathering between us.

"Hey now," Quinn said darkly, tilting his head to see around a guard built like a bull on steroids. "What's that about?"

A woman wearing the royal crest snatched the paper off the arrow, skimming the message. "It's for Helena."

Quinn and I both froze, then turned slowly to look at her. Solange did the same across the way.

"A tribe wants a seat at the Blood Moon council. It's signed by Saga."

"Who the hell's Saga?" Quinn demanded.

There were a lot of shrugs and curious stares.

"Mom doesn't choose who sits on the council," I added. "We didn't even call the Blood Moon." No one knew who called them; they just happened every hundred years or so. I held out my hand. "Give me the message. We'll get it to her."

I tucked it into the inside pocket of my coat, next to an ebony stake I'd found in a family chest in the attic. The crowd dispersed, muttering and shooting us dark looks. A few hovered, hoping for more drama. Don't let the emo brooding vampires fool you; most vampires love gossip and melodrama as much as blood. The older they are, they more they seem to crave it. Which only partly explained why my life seemed to resemble a soap opera lately, and not even the sci-fi space opera type, which might have been cool.

The black-haired stranger murmured something in Solange's ear before walking away. We still hadn't glimpsed his face, but we knew he was a vampire. He'd moved to block Solange faster than any human could have.

"Who was that, Solange?" Quinn asked as she approached us.

For all his wild oats, Quinn has a puritanical streak when it comes to our sister. We all do.

"His name's Constantine."

"And?"

"And nothing."

"What about Kieran?" I demanded.

She rolled her eyes. "I was talking to the guy, not pole dancing for him."

We both winced. I actually put a hand over my eyes in self-defense. "Don't ever say that again."

She just laughed. "Let's go."

She had her own bike waiting on the other side of the trees. It took us just over half an hour to get back to the farmhouse and Mom was already on the porch when we got there, fangs out. Dad was on the bench drinking brandy. He drank brandy only when he was trying not to fly into a fit. Mom never bothered to stop herself. They reached us before we'd even gotten off our bikes, the dogs circling, tails wagging.

"We got a call. Someone shot at you?" Mom had Solange by the shoulders, looking her over.

Solange squirmed. "Mom, I'm fine."

"It was a message arrow," I added quickly, taking the paper out of my pocket and handing it to Mom. "It was never meant for Solange."

"Oh," Mom said.

"Mom?" Solange said.

"Yes, honey?"

"Ouch."

Mom let her go. "Sorry." She half smiled. "We were worried."

Dad ran a hand over Solange's hair, also smiling. "It's encouraging to know you can go a whole night without getting shot at."

She snorted. "Makes for a nice change. You know what else would be nice?"

"What?"

"Since I already have, like, three guards tailing me all the time, *not* also having my brothers hovering everywhere I go would be a treat."

Quinn and I gave identical snorts.

"No deal," Dad added mildly. "Let's get inside."

We went to the kitchen, where Uncle Geoffrey and Marcus were helping Bruno unpack a new shipment of blood. The blood was stored in various refrigerators and some of it was transferred to plastic water bottles before being redistributed. The coppery smell permeated the house. My fangs poked out of my gums a little. It was like being inside a bakery while they baked every kind of cake imaginable.

Mom and Dad sat at the table and unfolded the note. Mom frowned. "Who the hell's Saga?" she demanded.

Uncle Geoffrey glanced at Solange. "How are you feeling?"

"Fine." She smiled without showing her extra fangs. Her irises were rimmed with red and fanned with veins like rays of sunlight.

"You look a little pale." He tossed her a bottle of blood. "Drink up."

She took the bottle with a sigh.

He just raised his eyebrows. "I told you, you need more blood than the others did."

"I know," she grumbled. She unscrewed the cap and lifted the bottle to her mouth. She paused, then recoiled sharply. Before she could take a sip, Mom, who was closest, leaped over a chair and knocked the bottle out of Solange's hand. Solange blinked, her chair sliding across the wooden floor. The blood arced over the walls. It smelled wrong—too sharp, too acidic.

Mom's mouth was grim, her nostrils flaring.

"Poison."

CHAPTER 1

◆

Lucy

I never would have thought I could have so much fun in a sweaty gym, running combat drills until I wanted to throw up.

In a Helios-Ra school, no less.

I mean, these were the guys who had previously devoted themselves to taking out my best friend and her entire family. Plus, they kind of acted like they thought they were superheroes. Not that I wouldn't love my own theme song and cape.

Still. It was a matter of principle. Drake family good. Vampire hunters bad.

Except that right now a vampire hunter from Helios-Ra Academy was not only dating my best friend's brother, she was also teaching me how to take out vampires. Not the Drakes, of course— but the *Hel-Blar*, who attacked anything human or vampire, and the other vampires who either wanted the royal throne for themselves or just didn't want Helena Drake to have it. Whatever. They were going down. Preferably on the end of my very pointy, steel-tipped staff.

Hunter's boot nearly clipped my jaw. I stumbled back out of reach, impressed. "Dude. You're bendy." Which didn't seem entirely fair since I was the one who did yoga. Mom and I had a new compromise: for every nonorganic, non-fair-trade, non-dark-cocoa chocolate bar I ate, I had to do a round of sun salutations.

After the kind of summer I'd had, I was doing a *lot* of sun salutations.

Hunter attacked again, moving slower so I could see what she was doing and choose a counterattack. Then she repeated it and sped it up. I blocked her blow, the force reverberating through my bones and practically into my teeth. I followed the momentum, pushing against her arm. She didn't drop her stake, but I knew she would have if she were a normal girl and not the valedictorian of Vampire Hunter High. She hated it when I called it that. She said it made them sound like a bad B movie.

Duh.

"That's good," Hunter said, panting. "Keep grinning at your attacker like that and they'll think you're way creepy. And mental."

I grinned wider. "I totally love this. Who can I punch next?"

She stopped and laughed. Her long blond hair was tied back, and I was gratified to see the collar of her shirt was damp with sweat too. I didn't want to be an easy mark. Ever. "About that. I know you like punching people in the nose, but it's much more effective if you aim for the throat or the eyeballs. Even vampires can't see where you are if they have no eyeballs."

"Cool. And gross."

"And you should get contact lenses."

I blinked behind my dark-rimmed glasses. "Why? I hate sticking my fingers in my eyes."

Hunter didn't say anything. She just reached out and gripped my elbow, spinning me around with one jerk so that my back was facing her. Then she used her other hand and quickly, casually flicked my glasses right off my face. They slid across the shiny wooden floor. Everything went blurry.

"Show off," I grumbled. Then I had to crouch down and feel around for my glasses, which was totally embarrassing. "All right," I said, shoving them back onto my nose. The walls of mirrors reflected three of me, all looking disgruntled. Then I leaned on my staff and I suddenly looked like I belonged in a fantasy novel. I wished Solange would answer her damn phone so I could tell her about it. "You proved your point. In fact, I'm going to get laser eye surgery as soon as possible."

"That's usually what we do too," Hunter admitted. "It's just safer." She tossed me a towel and we wiped our faces. I hurt all over and my lungs burned. And I still loved it. Next thing you knew, I'd be lifting weights and drinking protein shakes. And I'd know the difference between my quads and my glutes.

Clearly, growing up with vampires had caused irreparable psychological damage.

The campus stretched out around us, visible through the one wall of windows. There was a pond, lots of grass, and several Victorian-style houses and barns doubling as dormitories, teacher lodgings, and training areas, all grouped under the watchful eye of the Violet Hill mountains. According to Kieran, Solange's boyfriend, the garages are full of motorcycles. I wondered if I could get someone to teach me how to ride one. Then I wouldn't have to rely on Nicholas to take me to all the good vampire hideouts and the royal courts.

If I was ever allowed back in, of course.

They all seem to think I'm way delicate. I really don't know where they get that from. When my parents came back from their annual visit to the ashram with my cousin Christabel in tow, Solange and Nicholas's parents had felt the need to tell them everything.

Even though that was obviously the worst idea ever.

Dad took one look at the little scar on the back of my neck from when Solange and I were attacked by *Hel-Blar* vampires and he freaked right out. He now has an ulcer, which, apparently, is all my fault. But really it's Helena and Liam's fault for telling him in the first place. I never would have done anything that dumb.

Add in my mother's bonding with me over Nicholas being my first "official" boyfriend (no one counts Julian, not even Mom, because he was a jerk) and her chasing me around the house with safe-sex pamphlets and dress designs for the prom. It's October. Prom's not until May. And, really, how do you take a young vampire to the prom? Nicholas won't even sit in the same car with me because the smell of warm human blood is still too tempting. He just turned a little over a year ago, and it takes time to get all those appetites under control. I think of it like a case of perpetual PMS, where you just feel inside your bones that if you don't get a hot fudge sundae right away, you might actually kill someone.

Anyway, I distinctly remember my mother saying that prom was a Neanderthal throwback to debutante balls that signaled young ladies were eligible for marriage. Now all of a sudden she's talking about growing orchids in the greenhouse so I can have a pesticide-free homemade corsage. I told her if I had to do sun salutations every time I eat chocolate, she has to do them every time she brings up the prom or anything lame like that.

Any wonder I'm having so much fun having the crap kicked out of me by a vampire hunter?

A girl in a red ponytail was jogging around the track below us, smiling. If I wasn't careful, that would be me. I felt the sudden need for a chocolate bar.

The sun was starting to sink behind a line of pine trees, leaving streaks of lilac and fire. The shadows were so long, they looked like dark fingers reaching out to touch everyone and everything.

"I should get home," I said regretfully.

God. I was regretting having to leave Helios-Ra.

I had to get my priorities back in line.

Which would be easier to do if I could go over to the Drakes' and hang out with Solange. But I had a curfew now, which sucked, and Solange was acting weird, which sucked more. And one of the many new rules implemented since my parents' return was that my cousin and I had to be home before dark, period. If we wanted to go out after sunset, one of them had to drop us off and pick us up.

Never mind that I totally knew more about fighting vampires than my peace-loving parents. Or that Logan's girlfriend, Isabeau, had given us two full-grown, trained Rottweilers to protect us, plus the Drakes sent their human bodyguards by a couple of times a night. I named them Van Helsing and Gandhi. The dogs, not the bodyguards.

We told Christabel that Violet Hill wasn't safe at night, that there was some kind of gang war. It was easier than telling her the truth: that there were still too many *Hel-Blar* vampires in the area who were getting closer and closer to town. They were attacking livestock and, sometimes, people. They even freaked me out, and I'd grown up with vampires. They were feral, had a mouthful of fangs, and stank of rotten mushrooms and stagnant pond water. They didn't know any logic or master but the hunger. An ordinary vampire had to bite you, drain you, and feed you their blood to change you. A *Hel-Blar* just had to bite you. Rumor had it their saliva alone was contagious, not just to humans but to other vampires as well. Regular vampires didn't bite other vampires; it was considered revolting and in bad taste. Literally. Once a vampire had ingested human blood, it had no nutritional value to another vampire. It was just rude, however you looked at it.

So the *Hel-Blar* were definitely the uninvited guests at the party. We avoided them as best as we could, but that was becoming difficult. There were more of them than ever before, thanks to vampire politics gone wrong. But at least they mostly came out at night, even the older ones who could theoretically survive sunlight.

Which is why Christabel and I had a curfew now. It wouldn't

have been so bad if I could have gone to the Drake farmhouse. My curfew didn't exclude me from visiting them.

But Solange did.

And frankly I was getting sick of her emo suffering.

If she was sulking, she could damn well do it with me in the room. That's what best friends were for. And if she was feeling guilty because I'd gotten a tiny cut to the back of the head, she could just get over it. As soon as I was able to drive over there and thump some sense into her, I would. Right now we did all of our arguing through texts and e-mails. Hardly satisfying.

I tossed my damp towel into a laundry basket, grabbed my bags, and followed Hunter down the stairs. A few younger students passed us on their way into the gym. They stared at me like I was a museum exhibit. I only barely resisted the urge to yell "Boo!"

"What's with them?" I asked Hunter.

"Are you kidding? You're famous."

"*I'm* famous?" She must be joking. The Drakes were famous. Hunter was famous for stopping a Helios-Ra teacher who'd been poisoning students. I was just the mouthy best friend. "Give me a break. You're the one who took down a teacher."

"Yeah, but you're in with the royals even though you're human." Hunter shrugged as we hurried down the path toward the parking lot. I was running a little later than I'd thought. Cue parental breakdown now.

"Please. The Drakes were banned from court for, what, a century? Two? All of a sudden they're a big deal? You're dating one of them—you have to know it's not good for them to think that."

She grinned. "Yeah, Quinn's ego doesn't need the boost."

"They will be completely insufferable if humans start acting like groupies." I raised my eyebrows. "I am not a groupie," I pointed out fiercely.

"I know." She held up her hands placatingly.

"Okay then." I rummaged around for my keys.

"You *are* the first nonstudent ever to be allowed on campus for classes in over fifty years, though."

"Go me." I unlocked the door and slid into the driver's seat. "Heard from your grandpa yet?"

"No," she replied quietly. "He's still not talking to me." He was old-school Helios-Ra and he just couldn't stomach the fact that his vampire-hunter granddaughter was dating a vampire, Drake or otherwise. I felt bad for her. He was the only family she had. She just shrugged and tried not to look like it was bothering her. "Be careful," she said.

"Always am."

She snorted so loudly I was surprised there wasn't a small tornado. "Lucy, I've only known you for a few weeks, but careful is one thing you're not."

"Yeah, yeah. You all need to get a new speech." The engine sputtered a little but eventually turned over. Frankly, it was a miracle every time it started. I should so use that on my dad to convince him to buy me a new car. You know, for safety's sake.

I waved at Hunter and sped off down the driveway, stopping to punch in my number code so the security gate lifted. Despite the events of the last few weeks, the drive home was uneventful. I passed the usual farms and pumpkin patches and apple orchards. The mountains loomed impressively, the snowcaps looking almost purple at this time of night. Speaking of which, twilight was hitting fast and hard tonight. I dialed home on my cell phone. Christabel answered.

"I'm just down the street," I told her. "Tell my parents not to freak out."

"They just called," she said. "They're in town. Your mom's making your dad go to some Buddhist relaxation meditation thing."

"Did you tell them I was home?" I turned onto our street.

"I told them I saw your headlights in the driveway."

"Thanks, Christa. Be there in five." I switched off and counted to three out loud. "One . . . two . . . three." The phone rang, right on cue. I answered it, rolling my eyes. "I'm in the driveway, Mom," I said, pulling up to the garage. "Tell Dad to stop hyperventilating."

"Are you okay?"

"I'm fine. I learned how to punch someone's jugular."

"I'm so proud." Her tone was as dry as stale crackers. "Look after your cousin."

"Mom, she's two years older than I am. She can take care of herself."

"She's going through a hard time, Lucky." Even the phone crackled disapprovingly at her use of that hated nickname.

"I know," I said quickly. "I only meant that I'm sure she's fine."

"Okay. We won't be home too late. Don't eat ice cream for dinner."

"I won't," I promised. I meant it, too, but only because Mom bought us tofu ice cream. Yuck. Even more gross than drinking blood, if you asked me.

The porch light was on and I could see Christabel behind the living room curtain, curled up on the couch with a book. The girl read more than anyone I'd ever met. Even when we were little, she preferred the library to the beach. The slamming of the car door echoed, disturbing old man Jeffries's incontinent poodle across the road. She barked at me through the window. Gandhi barked back once from inside our house; the poodle whined and fell silent.

I glanced around before heading toward the house. I hated that all of a sudden the night felt dangerous, suspicious. I used to love sitting out in the garden and watching the stars, but now I had to worry about being mauled to death by *Hel-Blar*. A shudder in one of the bushes made me pause. My heart hammered loudly, slowly. I sniffed but couldn't smell mushrooms or mold. Still, maybe the *Hel-Blar* had learned to use cologne. I couldn't smell that either, though. I reached for the vial of Hypnos Solange's uncle Geoffrey had given me. It wasn't inside my sleeve. It was in my bag. I'd forgotten to reattach it after my class with Hunter. Stupid.

I reached for another weapon. At least my purse was handy and well stocked.

I nearly staked a stray cat.

He hissed at me, back arching, fur like iron spikes. I stumbled back, swearing.

"Sorry!" I told him. "Life is probably hard enough, living out of garbage cans and hiding from dogs, without some girl waving a pointy stick at you. I promise I'll leave you some milk, okay?" He hissed again, then sat back and licked his butt. Charming. "I don't know if that means I'm forgiven, but could you do that somewhere else?"

I turned away, my palms damp from the adrenaline surge. All this fear was contagious and I didn't like it one bit. I wiped my hands on my leggings.

"Were you just apologizing to a cat?"

I didn't have time to recognize the voice. I only heard noise where there shouldn't have been any. More adrenaline sparked through me and I felt like my insides had just been electrocuted. I leaped off the porch, somersaulted in the grass, and jumped to my feet, slightly dizzy.

Right in front of my smirking boyfriend.

I didn't lower my stake. Instead I waved it menacingly. "You scared the crap out of me, Nicholas."

"And that was your gut reaction?" he teased, arching an eyebrow. "Gymnastics?"

"Shut up," I grumbled. He just grinned. He was wearing dark jeans and a black shirt with a black tie. He looked good, as always. The adrenaline turned into a much more interesting chemical reaction. "Hi."

"Hi." He closed the distance between us, avoiding the pointy end of the stake still clutched in my hand. "Are your parents home?"

"No."

His grin turned seriously delicious. "Good."

And then he leaned in to kiss me. I met him halfway, with a grin of my own. His lips were gentle, soft. His arms slid around me, one hand digging into my hair, the other resting on my hip. I leaned in closer, nibbling at his lower lip. He sucked in a breath that made me feel wild and beautiful even though I was still kind of flushed and sweaty from the gym. Vampires didn't need to breathe; they just did it out of habit, especially young ones like Nicholas. Whenever he made that strangled sound, I knew I was doing something right.

And then I really couldn't gloat anymore because the kiss went dark and deep and I couldn't think at all. I felt the kiss everywhere—on my lips, in my belly, even in my toes. I tingled. I ached. There was nothing but his mouth and his hands. Suddenly the night felt infinitely more dangerous and infinitely more beautiful. It was all shooting stars and moonlight.

And then he pulled away and I had to struggle to find my breath again.

"Ready?" he asked, his voice a little rough.

"Huh?"

"Ready to go inside?" he explained, one corner of his mouth lifting up. It was surprisingly distracting.

"Inside?" I repeated dumbly.

"Movie night, remember?"

I swallowed. My knees felt weaker than they had after four laps around the evil jogging track at the Helios-Ra campus. "Right."

"Lucy?"

"Yeah?"

"Your house is this way." His pale eyes laughed at me.

I'd been heading for the garage door.

I shoved him, laughing. "Oh, shut up."

CHAPTER 2

•

Christabel

Lucy and her boyfriend were laughing when they came into the living room, where I was reading *Jane Eyre* for the six hundredth time. It was my security blanket, characters I knew and loved, red bedrooms full of ghosts and the dark moors. Van Helsing was asleep on the other end of the sofa, his huge, heavy head on my foot. He'd gotten up to look out the window and sniff the front door when Lucy came home and then went right back to his favorite napping spot.

"Hey," Lucy said. "Thanks for covering for me with the parentals." Gandhi trailed after her, sniffing the hem of Nicholas's pants and wagging his tail. For ferocious guard dogs, they sure had no problem with boyfriends.

"It's barely eight o'clock at night and they're all freaky that you're not home yet. It's not like you live in the ghetto." I paused, folding the top corner of the page to keep my place. My dad used to wince every time he saw me do that, but I think books should be loved to pieces. They should be as worn and soft as flannel. "Does Violet Hill even *have* a ghetto?"

"Not exactly."

"Then what's up?" Besides the fact that my mother was trying to kill me. There was no other explanation. Not only had she sent me to Violet Hill, the weirdest little backwoods town in the middle of nowhere, but she'd done it one month into my last year of high school.

In a place where everyone else had grown up together.

In a place with virtually no bookstores (at least none with more than one floor and windows *not* crammed with crystals and incense), one movie theater, and more vegan juice bars than coffeehouses. It just sucked.

I already missed home. I missed the anonymity of the crowded streets, libraries with rare books, and the fact that you could hop on the subway and end up anywhere.

Most of all I missed my mom.

I knew it was for the best. She needed treatment; she was getting worse and I just couldn't take care of her anymore. When my uncle came to stay with us after his hippie van broke down, I could read it in his face. He was worried. I didn't tell him that was the best Mom had been in weeks. After she got fired from her job at the office supply store, she lost nearly a week to a case of cheap wine. At least she drank the cheap stuff. Not that she had any choice—it wasn't as if she could afford the expensive stuff. Anyway, she tried. She really did. But she just couldn't seem to get better on her own. And Uncle Stuart was one of those peace-and-love family types. Before I knew it, my bags were packed and I was in the back of the patchouli wagon on the way to Violet Hill.

Lucy shrugged. "You know parents." She had no idea. "We're going to watch movies. Are you in?"

I shook my head, getting to my feet. "I'll go read in my room."

"I know for a fact that you've read that book a hundred times," Lucy pointed out.

I read a lot. I love books. If they came in a bottle, I'd be a drunk too. I'd bloat myself on the wine of Wordsworth, the gin of Charles Dickens, the licorice liqueur of Edgar Allan Poe.

I bet you can already guess I don't have a boyfriend. But to quote *Pride and Prejudice* for a moment: "Adieu to spleen and disappointment! What are men to rocks and mountains?"

Besides, guys are scared of me. Oh, I catch them looking sometimes. I have long, curly reddish-blond hair, and for some reason it mesmerizes them. I may as well be wearing a bikini. But then they see the ripped jeans, the combat boots, and the Edgar Allan Poe poem I'm reading (because I love it and not because it's homework), and all of a sudden all the long blond hair in the world just isn't enough.

Of course, Simon, my best friend back home, says it's got nothing to do with any of that. He claims it's because I stare at guys as if they're stupid. Can I help it? Am I supposed to giggle and flirt when they say something dumb? Simon says yes. I say no.

Thus, no boyfriend.

Also, I use words like "thus."

I can't help it. I love old books best of all, with their wordiness and intricate descriptions of gas lamps and pickpockets. I like historical fiction and poetry too. Not those trendy vampire books though; they just get on my nerves. But Bram Stoker's *Dracula*'s all right. *Jane Eyre* is my favorite book of all time. And I've been cultivating a very satisfying literary crush on the poet Percy Bysshe Shelley. I love that his wife, Mary Shelley, who wrote *Frankenstein*, kept his heart after he died in a handkerchief on the mantel and fought with fellow poet Byron over who should get to keep it.

I mean, really. What guy could compete with that?

Especially in this little hick town.

"You don't have to go," Nicholas added. He was so still, I'd almost forgotten he was there. He smiled his serious smile. "If you stay, Lucy's bad movie choices will be outnumbered. I might actually get to watch something other than a John Hughes or zombie movie."

"Hey!" she exclaimed. "B movies are an art form."

"Sorry." I smiled back at him apologetically. I'd watched enough movies with Lucy to know some cute guy would be either shirtless or mangled to death in a deserted cabin in the woods. The one time I tried to get her to watch *Pride and Prejudice*, she hadn't been able to sit still. Granted, it was the six-hour version, but come on. What's not to love?

I went down the hall, hung with gilt-edged paintings of various Indian gods with multiple arms. My room was the same as the rest of the house: simple wooden furniture; a handmade quilt on the bed; and a clutter of carved wooden boxes, incense holders, and yoga magazines in baskets. There was even a macramé holder for the spider plant in the window. But there was lots of space for my books and nothing smelled like stale wine. It was nice. Even with Van Helsing's doggy breath. He liked to follow me around.

It was also eight o'clock on a Friday night, and there was no reason in the world why I should be locked up while Lucy and Nicholas made out in the next room. I used to spend summers here roaming around with Lucy. I should be able to find my way even after all this time. After Dad died and Mom went to pieces, I wasn't able to leave her alone for an entire summer. She'd have forgotten to eat or pay the rent or take out the garbage. And then our secret would have been out. It was just easier if I stayed home. And I didn't usually think about this stuff. I just did what needed doing and got good grades so no teachers or social workers would notice us.

Maybe I hadn't been to the mountains in a few years, but I didn't believe for one minute that Violet Hill was so overrun with crime that I'd be in danger. As if there were a lot of hippie gangs roaming the streets, wearing hemp clothing and pushing organic fruit smoothies on unsuspecting bystanders. Please. I was from the city. I'd once taken the subway alone past midnight. Not smart, granted, but I think I can handle a hick mountain town.

But no need to rub anyone's face in it. I'd just slip out my window, go for a walk, and come back before my aunt and uncle returned. I was even on the ground floor, so I wouldn't have to shimmy down some tree. I tossed my book on the bed and put on my jacket and the black knee-high moccasins I'd found in the closet. They weren't as badass as my combat boots, obviously, but I loved them. And they were quiet, so I wouldn't give myself away clomping.

I pulled my window open, the cool October air ruffling the curtains. My room looked out over the backyard with the brick patio, the huge vegetable garden, and the twinkly fairy lights strung through the apple trees. Fields stretched out to the edge of the woods. I wouldn't go into the dark forest; I couldn't remember if there were bears or mountain lions around here. I was far more scared of that possibility than random violence in town.

I dropped my leg over the side and bent down, squeezing myself over the window frame. A nail caught my jeans as I dropped down into the grass, tearing them. At least they were already ripped at the knee. The stars were dizzying overhead. At home we were lucky to see the Big Dipper. But here stars were everywhere, seeming to fall into the forest or come out of the mountains. Inside my room, Van Helsing whined. I poked my head back in.

"Go out the doggy door in the back, dummy," I told him. I snapped my fingers and pointed to the open bedroom door behind him. He licked my finger and then hurtled down the hall like an elephant. I turned around, grinning.

And then suddenly I was falling back against the house, a hand closed over my mouth, a tall, lean body pressing me into the wall. My heart thudded with that slow, sick rhythm of fear, like a wet drum being played. Clearly, I'd been wrong.

It really wasn't safe out after dark.

"Don't scream," a male voice said, almost sheepishly. "Please?"

Now I was confused. He seemed my age, with dark hair and what my novels would call an "amiable manner."

Even if he did have me trapped between his body and the bricks.

I tried to kick him, just out of principle. I wished I were wearing my steel-toed boots. He evaded me easily.

"I'm Connor Drake," he said, as if that meant anything. "I'm Nicholas's brother," he elaborated when I didn't look particularly comforted. I vaguely remembered playing with a herd of brothers when I was little. "I'm not going to hurt you," he promised. "Really."

"Then let go!" I screeched against his palm. It sounded more like "Thennmffllg!"

"Oh, sorry!" He dropped his hand. "Don't yell, okay?"

"Not okay," I shot back. "Are you nuts?"

Van Helsing charged around the corner, kicking up clumps of dirt and grass. I smirked at Connor. I hoped the dog bit him right in the ass. Instead, he sat on Connor's foot and drooled.

I sighed, disgusted. "Honestly."

Connor pet his head. "He knows me."

"Well, I don't," I grumbled. "Do you always accost girls?"

"It's not safe around here at night."

I looked at him pointedly. "I'm getting that."

"Sorry." He shrugged. Now that I had time to look at him, I saw the family resemblance. He had dark hair like Nicholas, and the same lean beauty. His eyes were blue, even in the faint glow of the twinkly lights. He was wearing jeans, a black T-shirt, and some sort of leather cuff on his wrist. He was really hot. Deranged, but hot. And not my type. I usually went for the bad boy. And this guy, despite lurking in the bushes, was clearly nice.

"I'm going inside now," I announced, daring him to contradict me.

He shoved his hands into his pockets. "Okay."

I half turned to eye the window. Logistics were going to be a problem. If I crawled back inside, not only would it be extremely undignified, but I'd end up sticking my butt right out at him. And he so didn't deserve a look at my ass. I edged out of reach, moving as slowly as ivy creeping up a garden wall. "I'll go around front."

Van Helsing trotted at my side, furry traitor that he was. Connor trailed behind us, affable and yet somehow menacing at the same time. It wasn't that I was scared of him, not really. I remembered him now. He'd been gangly, all elbows, his nose always buried in a comic book. But I'd been lectured about curfews and prowlers and danger since I'd arrived, so the fine hairs at my nape stirred, like a cat's hackles rising for no discernible reason.

I cleared my throat. I was being ridiculous. "What are you doing here, anyway?"

"I need to talk to my brother."

"Oh."

How did one make small talk that didn't involve insults or threats with someone who'd just leaped out of the bushes and grabbed you? He was lucky I hadn't pepper sprayed him. I'd been here only a couple of weeks and I'd already lost my edge. Not cool.

I worried about that until we reached the porch. The cedar

planks were gray with age and sagged alarmingly in the middle. And near the rails. It was pretty much going to collapse any minute now. I climbed the stairs gingerly. Connor put a hand on my elbow to steady me.

It was stupid of me to think about Mr. Darcy.

I pulled free and hurried to the front door. And nearly concussed myself. The sudden stop sent a small shiver of pain through my arm and made me stumble. It was locked.

I knocked loudly, grumpily. I could practically hear Connor grinning behind me. I kept my back to him even though my neck prickled.

CHAPTER 3

◆

Lucy

I flung the door open, Nicholas crowding behind me.

"Did you even check the peephole?" he grumbled.

"*Yes,* already." I shook him off. "What, you think vam—uh, very bad guys—knock now?" I blinked at Christabel, confused. "What are you doing out there?" Van Helsing muscled past me. He didn't look alarmed, so I wasn't either. Gandhi came to snuffle at Connor before wandering off as well, bored. "And what are you doing here?" My heartbeat fluttered uncomfortably. "Is Solange okay?"

Connor nodded quickly. "She's fine."

"Good. 'Cause only I get to kill her."

Nicholas's hand was a comfort on my lower back. "She just needs some time to herself."

"Please. That would work on anyone but me. I was

grandfathered in." I scowled. "Plus, that's what people say when they break up with someone."

Christabel came inside, practically plastering herself against the wall, as if Connor were contagious.

If she only knew.

I waited until she'd gone back to her room. I folded my arms, pivoting to block the exit. "So what's going on?"

"Nicholas and I need to get home."

I narrowed my eyes. "Fine. Just as soon as you tell me what the new undead drama is."

Connor shifted, looking uncomfortable. "It's supposed to be secret."

I'd always been part of the family. I was *one* of their secrets, for crying out loud. But ever since my parents had gotten back from their trip, I'd been getting weird vibes. I wasn't staying at the farmhouse anymore, so I couldn't eavesdrop. I was getting left out of things. Even Solange was avoiding me. I swallowed hard, terrified I might cry in front of them.

Nicholas kept his hand on my back. He was the only one who wasn't acting weird, which, I supposed, was kind of weird in itself. He was the only reason I was keeping my shit together. I was used to being part of the Drakes. I didn't know how to be this other Lucy. She was miserable.

But when I was with Nicholas, I could forget about all of that, or at least not obsess over it. He made the hurt feelings fade a little. He might be arrogant and bossy, but he didn't hide the important stuff from me.

"We shouldn't be seen here," Connor added. He was right. The front door was open. Anyone could see us and overhear our conversation.

I backed up a step, forcing Nicholas back as well since he was still behind me. "Then come inside."

"Oh, man," he muttered. "Lucy, don't do this to me."

"Don't *you* do this to *me*!" I retorted hotly.

"Mom said we weren't supposed to drag you into this stuff anymore."

I scowled. "That's not fair."

"Neither's being eaten by a *Hel-Blar*," Nicholas pointed out. To Connor he added, "Just come in. Lucy will find out somehow anyway. At least this way she can't take us by surprise."

Connor shut the door behind him. "Fine, but if Mom finds out, I'm blaming you."

Some of the pressure eased off my chest.

Connor sniffed the air and took a step back, swallowing. "Could you be a little less fragrantly relieved?"

My eyebrows lowered at Connor. "Are you trying to say I smell bad? Nice moves with the girls there, genius."

Connor rolled his eyes. "As if I'd hit on *you*."

"Hey! I'm cute." I poked Nicholas. "Tell him I'm cute."

"She's cute," Nicholas repeated mildly. "But you can't have her."

Connor rolled his eyes even harder. "Give me a break." His nostrils flared. He stared at Nicholas. "How do you do it? This house is tiny."

He shrugged but I saw the muscles standing out on his neck. I knew what that meant. "He wears nose plugs sometimes," I explained. Nicholas nudged me. "What? Why is that a secret?"

Connor peered down the hall. "Did you tell your cousin?"

"Of course not."

"She shouldn't be going out alone at night right now. We don't have the *Hel-Blar* infestation cleared up yet."

"I know. We've already told her not to go out, but she's not stupid. She hardly believed Violet Hill is overrun with gangs."

"Was she sneaking out to meet some guy?"

I snorted. "She's saving herself for Mr. Darcy."

"So what's going on that you came all the way over here instead of calling?" Nicholas asked. He had that intense expression I loved so much, all brooding and serious.

"Give me your phone first." Connor held out his hand. Nicholas passed it over. Connor glanced at me. "Yours too."

I blinked, then fished mine out of my knapsack on the floor behind us. "Why?"

"I'm not convinced Mom hasn't had our phones bugged," he said, scrolling through the options and hitting a bunch of buttons. I had no idea what he was doing. "I'll leave the GPS tag, but I want to make sure no one's eavesdropping." He gave us back our phones, after pulling them apart to look at their insides.

"So?" I pressed. "What now?"

"The last blood supply delivery to the house was poisoned."

We both stared at him. The Drakes had been dodging assassination attempts since just before Solange's sixteenth birthday. And after Helena killed Lady Natasha and became queen, a whole new kind of assassin descended, vying for the throne.

He nodded grimly at our expressions. "Solange nearly drank some."

"What? Is she okay?" I demanded. I didn't wait for an answer, just hit speed dial on my phone.

"She's fine," Connor told me. "Really."

The phone rang and rang in my ear. I switched it off, disgusted. "She's not answering."

"She's fine."

"Then she should *answer*."

"She's okay. Mom and Dad went off to make sure all of the tainted supply is dealt with, and Uncle Geoffrey is testing the bottle Solange nearly drank. Luckily it wasn't the first of the night, or she might not have been slow enough for Mom to smell something off." Newborn vampires weren't exactly known for their delicate appetites or refined manners when first waking up. "But now Mom and Dad want to post more guards, assuming that's even physically possible. And I don't know about you, but I need more guards like I need a suntan." He looked disgusted, the way he did over shoddy computer programming or sci-fi movies not getting proper critical acclaim. "Han Solo wouldn't need guards. Neither would Malcolm Reynolds. Or Picard."

I had to grin. "You do realize you're not the captain of an intergalactic spaceship?"

"Just like you realize you're not really a superhero?"

I cracked my knuckles. "Hunter's showing me new tricks."

"That's all we need," he groaned. "Anyway, Dad wants us all back at the house," he added to Nicholas.

"What about—" Nicholas went still so suddenly that I cut myself off midquestion. "What?" I whispered.

But he relaxed, nodding to the driveway through the window, just before headlights speared between the trees. "Car."

I glanced out just as my parents' car rumbled down the dirt lane. "Crap."

"We'll sneak out back," Nicholas said. Lately my dad went a funny color when he came home at night to find Nicholas on the couch with me. Nicholas kissed me, quick and hot as a shooting star. Connor just headed down the hall.

"This isn't over!" I called after them.

Like hell they were going to leave me out of this.

◆

I stomped into my room, muttering under my breath. I decided to change into my comfiest pajamas; they helped me think. I opened the drawer and reached for the plaid flannel pants. Shrink-wrapped condoms fell onto the rag rug. "Unbelievable." I marched back down the hall. "Mom!" I heard them in the kitchen, boiling water for chamomile tea. Ever since his ulcer, Mom made Dad have a cup every single night. He couldn't seem to convince her that a bottle of organic beer was just as healing.

"Stop hiding condoms in my stuff. It's like some twisted Easter egg hunt in there."

Mom was at the kitchen table, a china cup in her hand. Her long hair hung in two braids, lightly sprinkled with gray. She wore a silver bindi and a tight T-shirt with a lotus embroidered on the front from the local Tibetan store. "I just want you to be safe, honey," she replied calmly.

"I've counted eighteen of these so far," I shot back. "How much freaking sex do you think I'm having?" Especially with a curfew of roughly seven o'clock at night, which was about the time Nicholas woke up. It's not like we can hang out at school.

Dad blanched, setting his cup down so fast his tea sloshed over his hand, scalding him. I don't even think he noticed. "Who's having sex?"

"No one, Dad." I stole an oatmeal molasses cookie from the plate in front of him while he was too busy hyperventilating to notice.

"You're sixteen," he said, half-accusing, half-terrified.

"I know, Dad."

"That's too young for sex!"

"I'm not having sex!" This was getting embarrassing, even for our family, who talked about everything. Besides, Nicholas and I had been together for only a month or so. He was trying to not drink from my jugular, not trying to get into my pants. He was more squeamish about drinking my blood than I was. When Dad just blinked at me, his skin the approximate color of a frog's belly, I shot Mom a reproachful glare. "See what you did?"

"You're sixteen," Mom said serenely, as if this weren't mortifying. "I just want us to be realistic."

Dad scrubbed his face. He had a long strand of crystal mala beads around his neck. "I'm going to need to get a gun, aren't I?"

"You don't believe in guns," I reminded him. "Remember? That big political march last year? Gurus, not Guns?" They'd om'ed for a record twenty-three hours straight on the lawn outside city hall.

I lasted an hour before I got bored. Plus, I really like miniature crossbows and UV guns, so I felt a little hypocritical. I met Solange for ice cream instead.

"That was before I had a sixteen-year-old daughter," Dad said, his hand pressing on his ribcage, a clear indication that his ulcer was bothering him. I kissed the top of his head. His ponytail was longer than Mom's.

"Drink your tea, Dad." Then I pointed sternly at my mother. "I mean it, Mom. No more condoms."

"I want you to see my gynecologist."

"*Mom!*" I turned on my heel. "Conversation over!" I slammed my bedroom door shut behind me in case she considered following me for a mother-daughter chat. I loved my mom but I did *not* want to talk about sex.

Frankly, I had bigger problems.

Sex paled in comparison to the myriad ways Solange and all her irritating brothers could get themselves killed without me. I deserved to be part of their clandestine plans. I'd earned it. And I was sure they'd need a human touch at some point. And if they asked Hunter to help instead of me, I'd stake every last one of them myself.

Mom says jealousy is unattractive.

So's a broken nose.

I'm just saying.

I dropped onto the bed, sighing. Emo best friend, crazy mother, and feral vampires in the woods.

Just another Thursday night in Violet Hill.

CHAPTER 4

•

Christabel

"You are *not* bringing a book to a bonfire party at the beach," Lucy said from the doorway to my room. She was wearing a long skirt with a tank top and a jean jacket decorated with a huge pink silk rose brooch.

"Nope," I agreed. I was wearing my usual torn jeans and combat boots. "I'm bringing two."

"How are you even going to read in the dark?"

I waggled my battery-operated booklight at her before dropping it into my favorite black knapsack. I'd written bits of poetry all over it in silver marker. "The only reason I'm even going is because you won't stop bugging me about it."

"Careful, all that enthusiasm will wear you out," she said drily.

I slung my bag over my shoulder. "How did you convince your parents to let us out after dark?"

"Nicholas and his brothers will be there. And dozens of people from school. Plus, I told them you needed to get out and do something normal."

I stared at her. "You blamed this on me?"

"Hell, yeah." She shrugged unrepentantly. "Anyway, I'm right. And I promise, beach parties are way cooler than the lame field parties where drunk idiots grope each other."

"You guys actually have field parties? Cars parked in a circle with their headlights on and everything? I thought those were only in the movies." I really missed the city. We had normal parties in people's living rooms.

"At the beach we have bonfires, and you can see all the stars, and the lake always looks like it's full of glitter. You'll love it."

"It doesn't sound entirely horrid," I admitted.

Aunt Cass was in the front hall trying not to look worried. Her jeans were covered in mandala patches. "Be careful, girls."

"Mom, it's just a party," Lucy said. But there was something in her tone. I suddenly felt as if I were missing out on the actual conversation.

Aunt Cass's smile was forced. "I know." She handed Lucy a batik bag. "I packed snacks for you. And water. You know how I feel about soda."

I had to grin. She didn't mention alcohol like normal mothers.

Lucy didn't take the bag, though; she just narrowed her eyes suspiciously. "Do you swear there are no condoms in there?"

I coughed. "What?"

"Mom's obsessed," Lucy replied without looking at me. "You know, because I'm sixteen and a big old slut."

"Lucky!" Aunt Cass exclaimed. "That's not it at all and you know it." She sighed, rummaged through the bag, and withdrew a handful of packets she stuffed into her back pocket. Then she handed the bag back. "Here."

Lucy grumbled all the way to her car. There were fake flowers glued to the roof inside. It was like driving with a ragged garden as a hat. She turned the ignition and loud music thrummed around us. I checked my cell phone as we went down the driveway, even though I knew my mom wasn't allowed to have outside contact for another month at least. She was allowed to write me letters, but I knew she wouldn't. And the staff would've kept any of mine until she was out of lockdown or whatever they called it. It was weird not to have contact, not to check that she hadn't passed out on her back or left a candle burning. Not to help her stumble to the bathroom. Not to hold her hair and pass her tissues when she fell into a weeping fit about what a bad mother she was.

I didn't have anything to do but go to a party.

A Jeep pulled out of the woods behind us, headlights flashing. Lucy stuck her arm out of her window and waved.

"It's Nicholas," she explained loudly, over the music. She squinted into the rearview mirror. "And Quinn, I think. I can't tell from here." The car swerved toward the ditch. I grabbed the dashboard.

"Hey, pay attention!" I squeaked.

She yanked on the wheel. "Sorry." She winced sheepishly. "The Drake boys can do that to a girl." We drove past orchards, a scraggly looking vineyard, and lots of pumpkin patches. We went past the only street into town and took a dirt road instead, winding around a sleepy neighborhood toward the lake. We parked next to an ice-cream stand, closed up for the season. I saw the fires already burning on the beach and the glitter of the lake. We could have been stepping into a painting, or better yet one of those poems about fairy queens and mermaids. The smoke made the air feel dangerous, like a rusted sword that looks innocuous but could still cut right through your skin.

"'I shall wear white flannel trousers, and walk upon the beach. I have heard the mermaids singing, each to each. I do not think that they will sing to me,'" I quoted T. S. Eliot under my breath.

"Told you," Lucy said smugly, unperturbed. She was as used to me quoting poems as I was to her quoting old John Hughes movies. "Sometimes, my friend Patrick brings his drum." She went around and popped open the trunk, pulling out a guitar case as the Jeep screeched to a halt beside us, kicking up dust and pebbles.

"I didn't know you played," I said.

"I had kind of a stressful summer," she answered. "So Mom gave me her old guitar. She decided I needed a creative outlet. Didn't she give you her 'creativity heals' speech?"

"Thank God, no. But she knows I write poems."

"Don't leave them out—she'll put them on the fridge."

"What am I, six years old?"

"She put one up a few months ago."

I blinked. "What? How?"

"I think your mom sent it to her."

"My *mom* sent her one of my poems?" I wasn't sure what to think about that. My mom knew I still wrote?

Nicholas unfolded from the front seat, grinning. "No folk songs," he teased Lucy, reaching out to carry the guitar for her. She elbowed him. He glanced at me. "Her mom keeps teaching her all these old hippie songs."

"That's all she knows. I'm in a whiskey beatnik mood anyway," she informed him loftily.

"Is that even a type of music?" I asked.

"Sure, it's when I make my voice all scratchy and interesting."

"Actually, she's pretty good," Nicholas's brother admitted. "For a brat." I thought he was Connor at first; he had the same blue eyes, the same jaw. But his hair was longer and the smile was all wrong. It was way too charming, for one thing.

"Christabel, do you remember Quinn?" Lucy asked as we started to climb down to the beach. "He's Connor's twin. And he'll flirt with anything with boobs, so be careful."

"She's just jealous because I don't flirt with her." Quinn's smile was lazy. "She's territorial when it comes to us Drake brothers."

I remembered all too well. Even when she was little, Lucy used to kick anyone playing with us who even looked at them wrong. I could never figure that out. It wasn't like they were defenseless. For one thing, they outnumbered everyone else. Plus, their mother was kind of scary.

Quinn deserted us when we reached the sand, heading straight for a girl with long blond hair. Nicholas put down the guitar and reached for Lucy's hand instead. The first fire was way too crowded; people bumped elbows and spilled drinks on one another. Others danced to tinny music trying bravely to blare out of cracked speakers. The lights of Violet Hill hung like lanterns through the trees behind us, drifting up the mountain before they went out entirely. Several different kinds of smoke braided together and hung thickly in the air. I drifted over to a smaller fire and sat on a bench, the red paint peeling away in strips.

I barely had time to pull out my novel when someone sat next to me on the ground, kicking sand over my boots. "Does your T-shirt say 'Heathcliff is a prat'?"

I started. Connor Drake was suddenly taking up most of the space, his long legs nearly in the flames, his body crowding mine. He had a habit of taking me by surprise. His hair fell into his eyes, which were blue, even in the wavering, uncertain light of the fire. His smile was crooked and slightly self-deprecating, so different from his brother's. It was hard to believe they were twins. He just screamed "good guy."

"Isn't Heathcliff the one girls get all giggly over?" he continued while I just sat there and stared at him like an idiot. I wasn't usually this moronic around guys. I hadn't been like this last night when he'd scared the crap out of me. I'd been too busy trying to pretend my heart wasn't trying to squeeze through my rib cage. Now I couldn't stop trying to figure out what exact shade of blue his eyes were; not quite turquoise, as pale as a robin's egg, but more like sapphires. Or cerulean? I had to stop myself from leaning forward to have a better look.

What the hell was wrong with me? I went for guys with tattoos and sneers.

"You've never read *Wuthering Heights*, have you?" I finally asked before the silence became this ridiculous thing that crushed us.

"No." He leaned back against the bench, angled away from the crazy girl cataloging his eyeballs.

"Well, Heathcliff's an ass. He's not a romantic hero *at all*. I mean, he hangs a puppy off the back of a chair!" I sounded as if I knew Heathcliff personally, but I couldn't help it. I took this stuff seriously. "Good book though," I conceded. "And at least he doesn't jump out of bushes and grab girls just for fun."

Connor winced. "Oops. Sorry."

A grin twitched at the corner of my mouth. He was kind of disarming, in a lean, intelligent way. You just knew he was a genius under all the casual slouching. He had that look: good heart, smart head. "It's okay," I said.

One of the girls from across the fire leaned forward. Her cleavage threatened us from all the way over there. Even her lip gloss was vaguely aggressive. "Are you one of the Drake brothers?" she asked breathlessly. I nearly asked her if she had asthma and needed an inhaler.

Connor nodded.

"Is it true that Lucy's dating your brother Nicholas?" she pressed, sounding doubtful. I narrowed my eyes. If she was about to insult Lucy, she'd get more than she bargained for. I wasn't nice like country folk. I once made a guy cry on the subway.

"Yeah," Connor confirmed, not looking particularly interested. If the girl leaned over any farther, she'd fall right into the coals. I wondered briefly if he realized she was flirting with him. "He's definitely into her. We all are," he added pointedly.

The girl and her friends giggled. Connor glanced at me and

leaned slightly toward my knee. He seemed disinclined to make them giggle further. He looked like he actually wanted to talk to me instead.

"You know those girls are flirting with you, right?" I whispered.

He blinked. And then he squirmed. "They are not."

I laughed. "Are so."

He looked utterly flummoxed. It was adorable.

"Save me," he hissed.

Even more adorable.

"I'm serious," he added.

"So what are you doing here, then?" I asked, still laughing. Even the guy hanging out by the water's edge looked briefly interested in Connor. He might not be my type, but I wasn't blind. I could see the appeal. "You don't go to school in town, right?"

Connor shook his head. "I was homeschooled. I took my equivalency test when I was sixteen."

Knew it. He was one of the smart ones. Suddenly he was even cuter, even if he hadn't read *Wuthering Heights*.

"Do you like Violet Hill?" Connor asked as we watched a girl twirl devil sticks over her head. She could have traveled with a circus with her multicolored dreads and all the silver studs in her face. She was cute, as if she belonged in *Alice in Wonderland*. She was the part of Violet Hill I actually liked, and I told Connor that. "And I like all the art and the photocopied zines in the cafes," I admitted. "But you don't have enough bookstores. And your library is tiny."

"You say that like we sacrifice babies." He laughed. "And there are at least four bookstores in town."

"Yeah, but they're mostly full of vegetarian cookbooks and crystals. Which is fine, but I have Aunt Cass for that kind of thing."

"I know how you feel. Getting decent comics or computer parts is always a challenge."

I groaned. "Don't remind me. My laptop has PMS."

He chuckled. "I can take a look at it, if you want. And Guilty Pleasures in town has a second floor full of novels," he added. "The first floor's all chocolate and Johnny Depp memorabilia. There's also a poetry stall in the farmer's market on Saturdays."

"Okay, *that's* cool." I felt a small seedling of hope that I'd survive the year.

"I can take you," he said, somewhat shyly. "If you want."

"Okay. Sure." The seedling turned into a rosebud. It would be nice to have a friend here, even if he didn't go to our school.

The wind shifted slightly, fanning the fire and shooting delicate sparks. I couldn't smell the lake anymore, or the smoke, just Connor. It was something spicy and sweet, like black licorice. I wouldn't have thought he wore cologne. And usually I hated cologne. But this one was different. I inhaled surreptitiously. There was something else, like sugar melting or a bakery first thing in the morning. And cinnamon? No, not cinnamon. Something else.

Now I was *sniffing* him?

Clearly having all this free time to sit around at parties wasn't good for me.

He sat up suddenly, rising into a crouch. Something about the way he moved made my heart race. I couldn't help but think about wolves and tigers and animals with a lot of teeth. Adrenaline and something that made me feel like blushing warred inside my body, confusing me. This was poetry, this push and pull, this mysterious need.

Clearly there was another side to Connor.

He stood up, oblivious to the fact that I was apparently losing my mind.

He tilted his head as if he were listening to something I couldn't hear, something beyond the chatter of voices, the crackle of the fire, and Lucy's friend playing his drum.

"I have to go," he said quietly and maybe just a little regretfully. "Stay by the fire." He'd leaped over the bench and was prowling through the crowd before I could say anything.

"'We have lingered in the chambers of the sea, By sea-girls wreathed with seaweed red and brown, Till human voices wake us, and we drown.'" I quoted T. S. Eliot again, feeling bewildered.

CHAPTER 5

◆

Lucy

It was almost normal.

I was hanging at the beach with my boyfriend and he was holding my hand and he kept giving me those smoldering sidelong glances I loved so much. Not that I'd admit it to him, but he could probably hear my heart rate change. Sometimes having a vampire boyfriend had its disadvantages. He smirked, as if to prove my point.

We stayed at the edge of the crowd. I knew what it meant when he clenched his jaw in that particular way: temptation. There was lots of space, though, and the wind off the lake blew away most of the scents that made him hungry, like warm skin and blood and the sweat of the girls dancing.

My life's just weird.

Still, it was a beautiful night. It was crisp and just a little bit misty at the edge of the water. The moon hung sideways, like it was going to fall into the lake and drown if the wind blew too hard. The stars glittered, too many to count. My friend Nathan caught my eye and made the face he always makes when he thinks someone's gorgeous. He fanned himself dramatically. I just laughed.

It would have been perfect if my best friend would get over herself and get down here.

"So, Solange seriously isn't coming?" I asked, disgruntled. "Not even for, like, half an hour?"

Nicholas shook his head gently. "Luce, she can't. She's not . . . subtle. She can't even retract her teeth properly right now," he added quietly.

"She's really starting to piss me off."

"Believe me, I know." The muscles in his throat spasmed when he swallowed. "Could you do that weird yoga breathing your mom taught you to calm yourself down?" he asked, even as he dipped his head to nuzzle the side of my neck. I tingled all over, my breath going shorter—which was the opposite of calm yoga breathing. His mouth was soft, tickling under my ear. My knees suddenly felt wobbly. I shifted slightly; if I was going to go all embarrassingly mushy, so was he. I slid my hand up his arm, the cool muscles moving under my palm. He was in short sleeves as usual, since vampires rarely got cold. He only wore a coat out in public in winter so as not to draw attention to himself. As if that beautiful, serious face didn't draw enough attention.

I touched his shoulder, skimming my fingers up to dig into his hair, smiling devilishly.

"It's not a competition," he whispered against my lips.

"Show's what you know," I whispered back, kissing him until he pulled me closer, his hands on my hips. His tongue touched mine and my smug triumph turned into something else entirely. He was yummier than chocolate.

Someone whistled, the sound piercing through the very tiny space left between our bodies. Applause followed. I opened my eyes to half my classmates watching us. Nicholas swore softly under his breath.

"So much for stealthy," I said cheerfully.

He turned toward the cliff, tugging me behind him. His teeth gleamed.

"Are you okay?" I asked.

He nodded. "Just give me a minute." He was very pale, as if he were made of seashells and pearls. It was deceptive. Nothing cut deeper than a broken seashell, despite the delicate opal shimmer.

I put my hands in my pockets and turned on my heel, watching the fires gleam on the still lake and the elongated shadows of my friends in the sand. Nicholas was more private than I was, and he always wanted to do his vampire-struggle thing alone. I was finally learning to let him, even though it went against all of my instincts not to get right up into his face to see if I could help him. Or at least bug him until he was himself again.

I saw Quinn and Connor both detach themselves from the party and come our way, just as Nicholas swore again, differently this time. When I glanced back at him, his head was tilted, his eyes fierce. His fangs were fully out again. "Someone's coming," he said.

Quinn and Connor reached us before I could say anything. They both looked grim. Hunter ran through the sand behind them, scowling.

"I said, wait up," she muttered. "Hey, Lucy."

"Hey, Hunter." She was wearing a short sundress and sneakers. She looked like any other girl at a bonfire, but I knew she had at least eight different weapons stashed all over her. I had a stake in my boot and two more in the inside pocket of my jacket. Nicholas's nostrils flared.

"*Hel-Blar*," he spat. "Coming down the cliff, behind that cave."

I couldn't smell the wet mushroom, green swamp smell of a *Hel-Blar* vampire, but then I had a regular, boring human nose and the wind was blowing off the lake. I smelled only smoke and water and, if I inhaled hard enough to make myself dizzy, a faint whiff of Hunter's shampoo.

"Stay here," he added. He and his brothers were gone in a blur of pale skin and pale eyes before we could answer.

"Yeah, right," I said anyway, knowing he'd hear me.

Hunter suddenly had a stake in one hand and a dagger in the other hand. She didn't even dignify their order with a response, just started running. The stench didn't hit us until we rounded the cliff side. Quinn was clinging to the exposed roots and tall grasses, dirt raining down. He grabbed the blue-skinned vampire by the ankle and tossed him down to his brothers, waiting below. Nicholas staked him, ashes billowing around their ankles.

From the dark cave beside us, Hunter and I heard a yelp, followed by a shriek.

"What the hell, man?" a guy bellowed.

"Another one," Hunter said. We both advanced toward the mouth of the cave. Hunter broke a light stick she pulled from her bag and tossed it inside. The green acidic glow made me think of aliens and sci-fi movies.

And then there wasn't time to think at all.

A *Hel-Blar* had a couple cornered in the back of the cave, fish bones and broken glass around their feet. In such a cramped, humid space, the odors were nearly visible—slimy rotting mushrooms and the scum on old water, the kind not even insects will visit. A girl clutched her shirt closed with one hand and hyperventilated. The guy was trying to look brave, but when he saw the blood on his arm, his eyes rolled back in his head. At least it didn't look like teeth marks. The way his shirt was torn, he'd probably been thrown into the cave wall.

"Keep it together," Hunter barked in that military-school voice of hers. His back straightened before he consciously thought of it. The *Hel-Blar* snapped his teeth together, all of them wickedly pointed and as sharp as needles. He wore an odd, twisted copper collar around his neck. Since when did *Hel-Blar* accessorize?

"What is that thing?" the girl squeaked.

"Just a drunk raver kid, all dressed up," Hunter answered. "Stay where you are," she snapped when they stumbled forward. The *Hel-Blar* snarled.

I picked up a handful of pebbles and threw one at his head. It bounced off his temple and he whipped his head around. I just grinned, showing all my teeth like any good predator, and threw another rock. I kept throwing them until he snarled again, saliva dripping on his chin—and leaped for me.

Okay, so the plan worked better in theory.

Because no matter how prepared I was, or how many times I'd had a vampire leaping at my face, some facts remained the same. They were faster than me. Always.

"Duck!" Hunter yelled as I stumbled back. I went down, hitting my knee hard. Pain bloomed. I'd have a wicked bruise by morning.

You know, if I didn't get eaten.

Hunter threw her stake with the kind of ease and accuracy one might expect from a straight-A student at a vampire-hunter high school.

Thank God.

The momentum of the stake biting into his chest stopped the *Hel-Blar* in his tracks. He flew off his feet, clutching at the wound. Thick blood oozed between his fingers. The stake had done enough damage to slow him down but it hadn't penetrated through his rib cage into the fleshy heart underneath. So he wasn't dead.

Yet.

I took advantage of his pained yowling and threw myself forward with my own stake. I thrust it into the wound next to Hunter's stake. Then I leaned back and used the heel of my boot like a hammer to shove it through clothing, skin, and in between bones. Hunter jumped over his decomposing body to usher the couple away. The *Hel-Blar* disintegrated into dust and a pile of mushroom-scented clothes.

I crab-walked backward to the cave mouth and then pushed to my feet, panting. Nicholas dropped down from the cliff edge in front of me. I screamed before I could stop myself, choking on adrenaline as he rose out of his crouch.

"Are you okay?" he asked.

I nodded, coughing. My body was trying to sort through all the stimuli and was momentarily stunned. "I'm fine," I finally managed to croak.

"What was that?" the girl asked shrilly. "It was, like, some monster, did you see that? Where did he go?"

"We scared him off," Hunter assured her.

"That thing was not human," the guy insisted.

I made my expression calm and unimpressed. "You're drunk," I said. "You're seeing things."

He rubbed his face. "Uh . . ."

His girlfriend pulled him backward. "Can we go? I want to go. *Now.*"

They wandered away, back toward the fires and the people. Hunter let out a breath. "That was way too close," she said, taking out her cell phone. "I'm calling it in."

Nicholas pulled me against his side. "Are you sure you're okay?"

I nodded. "We dusted him," I said, a little proudly.

"I—" He cut himself off abruptly. He, Quinn, and Connor all whirled back toward the cliff.

"Coming around the back," Quinn said so softly I barely heard him. Hunter hurried to hang up her phone, but they were already moving out like some vampiric fan. We had to run to catch up again.

"So not fair," Hunter muttered. "I work out all the damn time and he's still faster."

"I know," I agreed, huffing. "Sucks." I wasn't even as fast as Hunter. For one thing, I still couldn't run and talk at the same time.

The moonlight made the *Hel-Blar* look strangely beautiful, as if she were made of opals and lapis lazuli. Nothing could make the smell beautiful, though.

Before Nicholas and the others could cross the rocky peninsula to reach her, two figures dropped from the hill above. The guy kicked the *Hel-Blar* in the neck with his steel-toed boot, ivory lace fluttering from his cuffs when he put a hand out to steady his landing. The girl followed, landing with her arm outstretched, stake plunging into the *Hel-Blar's* chest. Ashes drifted down and disappeared into the lake.

Nicholas's older brother Logan and his girlfriend, Isabeau, grinned at each other.

"Heads up," Hunter said suddenly. We followed her gaze. At the top of the cliff was another *Hel-Blar* and Isabeau's giant gray wolfhound, Charlemagne. They were both snarling.

"*Merde,*" Isabeau said when the *Hel-Blar* approached her beloved dog. "I will kill him."

She was running toward the hillside when a strange sound ululated from the woods. It was a cross between one of those old-fashioned hunting horns and a broken flute. It was haunting but sharp enough that I wondered if there was blood coming out of my ears. We all winced, especially the vampires, with their sensitive hearing. Quinn swore, in extreme detail.

The *Hel-Blar* screeched, clutching his ears. Then he looked around, as if he was frightened.

I'd never seen a *Hel-Blar* frightened like that before.

It didn't bode well.

He snapped his teeth before running away from us, from the dog, and from the unprotected students laughing on the beach.

That was something else *Hel-Blar* never did: run away from food. And that's what we were to them.

"What the damn hell was *that?*" Quinn demanded.

We looked at one another, bewildered.

"I've never seen that before," Hunter said. "I thought *Hel-Blar* were all about the mindless feeding."

"So did I," Nicholas muttered. "I hate it when they change the rules. And why are they all wearing those collars?"

"*Attend-moi,*" Isabeau called up to Charlemagne. He waited patiently at the top of the cliff.

"Isabeau!" I exclaimed. "You're back."

She wiped her stake clean in the sand and smiled her rare, reserved smile. "*Oui.*" Her French accent was just as thick and she still wore the same kind of tunic dress, with the chain mail work over her heart. Bone beads dangled in her hair. "I have been here for a week now."

"A *week?*"

"Solange asked for me to come."

"Oh." I was not going to be one of those jealous best friends too insecure and stupid to share. I was evolved and I did yoga and I was better than that, damn it.

Nope.

Hurt pinpricked through me. A hard lump of dread was forming in my belly, as if I'd swallowed a peach pit. In a certain kind of story, I'd grow a tree from my belly and peaches would fall out of my mouth when I spoke.

Instead, I just felt like I was going to be sick.

I tried to keep my smile firmly in place. "Oh," I said again.

Nicholas stepped toward me but I took a step back. I didn't want sympathy. It was mortifying. Logan just looked at me for a long moment before slinging his arm over my shoulders. "Come on, Lucy, tell me whose nose you broke this week."

"No one's. Maybe yours right now," I grumbled. "I didn't know you were back, either." I'd missed him too, with his frock coats and wicked smiles. He wore a bone bead like Isabeau wore in her hair, but on a leather thong around his wrist. He'd been staying with Isabeau's people, the Cwn Mamau, getting to know their ways since he'd been initiated into their tribe. Isabeau was a Shamanka's handmaiden and knew all about the magical aspects of being a vampire, the stuff the Drakes had never really believed in until Solange turned sixteen. I liked her. It's not that I didn't want Solange hanging out with her. I just didn't want to be left out. And this was just further proof that I wasn't an honorary Drake anymore.

Thinking about that made me kind of nauseous.

I texted Solange.

You're meeting me tomorrow night. 9 pm. Oak tree.

We met at the oak tree only when we wanted to be certain of privacy. That tree had heard more stories about cute boys, mean boys, and parental interference than anything else on the planet. It was on Drake property, so it would be safe enough, and I'd take Gandhi to protect me on the car ride over to appease my parents.

"We tracked those three from the woods," Isabeau was telling the others. "And one who tried to eat a dog."

I could just imagine what Isabeau had done. Dogs were sacred to her tribe. *Cwn Mamau* meant "Hounds of the Mother." There probably weren't even ashes left.

"They must be getting desperate," Hunter remarked grimly. "I'll put an anonymous call in to get the cops to bust up the party. It's obviously not safe here."

"I'll wait with you," Quinn said.

"Take my motorcycle." Connor tossed him the keys. "I'll catch a ride with Nicholas."

I nodded. "I'll get Christabel."

I ran to the edge of the water by the farthest bonfire. I knew she'd be there, away from the crowds and as close to the lake as she could be without actually being in it.

"We have to go," I said.

She turned. "Oh. Okay." She frowned at me. "You look weird. Did you and Nicholas have a fight or something?"

"No, but someone called the cops on the party and I'd rather be out of here before they show up."

Lucy

"Good plan." She grabbed her knapsack and followed me. I stopped to warn Nathan about the cops. He scrambled for his stuff and by the time we'd climbed the steps to the parking lot, we could see the frantic whispering travel from fire to fire. Nicholas and Connor were waiting for us in the Jeep. Nicholas was on his cell phone. I hopped into the car and pulled out before Christabel's door properly closed.

CHAPTER 6

◆

Connor

"What the hell was that?" I asked, flipping my laptop open. I'd rescued it from the motorcycle pack before Quinn took off with Hunter. He hadn't even bothered to tease me about it, which just proved how much the *Hel-Blar* had rattled us. *Hel-Blar* didn't back down, ever. And they didn't cower. Ever.

So much for a night on the beach with Lucy's pretty cousin.

Nicholas glanced at me, hitting the accelerator. "Are you Googling whistles?"

"I'm Googling every damn thing I can think of," I muttered, typing quickly. "Because that was just weird."

"I don't think they sell magic whistles on eBay."

I snorted. "You'd be surprised."

"Damn it, Lucy," Nicholas muttered suddenly. "She's going way too fast."

I looked at him incredulously. "Dude." Nicholas was notorious for driving too fast. He'd crashed his tricycle when he was five years old, trying to drag-race Quinn.

"Well, she is," he insisted. "How are we supposed to protect her?"

The fields and orchards of Violet Hill gave way to thick forests of pine and oak. The shadows blurred. One blurred differently than the others.

"On the right," I said, rolling my window down. We were going fast enough that the sky looked full of shooting stars. It was too fast to differentiate scents; it was all pine and mountain-fresh wind. No hint of mushrooms. A howl shivered between the trees.

"Probably that wolf," Nicholas said.

"Probably." I went back to my laptop. The Internet connection flickered off and then came back on. While I liked the solitude of living in the middle of nowhere, the Wi-Fi sucked. "I need to boost—"

And then Nicholas hit the brake so hard, my computer flew into the dashboard.

"Hey!" I yelled, grabbing it before it bounced back and knee-capped me. "This thing's expensive."

Nicholas swore under his breath. I looked up. I knew he didn't care about my computer, not enough to swear like that.

The shadow we'd seen at the edge of the trees was in the middle of the road, wearing the remains of a ragged dress, mud, and not much else. She was hunched over and snarling, trying to shield her unnatural red eyes from the glare of the headlights.

"Hit the high beams," I said.

The light turned into spears of brightness that would have made even my eyes water. We might not be as sensitive as the *Hel-Blar*, but our pupils weren't made for light either. Her blue skin was like crushed blueberries, her teeth needle-sharp. There was blood on her chin, running down her throat where the light glinted off a metal collar.

"Should I run her over?" Nicholas asked, bewildered.

I was just as confused. She wasn't attacking. And she was too skinny to be a threat, but she was also covered in blood. She'd kill someone before the week was out, that was a certainty. The *Hel-Blar* weren't just feral, they were crazy.

But we weren't assassins.

Mostly.

And then she did something else *Hel-Blar* never did.

She ignored us.

She ignored two Drake brothers—the hell I was going to refer to us as princes—and stared at the tree line, cringing.

"Something is scarier to her than her hunger," I muttered.

"That is *not* good," Nicholas muttered back, hitting speed-dial on his phone. I heard Lucy on the other end.

"You all right?" Nicholas asked.

"Yes," I heard clearly.

"Then drive, don't look back. Just drive!" He hung up before she could reply.

A woman stood in the cedars, barefoot but wearing a leather vest covered in weapons. One of them looked like a cutlass from here. She was pale blue, like a sheen of watercolor paint, not dark-bruise blue like the *Hel-Blar*. Her skin was chalky but her veins were so prominent it was like she'd been painted in woad like an ancient Pict or the guys from the *Braveheart* movie.

But she had a lot of teeth, even from here.

The *Hel-Blar* woman, still cringing, clutched at her collar, her nails leaving jagged, bloody welts behind.

Nicholas turned at the clicking of my keyboard. "Are you kidding? You're online *now*?"

"Well, do you know what the hell's going on?"

"No."

"Neither do I." I clicked through some of my private files but I wasn't even sure what I was searching for. His phone rang in his pocket. We both knew it was Lucy without having to look. He switched off the ringer. She'd kill him for that later.

But we had bigger problems than Lucy's mean right hook.

The vampire in the woods lifted a wooden miniature flute-style whistle and blew it once. It was the same sound we'd heard at the beach. Nicholas and I exchanged a grim glance.

The *Hel-Blar* shrieked. The sound was animal in its pain and it lifted the hairs on the back of my neck. I expected electricity to arc from the collar, but it didn't. Something else was happening to her, and whatever it was, it was painful.

Another whistle. She ran toward it, instead of away, bowing her head.

"What the f—?" The door cut Nicholas off, slamming shut behind him as he followed.

"Shit, Nick, don't go out there alone!" I scrambled out after him.

He was in front of the lights when the first knife cut into the hood of the Jeep. He jerked back and froze. Another knife hit the passenger door by my elbow.

"Not yet." The woman laughed, her red hair streaming behind her when she whirled and vanished into the forest. We hadn't even reached the other side of the road when the sound of clacking jaws skittered around us like hungry insects.

Hel-Blar. They rushed at us, stinking of mushrooms and death, fueled by a vicious need that could never be appeased. There were three of them—and none of them wore collars. There was also no whistle to call them off.

"Well, shit," I said reaching for a stake. I slid over the headlight, landing in front of Nicholas. We turned without another word so we were back to back.

Quinn liked to tease me because I watched so many sci-fi movies and read fantasy novels about quests and good against evil. Was it any wonder when a casual trip to the beach turned into this? They weren't fantasy novels to me, just an extension of my regular life. And at least in my books, good always won.

Well, mostly always.

A huge *Hel-Blar*, bloated on blood, rushed at me. He was tall enough that he clipped me on the ear with his fist before he was even in range of my side kick. I could have dropped to the ground but it would have left Nicholas open. My ear rang uncomfortably. Teeth clacked, way too close for comfort. I kicked again and caught him in the sternum. He stumbled back a step but didn't fall. It gave me just enough time to throw my stake. It didn't quite pierce his heart, so he just fell to his knees, wheezing and cursing.

I heard a crack behind me. Ash drifted in the beams of the headlights. There was blood on Nicholas's arm but it was his own.

"High ground," I said, and we launched ourselves onto the Jeep. It rattled as we went up onto the roof, boots clomping. The *Hel-Blar* I'd annoyed with my stake clambered up after us, saliva and blood frothing at the corners of his mouth. He grabbed Nicholas's ankle and yanked. Nicholas fell hard, half sliding off the roof. But he was a Drake, so he took out the second *Hel-Blar* with his boot as he landed. I took a moment to aim better and threw another stake, closer to the first. It hit true this time and mildew-smelling ashes dusted the hood.

Nicholas had slid into his open window. "Hang on!" he yelled at me, throwing the Jeep into reverse. I clung to the edges of the sunroof, legs dangling. The *Hel-Blar* turned around, snarling.

"Get in, Connor!"

I managed to get my legs up and dropped into the open sunroof, landing mostly on my seat. I cracked my elbow into the window and my tailbone on the seat-belt latch. Nicholas jerked into drive without any warning, and when we lurched forward I nearly broke my nose. I grabbed the dashboard as he hit the *Hel-Blar* with enough force to make a very wet sound followed by a crunch that could only be the breaking of bones.

"They're everywhere tonight," I bit out.

"Call Lucy back," Nicholas said, speeding away.

I stared at him. "Like hell. *You* call her back."

"Connor, just do it."

"You owe me," I muttered, then decided to text her instead. Lucy's temper could fry my eyeballs even through a phone line. I read her reply and snorted a laugh. "I'm not reading *that* out loud."

CHAPTER 7

◆

Christabel

Lucy was driving way too fast, as usual.

I stared at the lake, where I'd been brooding when she came to get me. I'd been trying not to think about my parents. It was hard not to. My dad had loved to fish. He drove out every weekend in the summer to sit in his rowboat in the middle of a lake just like this one, waiting for fish. But one morning when I was eleven, he didn't come back. His rowboat eventually drifted to shore three days later, empty. Mom started drinking that week and never really stopped. I turned to poetry, especially Percy Bysshe Shelley. He had been lost at sea, too, but when his body was found three days later, they burned it on a funeral pyre. Everything but his heart turned to ash. Sometimes I like to think that my dad's heart is still out there somewhere, like some precious underwater treasure.

There was the teeniest, tiniest possibility that I was incredibly morbid.

Lucy's phone rang. "Nicholas," I told her, reading the call display.

"Answer it," she said. I hit the button and held the phone up to her ear so she could keep her hands on the steering wheel. I couldn't hear what Nicholas was saying but her face changed.

"What? What do you mean? No way! Nicholas? Nicholas! Nicky, damn it!" Her hands clenched. "Hit redial, would you?" she asked through her teeth, switching on the high beams. I kept forgetting this was deer country and they might jump in front of the car without warning. The phone rang and rang. I eventually hung up.

"He's not answering."

"I think we need to turn around," she said.

"Why, did the cops get them?"

"No."

"Then what's wrong?"

"I don't know."

I frowned. "Lucy, that doesn't make any sense."

"I know," she admitted. She looked torn, easing her foot off the gas pedal.

"Ever been to jail?" I asked, mostly to distract her.

Lucy rolled her eyes. "Hello? Of course I have. Who do you think has to go bail out my parents when they lie down in front of logging trucks or climb trees to snuggle with endangered owls or whatever?"

"Right." Which was a better story than mine. I'd been only

once, and not to some small-town single-cell jail, either. Mom once got arrested downtown for a DUI. She lost her license. That was last summer, before Uncle Stuart unexpectedly dropped by and found his older sister passed out on the couch with vomit in her hair. Not exactly her finest hour. Then Uncle Stuart knew the truth and wouldn't be stopped from helping, no matter what we said.

I missed her. She didn't do that stuff on purpose. I knew she loved me. She was just weak. I felt kind of bad thinking of her that way, but it was true.

I shook off the mood before it could clamp its sharp teeth shut over my head. Mom was in rehab, getting better. When Lucy's phone rang, she yelped so loudly that she startled me into yelping too. Then we both laughed.

"What are you so nervous about?" I asked her as she fumbled for her phone. "Give me that." I glanced at the call display before she drove us into a tree. "It's your mom."

"Of course it is."

"She's texting. She and your dad are going to a late movie."

"Text her back that we're fine and on our way home."

When I was finished, I shook my head. "Honestly, it's a good thing you guys don't live in a big city. Your parents would be a wreck."

Lucy just snorted. I got that feeling again, like there was a layer under everything that I wasn't quite seeing. It made me want to pick away at it until it unraveled. She slowed her car down to an idle.

"I'm counting to ten," she decided, reaching for her phone. "And then I'm turning around if he doesn't answer."

"What's the big deal?" I asked.

"Um, his car is crap," she replied, a little too quickly. "Breaks down all the time."

I raised an eyebrow incredulously. "And you know how to fix it."

"Well, no, but I worry. You know, gangs."

"Right, the organic New Age flakes roaming the countryside with their ferocious flaxseeds. Give me a break, Hamilton."

Her phone trilled, announcing a text. She grabbed it from me so fast she accidentally scratched me. "They're fine," she assured me, sounding way more relieved than was warranted. What the hell was going on? She put the car back into drive, her shoulders visibly unclenching. I hadn't even known shoulders *could* clench. She relaxed even more when Nicholas's Jeep caught up to us, trailing behind like a clunky, muddy shadow. I glanced in my side mirror, frowning.

"Is that a *knife* in the hood?"

She glanced back. "Trick of the light. Told you it was falling apart."

It looked in pretty good condition to me.

"So," Lucy said before I could press her. "You and Connor?"

"He's nice, but he's not my type."

Lucy shot me a look, as if I were demented. "Are your eyes broken? Hot guys aren't your type?"

"Good boys aren't my type," I corrected. "I like an edge."

Her smile was more of a smirk. "Give him a chance."

"I'll totally hang out with him, don't get me wrong. He's decent. You know, nice."

Lucy winced. "Ouch. He's not dark enough for you?"

"Exactly."

She was still smirking as we pulled in front of the house. I had no idea why she thought it was funny. Nicholas raced in on squealing tires to park behind us. Lucy ran down the driveway to smack him on the shoulder. Hard.

"Don't do that again!" she exploded.

"You stopped the car," he accused, "when I told you to keep going!"

"So?"

"So, *you* don't do that again!"

I unlocked the front door, very aware of Connor ambling up the walkway behind me, which was stupid. Hadn't I just told Lucy he was too nice? "Are they fighting?" I asked, even though she'd already told me they weren't.

"Not really." He smiled. "Trust me, you'll know if they're fighting."

The dogs greeted us with wagging tails and drool, as usual. Nicholas followed Lucy into the living room. They both looked worried.

Connor turned to look at me, kicking the door shut. "Where's your laptop?"

"Oh, um, in my room." I hurried ahead of him, suddenly worried that I'd left a bra out on the bed or that there was underwear falling out of my laundry basket. Girls in poems never had to worry about that stuff. Luckily, my room was relatively inoffensive. The bed was unmade and there was a row of old teacups on the windowsill, but the closet door was shut and my diary was well hidden. Connor went straight to my desk and lifted the screen of my laptop.

"So what's it doing?"

I half smiled. "I have no idea. The Internet's not talking to me."

He flicked me a glance and half smiled back. "Okay."

His fingers flew over the keys and he bent his head, his hair falling over his forehead. "How much poetry do you have on here?"

My eyes widened. "You're not reading them, are you?" I never let anyone read anything I hadn't edited or fixed up.

"I won't," he promised. "You just have a lot of Word documents here. You should make sure you back them up."

"Oh. Okay."

"So, you're really into this poetry stuff, aren't you?"

I nodded. "Yeah. I can't help it."

"Who's your favorite?"

"John Keats right now, but only because of that movie *Bright Star*. I love Shelley too."

"They're all old dead guys, right?"

"Um, yeah." I shrugged. "But they were the best."

He grinned at me slowly. "You're a geek."

"Am not."

He snorted. "I know a fellow geek when I see one. I can quote *Firefly* and old *Star Wars* until you throw up."

I had to laugh. "Nice image. I still bet I can out-quote you, or at least out-trivia you."

"Please."

"Byron used to drink vinegar to lose weight."

"Leia's cellblock in *Star Wars: A New Hope* was AA-23."

"Charlotte Brontë's pen name was Currer Bell."

"On *Firefly*, Jayne's favorite gun is named Vera."

"*Pride and Prejudice* was originally called *First Impressions*."

"To throw off the media, one of the fake titles for *Return of the Jedi* was *Blue Harvest*." He leaned back in his chair, grinning. "Draw?"

"All right, tie."

He shut my laptop and tilted it back to show me the side with all the buttons. "So you can't connect to the Internet, right?"

"Right."

"It's just this switch here on the side. You probably accidentally hit it. Happens all the time."

"Oh. Thanks."

"Sure."

He looked comfortable and confident in a way I hadn't noticed when he was with his brothers. He was quiet, less flashy in his charm, but there was a glint in his eye.

I couldn't help but wonder if he was a good kisser.

He looked up as if he knew what I was thinking.

Which wasn't possible, of course. And had I really been wondering what it would be like to kiss him? A guy who lived on a farm in the backwoods of nowhere and quoted *Star Wars*?

"I'll get us drinks," I offered. "I know where Lucy hides her secret soda stash."

He mumbled something unintelligible that I took as an assent.

Lucy and Nicholas were still in the living room and were being very quiet. I averted my eyes. The last thing I wanted to see was my cousin making out. Van Helsing followed me down into the basement, which had walls of brick and wood paneling; all it was missing was green shag carpeting. The fridge was in the corner, bookended with shelves full of Aunt Cass's pickles and tomato sauce. I had to dig in the back, behind bags of tempeh and packets of pumpkin seeds. I knew there was ginger ale tucked inside a box purporting to house vegetable juice. I had to move aside bottles of wheatgrass and vitamins and a jar of something thick and red, like raspberry pulp. I tucked the soda cans under my arm and pulled out the jar, holding it up to the light. It was viscous and only let a little ruby light through. Van Helsing bared his teeth. I blinked at him.

"I know, it's disgusting, right? I wonder what Aunt Cass was trying to make."

I took it upstairs. "What the hell is this gross-ass thing?" I demanded, waving the jar. The lid wasn't on as tight as I thought, and a dribble of thick, red liquid oozed over the side. I nearly threw it onto a side table, next to a fertility statue carved out of turquoise. "Ew!"

Connor was in the living room now, and he and Nicholas stood up so fast, I barely saw them move. I jumped, startled. "What?" I asked.

Van Helsing growled. Gandhi came charging down the hall, also growling.

"Shit, Christa, back!" Lucy shouted, sliding across the wooden floor. She crashed into me and I hit the wall, then the floor.

A photograph tumbled off its nail and fell, glass breaking. Lucy whirled, knees bent, staring down at Nicholas and Connor, who had gone from moving too fast to not at all. They were so still, they looked like they were holding their breath. Van Helsing barked once. Nicholas flinched.

"Christa," Lucy whispered urgently when I sat up. "Don't move."

"What? Why?" I made sure none of the glass was about to poke me in the hand or the butt if I altered my position. "I'm fine."

"Just trust me." She swallowed.

I didn't trust Nicholas's smile one bit. Even Connor looked odd beside him, pale and sleek. Gone was the friendly hot-geek vibe. His eyes looked even more blue and he seemed taller for some reason. I wanted to get closer to him. I shifted, suddenly thinking all sorts of naughty things. Maybe there was a bad boy in there after all.

"Lucy." Nicholas's voice cracked.

"Christa, pass me the jar," Lucy said as Gandhi and Van Helsing angled themselves in front of us.

"You just told me not to move!"

"Just do it!"

I pushed into a crouch.

"Move slower!" Lucy added frantically when Nicholas tensed and Connor put a restraining hand on his shoulder. "Gandhi, stay!"

"Are you guys high?" I snapped, annoyed. I shoved the jar at her. "Here."

Lucy just angled her hand back, not taking her eyes off the

brothers for even one second. When she had a good hold, she put it on the floor right in front of her.

"Okay, no more drugs for you," I said. "Seriously. It makes you guys weird."

She ignored me and lifted the lid off. Then she used the toe of her boot to slide the jar across the polished wood toward Nicholas and Connor. The huge dogs pushed at us, ushering us backward into the kitchen before I could see what was going on.

"What the hell?" I asked.

She pushed her hair off her face, hands trembling lightly. The front door slammed and there was the rumble of a car engine starting, followed by the peel of tires on the road.

"Lucy?"

Her smile was tight. "Never mind," she said. "I think someone spiked our drinks at the party."

Somehow, I knew she was lying.

For one thing, I hadn't seen her take a single sip of anything the entire time we were at the beach. And I knew exactly how people acted when they'd had too much to drink. Not like this.

In the hall, the jar was empty.

CHAPTER 8

◆

Lucy

I knew Mom would knock on my door the minute she came home and heard the Smiths coming from my speakers. She'd given me all their albums the day I turned fourteen and swore they were the band that got her through high school.

"Uh-oh." She poked her head in. "I heard the music. That's not a good sign."

I was curled up on my bed, the only light coming from a candle and my laptop screen on my desk. I'd texted Kieran to come over so I could talk to him and then buried myself in chocolate while I waited. She picked her way around the clothes and DVD cases scattered over the floor. "What's the matter, Lucky Moon?"

I just shrugged and ate more chocolate. She sat on the edge of the bed and nudged me until I moved over and made space for her. She stretched out beside me and stared up at the sari material draped from the ceiling like a sultan's tent. My walls were purple and covered in framed pictures and the antique glass doorknobs where I hung all my necklaces.

"Oh, Mom," I finally said, feeling my throat burn. "It's all messed up now."

"What is, sweetie? Did you and Nicholas have a fight?"

"Why do people keep asking me that? Not everything is about boys."

"Okay. Is it school? I know it's not as exciting as boys and vampires, but I hope you're worrying about it a little. Don't you have midterms soon?"

"Mom."

"Sorry. Not school, clearly. What is it, then?"

"Solange."

She looked surprised. "You and Solange had a fight?" She *should* look surprised. The last time we'd seriously fought, it was over whether werewolves smelled like wet dog, and I'd pulled her hair. We were eight.

"Not really a fight," I explained. "But it's . . . weird now. They're all keeping secrets from me, and I'm barely allowed to go over there. And she never answers her phone!"

Mom paused for a moment.

I didn't like the look on her face. "What?"

"Maybe it's for the best."

I sat up. "*What?* It is *not!* How could you say that?"

She sat up too, drawing up her knees. The bells on her silver anklet sang softly. It was a sound that comforted me. Growing up, I always knew where my mom was in the house by the jingling of her anklet.

"Honey, I know you love the Drakes. We do too. But the fact is, you're human. They're not. You can't pretend otherwise."

I blinked at her. "You're the one who's always saying our differences shouldn't matter."

"I know." She took a deep breath. "And I'm so proud of you for being loyal and strong and seeing people for who and not what they are. But the Drakes are dangerous right now. Helena and I both—"

"Wait." I swallowed a thorny lump of anxiety. "You and Solange's mom talked about this behind my back? You're part of the freeze-out?"

"It's not a freeze-out," she insisted, wincing. "And I know you're hurt, but we're worried about you. We just want to keep you safe."

All of a sudden I really understood how Solange felt.

And it sucked.

"I can take care of myself," I said flatly.

"You're sixteen years old."

"So? I've been training with the Helios-Ra, and before that Helena showed me a bunch of moves," I insisted. "I can fight better than Dad."

She pursed her lips. "That's not exactly a winning argument, Lucky. We don't *want* you to fight."

"Well, neither do I!" Which was a lie. Right now I really wanted to break someone's nose. "But I'm fine. We're all fine." I wasn't about to mention the *Hel-Blar* at the beach or the incident in the hall with Christabel. "Mom, you keep saying I can't be like them, but I can't be like you, either. I'm just me," I said quietly. "And you can't suddenly take away half my family and expect me to be okay with that."

"I know." She scrubbed a hand over her face, looking tired and older than usual.

I went cold, as if my belly were full of icicles. "And you can't forbid me from seeing Nicholas." I'd wanted my voice to be strong and calm and grown-up, but instead it squeaked like a little girl's.

"We aren't," Mom assured me, half smiling. "I've been your mom for a long time. You think I don't know just how well that would work?"

I could almost breathe again. "Okay." I exhaled sharply. "Okay."

"Just think about what I said." She slid off the bed. "And clean your room and do your homework and eat your vegetables." She winked. "I just wanted to say something mom-ish that didn't involve mortal peril of some kind."

"Mom," I said quietly as she opened the door. She looked over her shoulder. "I'm not stupid. And I'm way more careful than everyone gives me credit for. So at some point you're going to have to let me be me and trust that I know what I'm doing. Just like the Drakes are going to have to stop making Solange the princess in the tower." I lifted my chin. "Because she's not Snow White or whatever. And if this is some kind of a fairy tale, then I get to be a wolf or a witch or a wild girl, *not* the damsel in distress."

◆

I turned my bedside lamp back on and paced the length of my room, waiting for Kieran. Next to my laptop was a bronze statue of Ganesh that Dad had given me on my first day of high school. Ganesh was an elephant-headed god from India who was believed to remove obstacles. I kept him on my desk because outside of the vampire world, I didn't know a bigger obstacle than homework. Which I should probably be doing right now, as Mom suggested, but who could concentrate?

Tired of waiting, I yanked open my window and stuck out my head.

My forehead bonked Kieran's and bounced off.

"Ow!" we both yelped, grabbing our heads.

"I always knew you had a hard head."

"Ha-ha," I grumbled, rubbing my hairline. "I was pretty sure yours was soft."

He was in his usual black cargos and T-shirt. He'd cut off his ponytail but wouldn't tell me why or how it happened. Which just proved there was a good story attached. I'd have to ferret it out later when I had time. I slipped into the garden and folded my arms expectantly. "What the hell's up with Solange?"

He frowned. "I thought *you'd* know. You're her best friend."

"Someone should remind her of that."

"She's still not talking to you?"

"Not really." The grass was cold under my bare feet. My toes curled in.

Kieran looked worried. "She's not really talking to me, either," he admitted.

I stared at him. "What? But you see her all the time."

He shoved his hands in his pockets and looked as if he were trying not to blush. "She doesn't talk much. She won't ever take off her sunglasses. And she only ever wants to make out. I can barely get her to say three words to me." He winced, disgusted. "God. Could I sound more like a girl?"

"Please. You should be so lucky."

Still, Solange just wasn't the type to be all about the kissing and nothing else. She was too reserved for that, too elegant. I was the one who probably liked kissing a little too much.

"That's not like her," I finally said.

"I figured." He shifted from foot to foot. "And I kind of need to talk to her. Which is hard to do, even with nose plugs." Vampire pheromones were notorious for making humans befuddled and bewildered. Just as Nicholas sometimes wore his so he wouldn't be distracted by the smell of my blood, vampire hunters wore them so they couldn't be brainwashed by vampire pheromones. I was so used to them from growing up around the Drakes that I was mostly immune. So far.

"Talk to her about what?" I asked.

"I'm . . . uh . . . well, I'm going to college to finish my training. Now that the Helios-Ra is in good hands, I want to be a real agent. I don't want to coast on my family name."

I'd forgotten that he technically wasn't an official Helios-Ra agent. He'd dropped out of the last two years of his training to hunt down his father's killer, who he'd mistakenly assumed was a vampire, and a Drake at that.

"Well, good for you, I guess," I said. "I suppose you're not so bad for someone who was trying to kill my best friend and her entire family."

"I *never* tried to kill Solange," he argued. He paused. "The college is in Scotland."

I blinked. "You're *leaving*?" Could this day suck worse?

He shrugged. "Maybe."

"Have you told Solange yet?"

He shook his head. "I haven't had a chance."

"I can't know this kind of thing if she doesn't know! There's a code. You have to tell her." I waved my hands frantically at him. "Right now!"

"Don't you think I've tried?" he asked, frustrated. "I told you, there's not a lot of talking."

"Ew. Get your tongue out of her mouth and talk to her, dumbass."

He glared at me. "It's not that simple."

"It is too," I insisted. "I'm dating a vampire; I get it. They're yummy."

He sighed, looking a little embarrassed. His ears were actually red. "Lucy, you're practically immune to pheromones. I'm not. And Solange's are stronger than any vampire I've ever met. She's . . . different."

I wanted to kick something. I should know exactly what was

going on, why and how Solange was different. No amount of yoga was going to neutralize the anger and hurt burning inside me.

I fisted my hands. "Okay, look. I'm going to see Solange tomorrow night and I'm going to figure out what the hell's going on. You better talk to her first."

"How?" he asked helplessly.

I rolled my eyes. "Use the phone, idiot."

"Oh." He blinked, as if he'd never actually considered that. Honestly, boys. "I guess I could do that."

I just shook my head. "Some vampire hunter. Don't they teach you anything at that school?"

"You tell me. You're practically one of us now."

I gaped at him. "Am not!" He just grinned at my agitation. I stepped on his foot. It wasn't exactly effective since I was barefoot and he had his combat boots on. "Stop it."

He glanced at his phone when it trilled discreetly. "I gotta go. Another bulletin."

"What now?" I asked, trying to read the screen. He flicked it off and slipped it into his inside pocket. Spoilsport.

"Murder and mayhem, the usual. We're being run off our feet. The *Hel-Blar* are organizing."

"Is that even possible?"

"The blood chills." He grimaced, agreeing.

"They were at the beach earlier."

"I know. Hunter called it in."

"We heard some kind of whistle. And it actually scared them. That's weird, right?"

He nodded.

"Know what it is?"

"No."

"Damn."

"Yeah. So watch your back, hippie."

"You too, 007."

CHAPTER 9

◆

Christabel

The cafeteria was all scuffed linoleum, French fries, girls squealing, and guys laughing too loud. But with the help of a good novel, I was in a parlor lit by beeswax candles, with windows wreathed in a damp, menacing fog rolling off the moors. The chatter of voices became the crackling of a fire and the strains of a waltz played on a pianoforte by a girl in a dark dress. The plastic bench underneath me was actually a velvet sofa.

"There she goes." Lucy interrupted my travels, her voice sounding as if it were far away.

But not far enough.

"Earth to Christa." She grinned, slapping her lunch tray down onto the table. Green Jell-O wiggled alarmingly. She didn't look hung over, despite how drunk she claimed to be last night.

"Go away," I mumbled, trying not to lose my spot. I struggled to smell the wood smoke, to feel the tendrils of mist.

"Never mind her," Lucy assured her friends cheerfully. She'd introduced us before but I hadn't really been paying attention. I thought the guy was Nathan and the girl Linnet. Linnet had beautiful dark skin and blue eyes and didn't say much. Lucy was convinced that if I sat alone at lunch I might waste away from loneliness. I couldn't convince her that if I had a book with me, I wasn't lonely.

And it was ironic that *now* she wanted to talk to me. On the way to school she kept the music so loud my ears rang. She wouldn't answer a single question about last night.

"She's always like that when she's reading," she continued. "And she's *always* reading."

I peered at her over the top of my novel. "Does your mom know you eat Jell-O?" Aunt Cass thought white sugar, intolerance, and cell phones were the devil. In that order.

Lucy shot me a conspiratorial grin. "If you tell her I eat white sugar, I'll tell her you're antisocial and depressed at school. She'll make you hug."

"She wouldn't," I said, even though I knew she totally would.

Nathan snorted. "When I came out, she made me hug her," he confirmed. "And she baked me a cake."

"She baked you a cake?" I echoed. "For being gay?"

"A stevia-sweetened, organic, whole-wheat cake for being brave enough to come out," Lucy said proudly. I had to admit, Aunt Cass was kind of awesome in her own way. Only she could reclaim a coming-out tradition from the pages of one of my favorite novels and turn it on its head.

"What did she call it?" Nathan shook his head fondly. "An affirmation cake or something?" His hair was short and spiky, bleached bone white. "Your mom's cracked."

"Yup," Lucy agreed cheerfully.

"My mom's not nearly as cool. She cried for three days straight. Think yours'll adopt me?"

"Probably."

I stole a French fry off Lucy's plate. They were definitely not allowed in the Hamilton household, like the contraband Jell-O. "How come Nicholas and Solange don't go to school here?" I asked.

"Oh." Nathan and Linnet both sighed. "Nicholas." It was the most I'd heard Linnet say. She was quiet as a cat.

Lucy rolled her eyes. "Shut up, you two." She smirked at me. "They're totally crushing on my boyfriend. Nathan saw him last night at the lake and he hasn't shut up about it all day."

"He is yummy," Nathan said. "There is a definite dearth of hot guys at this school."

"The Drakes are homeschooled." Lucy answered my question before Nathan could really sink into a tangent. Connor had told me he'd been homeschooled too. It must be some kind of family tradition.

"You're still bringing him to prom, right?" Nathan asked.

Lucy groaned. "You're as bad as my mom with the prom stuff."

"I just think he'll look good in a tux."

"Stop drooling." Lucy pointed her finger at him. "And get your own date."

"Oh, all right," he grumbled good-naturedly. "He has brothers, right?"

"Yes, like a gazillion of them. But I don't know if any of them play for your team."

"Well, find out, woman."

"What am I supposed to do, take a survey?"

"If you were a real friend," Nathan said primly, but his eyes twinkled.

"Got your little friend pimping for you, queerbait?" someone sneered from behind us. Nathan went red in the face. Linnet looked like she wanted to crawl under the table.

Lucy leaped to her feet, her fists clenched. "Shut up, Peter."

I turned my head slowly, flicking him the most disdainful glance I could muster, then I turned my back as if he wasn't worth my time. And he so wasn't. Peter just laughed with his friends. Bullies.

If there's one thing I hate, it's a bully.

I'd nearly had to deal with Social Services because a bully shot her mouth off at school after my dad died. Sara and I had to work on a school project, and when she came over, my mother was drunk. She told everyone at school the next day, and the day after that, until even one of the teachers was asking me if everything was all right at home. Sara didn't stop until I burst into tears in the lunch line in front of everyone. It wasn't until I flushed her favorite bra down the toilet after gym class that she finally left me alone.

"Just ignore them," Nathan said quietly.

Lucy was the color of pickled beets beside him. He, on the other hand, looked perfectly calm.

"Yeah, *Lucky*," Peter guffawed. "At least queerbait here knows when he's whipped."

I thought Lucy was actually going to jump right over the table, littered with empty chocolate milk cartons and lunch trays.

Apparently, since the last time I'd visited, Lucy had decided she was a ninja.

Only Nathan was able to stop her. He put his hand on her arm. "Don't," he said mildly.

"But . . ." She glared at Peter. "I really want to."

"Please. Just don't, Luce."

Peter and his winged monkeys got bored and drifted to another table. Nathan pushed away from his chair and stood up. His ears were red but his expression hadn't changed. Lucy hovered at his elbow, scowling.

"I don't need a bodyguard," he told her.

"Do too," she insisted mutinously. "And I could have taken him. I'm taking self-defense classes. I could have made him cry."

Nathan half smiled. "You're scary enough without the classes."

"Why does everyone keep saying that?" she wondered out loud.

"Can we just go now?" Linnet asked, still looking as if she wanted to cry. "People are staring."

Lucy put her hands on her hips. "So?"

"So, Nathan hates that."

Lucy deflated quickly; if she'd been a helium balloon she would have careened through the cafeteria. She still might. "Oh." She winced at Nathan sheepishly. "Sorry, Nate."

"It's okay."

She glanced at me. "Are you coming?"

I shook my head. "I'll catch up."

I knew Peter. He was in twelfth grade, like me, and he was a jerk. He belonged in one of those John Hughes movies from the eighties that Lucy loved so much. I slowed my pace as I approached his table, carrying my plastic cup full of soda. He was talking too loudly, as usual.

"What a loser," he half shouted. "We should key his car."

"He rides his bike to school," one of his friends said.

"Figures. Fag."

That did it.

I was so used to keeping my grades up and my head down so as not to attract the attention of the school counselor that I usually fumed quietly to myself.

Not today.

Maybe not ever again, if Mom's treatment went well.

After all, the worst had happened. Her secret was out. I didn't have to stay quietly in the background anymore if I didn't want to.

And right now, I really didn't want to.

I couldn't help but think about a story I'd just read about Percy Bysshe Shelley when he was at school. Someone picked on him until he finally jammed his fork through the guy's hand and into the table underneath.

If a cherubic blond poet in a cravat could kick ass, so could I.

Besides, I'd never gotten detention before, and there was something liberating about having that option. Plus, Nathan shouldn't have to deal with Peter's homophobic crap all year. Anyone could see Peter wasn't going to let up. Also, Peter's shirt gaped away from the back of his neck just enough. And there were a lot of ice cubes in my cup.

Perfect.

I tipped my drink, spilling the cold, sticky soda down the back of Peter's neck, making sure most of it dribbled into his shirt.

He screamed like a little girl at her first horror movie.

Even more perfect.

He pawed at his back while simultaneously scrambling to his feet, scattering his lunch tray and knocking over his chair. Everyone turned to stare. The silence cracked like an egg, spilling laughter. Someone clapped. Peter whirled on me, rage making him sputter.

"What the hell, you bitch!" He took a threatening step forward. He was really tall and as wide as an ox. And clearly used to people backing away from him in fear. When I didn't move, only lifted an eyebrow, he looked briefly confused.

I smiled, showing a lot of teeth, like an angry badger. "Oops," I said insincerely.

"You are so dead," he seethed while our audience kept laughing.

I tilted my head obnoxiously and batted my eyelashes. "Ooh. Scary."

He stepped in so close to me that I had to crane my neck back to look up at him. "New girl, you just made the biggest mistake."

"Seriously?" I asked. "Who writes your dialogue?"

When even his friends laughed, he reached for me. His hand dug into my arm, wrinkling my favorite T-shirt and bruising the skin underneath.

I kneed him right in the crotch.

He squeaked, doubled over, and then lost his balance entirely when I shrugged off his grip. One of the teachers rushed toward us, blowing her whistle. She did not look impressed.

I tried not to smirk but failed. She pointed at me. "You. Principal's office. Now."

I put down my empty cup, pulled my copy of *Jane Eyre* from the back pocket of my jeans, where I'd kept it safe from soda spills, and nodded politely. "Yes, Mrs. Copperfield."

Lucy was in the hall on the other side of the glass, grinning wildly and bouncing on her toes like a little kid.

I grinned back.

◆

The stern lectures, disapproving head shakes, and threats of spoiled school records were way more brutal than detention could ever be. And they were nothing compared to what my pacifist aunt and uncle would do when I got home. They didn't believe in violence, ever, for any reason. But then, they'd never met Peter. I had a feeling that fact wouldn't be worth much to them.

I managed, barely, to talk myself out of anger management classes and Peter *into* a tolerance seminar. I planned to use that later to diffuse any mention of being grounded. Not that I could go out after dark anyway. I mean, look at last night. We'd finally been allowed out and then Lucy and her friends got weird.

Also, the principal was impressed with my obviously beloved copy of *Jane Eyre* and my straight As. No one tells you that if you get really good grades, adults are sometimes willing to overlook a little badly placed attitude.

"Are we clear, Ms. Llewellyn?" The principal drummed his fingers on his desk. I wanted to tell him his tie clashed horribly with his shirt. Instead, I just nodded.

"Yes, Mr. Ainsley."

"I don't want to see you in here again."

"Yes, Mr. Ainsley."

"You're a bright girl, Christabel. I know moving to a new school in your last year can't be easy, but I'd hate for you to sabotage your future."

Oh God, the "future" speech. "Yes, Mr. Ainsley."

I think I said that about six more times before he finally let me go. Lucy was waiting for me at my locker. "That was so cool," she gushed.

I tossed my extra binders into my locker. "That guy just really bugs me."

"Last year he gave Nathan a black eye." Lucy scowled. "But Nathan's all 'ignore them' or 'kill them with kindness.'" She huffed out an impatient breath. "That just takes way too long."

"Dude," an eighth grader interrupted us, eyes wide. "Is it true you busted Peter's legs?"

"No."

Lucy grinned. "But it'll hurt for him to pee for the rest of the day."

"Cool," he returned. "He once held my head in the toilet." He looked at me adoringly, as if he had cartoon hearts for eyeballs. Awkward. I stared back.

"Go away," I finally had to tell him. He fled.

"He's totally crushing on you now." Lucy chuckled.

"Lucky me."

"And you're, like, the school hero." She was entirely too happy about it.

"Hero with detention." I shut my locker door. "Starting tonight."

"Already?"

"Yeah, there's some parent-teacher thing for the ninth grade. I have to help set up chairs or something." I wrinkled my nose. "Think your mom will freak?"

"About detention, no. About using physical violence to solve your problems? Definitely," she confirmed. "Oh, and there'll be a poster of Gandhi on the back of your door by tomorrow. The man, not the dog."

I blinked. "Um, why?"

"It's Mom's very unsubtle reminder that nonviolence can change the world, blah, blah, blah. You're supposed to imagine Gandhi looking at you the next time you lose your temper."

"Creepy."

"Yeah. I've had my poster since second grade. I used to have nightmares that he was so hungry he'd try to eat my head like an apple," she said, shuddering. "But you can talk her down some if you mention Nathan. She loves him."

"Cool."

She paused. "Oh, but I'm going to Solange's tonight."

"Okay." I wasn't following the abrupt topic change.

"So it'll be dark when you finally get out of here. These parent-teacher things don't usually start until seven thirty."

I rolled my eyes. "This curfew thing is stupid, Lucy. I'm from the *city*. You know, where there's actual crime and stuff?"

"I know." She bit her lip for a moment and then brightened. "You can take my car home. Mom's working today, so I'll just go over there after school and get a lift home with her. Dad's got the snowplow on the truck already, so no one's allowed to drive it. But I can take Mom's car to the Drakes'."

"Okay. Thanks."

She handed me her keys. "Are you kidding? I've been wanting to kick Peter since I was thirteen."

"About last night," I said. "What were you guys on?"

"Nothing!"

I knew she was hiding something. I could just tell. I'd had enough experience sorting through my mom's lies. "Lucy."

"I gotta go!" she practically yelled before turning on her heel and running down the hall. I sighed and went to math class. Peter wasn't at his desk. I should probably have felt bad about that.

Oh well.

◆

As it turns out, detention is boring.

I helped the janitor set out rows and rows of chairs, fetched plastic cups, and made punch, and when they'd exhausted the normal errands, I had to clean the whiteboards in all the classrooms. Even detention was wholesome in this backwoods town. On the plus side, by the time the parents started to arrive, I was allowed to go home.

The parking lot was filled with cars and parents in sensible shoes and sweaty, nervous-looking students. The sky was dark, with a thin line of lilac in the west. The mountains were already black, but I still felt them there, tall and stately. Most of Main Street was closed up except for the cafes and a bookstore. I would have stopped if I wasn't in enough trouble already. I rolled down the windows and the cool evening air was full of smoke and pine needles and apple trees. I loved October.

I did not love Lucy's car.

At a stop sign just outside town, it stalled. It didn't even have the decency to stop under a streetlight or by a restaurant where I could drink cappuccinos and wait for a tow truck. I got out of the car, turning up the collar of my jacket as a light rain began to fall.

"Perfect," I muttered. I popped the hood and peered inside. I had no idea what I was looking at. If the engine had been a haiku, I'd have been perfectly able to fix it. I slammed the hood shut again as the wind picked up. It smelled worse out here, like mud and rotting vegetation. Deserted roads and crumbling, abandoned farmhouses were creepy, way creepier than biker bars and that homeless guy downtown who threw soda cans at you when you walked by.

"I hate this town," I grumbled to myself, slipping back into the warm car. I reached for my bag to get my cell phone.

Just as someone reached for me.

"Lucky," a gravelly voice said.

I jerked back, my heart leaping into my throat and taking up all available space so that it was impossible to open my mouth and scream. I swallowed. "I'm not—"

"Sleep now." A puff of white powder wafted toward me. I coughed frantically. Was it anthrax? Some kind of drug? Who the hell did that? I struggled to let anger and fear burn through the fog settling like sticky spiderwebs over my eyes and my legs and my mouth.

And I could have sworn that the man was blue.

CHAPTER 10

♦

Lucy

I left a little early just to avoid more of my mom's well-meaning lectures and fretting. She knew I'd be safe on the Drake compound; it was nearly a thousand acres of protected lands and I'd been going there since I was a kid. I'd driven by two guards already. But everything was different now.

No one knew that better than me.

I assumed I'd be there first and would have to wait for Solange. She sometimes needed an hour or two after sunset to fill up on blood so the thirst didn't hurt so much. I had my iPod, homework I had no intention of doing, and Gandhi in the passenger seat—smearing the window with his big wet nose. I'd climb into the old oak tree and enjoy a rare, safe moment to myself at night, able to count the stars and make up my own constellations.

The main trunk of the tree was gnarled and thick enough to support three main branches. It looked as if the oak had split in three. One of those branches dipped all the way down to the ground, like a swing made of bark and green leaves and littering acorns all around. If you painted it with glitter, it wouldn't look out of place in a Tim Burton movie.

Solange was already perched in it like an exhausted cheetah. She was on a higher branch we'd never yet managed to climb, lying on her stomach, her long hair drifting down like a crow's broken wing. She was pale enough to look like starlight. And she was wearing sunglasses.

"What, are you a rock star now?" I teased, trying to keep the conversation light. "Wearing sunglasses at night?" I felt a new tension between us and I didn't like it. It was unrecognizable and hung oddly, like a dress that didn't fit.

She didn't move and didn't take them off. "My eyes hurt."

I knew she was lying. I hated that most of all. I dropped my bag and leaned back against the branch, looking up at her. I didn't smile. "Wow, you're a really bad liar."

She sighed, looking faintly pained and more like herself, before the cool mask settled back onto her features. "I'm fine."

"I didn't ask," I shot back drily.

She half smiled. "You're the only one not to ask me that every five minutes."

I folded my arms, feeling slightly vindicated. "Remember that."

"I'm sorry, Luce," she whispered, so softly I almost didn't hear her over the dry rattle of leaves and the tall grass as a light rain pattered around us. We stayed dry in our oak throne.

"I just don't get why you're shutting me out." I sounded hurt even to my own ears.

"Because I don't want to hurt you."

"Hello? You already have," I snapped. "So get over it and tell me what's going on."

She looked at me for a long, weird moment before rolling off the branch, dangling from her fingertips, and landing gracefully next to me. The branch barely swayed. She'd always been graceful, but since she'd turned into a vampire, it was like she was made of porcelain, hard and perfect. She'd have hated that comparison, but it was apt.

At least until she slipped off her glasses.

Even Nicholas didn't look that bad after we'd made out a little too long.

Her eyes were the same pale blue, but the whites were traced with red, like the veins of a leaf before it falls off the tree in autumn. It was strangely beautiful, in a menacing way. Christabel would have turned it into poetry. I just winced. "Oh, Sol. Does it hurt?"

"Not really. Not anymore."

"Do your teeth hurt?"

"A little."

She had three sets of fangs now, more than when I'd last seen her. Only the *Hel-Blar* were feral enough to have multiple sets of fangs; even most of the Hounds had only two pairs. Certainly none of the Drakes I knew of had any more than the usual single pair—including Solange's cousin London, and she was really beastly.

"Oh!" I exclaimed suddenly. "Did Kieran talk to you?" Because that was way more important than extra teeth.

"The Scotland thing, right?"

"Yeah, that." She didn't sound nearly as upset as I'd thought she would. "I mean, that's really far. For, like, two years."

Not that I wanted her to cry or anything, but some kind of reaction would have been nice.

She lifted her chin. Her eyes glinted like an animal's, like a wolf's. "I could make him stay."

Not *that* reaction.

I went cold in a way I'd never felt before. "Sol?"

She shrugged one shoulder and slipped her sunglasses on. "I'm just saying."

"Yeah, and it's kind of creepy."

"I can't help my pheromones. And I'm kind of tired of trying."

"Dude, if you start wearing a tiara and make everyone call you Your Highness, I will mock you."

She snorted out a surprised and entirely unprincesslike chuckle.

"Thank God," I said fervently. "You're back."

"Oh, Luce." Her shoulders slumped. "It's all so messed up."

"I know." I poked her, hard. "And you're not making it any better by being all secretive and emo. It's pissing me off."

"You know, there are some people who are afraid of me," she pointed out loftily, but she was smiling.

"Yeah, well, they never saw you laugh so hard spaghetti came out of your nose." I grinned back. "I own you, Drake."

We leaned against the trunk, watching a couple of bats weave and drop as they caught mosquitoes. The rain felt far away.

Solange made a face. "I hate those things."

"What, bats?"

"They're everywhere. It's like they're following me."

"Ew."

"Yeah." She was as pale as an opal, with thin, translucent veins like blue fire inside her wrists. She rubbed at them. "I don't want to turn blue," she said. "And I don't want Uncle Geoffrey taking more blood from me or running experiments and frowning the way he does when he's puzzled. I don't *want* to be a puzzle," she said hotly. "And I *really* don't want to smell like mushrooms."

I sniffed. "You smell like wood smoke and roses," I assured her. "Same as always."

"Promise you'll tell me if that changes."

"I will if you stop avoiding me. And I think the gagging would probably give me away."

"You're such a comfort to me, yakbreath."

"Right back at you, snotface."

We grinned at each other the way we had since we were four years old. Another bat dipped into view, a little closer than I liked. I leaned farther into the tree.

"Okay, one's cute. But that's my limit." The sound of leathery wings surrounded us. I pulled the collar of my shirt up. Even Gandhi looked disconcerted.

"Um, Solange?"

"Yeah?"

"Let's get the hell out of here!" I ran, ducking my head down. The tall grass feathered around my knees and the rain rattled in the dry oak leaves. The bats were like a dark thundercloud, about to release teeth and rabies and God only knew what else.

"If one of those things gets in my hair, I'm going to freak right the hell out." Gandhi was at my heels. Solange was a blur behind me, trying to keep pace, slowing down and speeding back up. She would have been waiting for me at the car already if she let herself go. And her lungs weren't burning like mine.

She stopped so fast, the grass flattened around her. I was on the other side of the car, my hand on the door. Solange turned so that she was facing the approaching bats, the way she'd have faced an opponent with a rapier. She was slender and standing sideways, to make a smaller target. I paused.

"What are you doing?" I asked frantically. "Get in the car!" I opened the back door for Gandhi. He at least, was smart enough to jump in.

"Wait," she murmured softly. The moon was a pearl behind the clouds, the light faintly blue and glinting off the embroidery on Solange's black tank top. The rain was cold in my hair.

And the bats were still coming straight for us.

I had no idea if bats attacked and I really, really didn't want to wait around and find out.

"I kind of hate you right now," I muttered at her. I couldn't just get in the car and leave her to fend for herself. I had to stand there and wait for my face to be gnawed on by tiny bats. Standard BFF rules.

Solange lifted her hand, palm out. She looked like a ballerina directing traffic.

The bats paused, hovered. The sound of so many wings made the hairs on the back of my neck stand up. The bats were still aloft but they didn't come any closer.

"How are you doing that?"

"I have no idea," she answered between her teeth.

She flicked her wrist and the bats whirled as one and flew away in the direction she'd pointed, toward the mountain. When she finally turned around to look at me, her eyes were huge. "Okay, that was weird."

I stared. "We could totally hire you to do special effects on Halloween." I shuddered. "Can we get in the car now?"

I didn't wait for an answer and launched myself into the front seat. I ducked down to look at her through the window. "Are you getting in or what?"

She looked uncertain. She bit her lower lip, the way she used to when she was nervous, forgetting she had fangs now. One of them nicked through her skin. Blood smeared like ghoulish lipstick. She licked it away.

"I don't think I should, Lucy."

"I have nose plugs." I kept a stash of them in my glove compartment for Nicholas. I reached over and flipped it open. I stopped. "In my car," I amended. "I forgot I'm driving Mom's. And—oh my God," I muttered when a condom fell out onto the floor mat. "My mother is out of control."

"Is that a *condom?*"

"Don't even ask." I slammed the glove compartment shut again. "And watch your stuff the next time you come over. She'll totally sneak them into your coat and your bag."

She blinked. "She's doing with condoms what my mom does with stakes?"

"Definitely. Okay, back to the matter at hand." I grinned. "You could stick your head out the window like the dog."

"I don't think so."

"Come on, Sol. Don't wimp out on me now—it's still early. And you owe me."

"Okay, okay." She climbed onto the roof of the car and smirked at me through the sunroof. "But I'll ride up here."

I shrugged. "You'll get wet."

"Better that than bugs up my nose."

"I doubt the cops will think so. And you're so paying any reckless driving ticket I get."

"We'll stay on the property. Head to the end of the lane by the marshes. We can walk from there. It's only half an hour or so."

I started the engine. "Cool. Who are we spying on?"

"What makes you think we're spying?"

"Please, all of our good slumber parties involve spying of some kind."

"True."

"So?"

"You'll see."

Gandhi wasn't too proud to hang his head out the window and try to bite the wind as we rumbled down the dirt road. After about fifteen minutes it narrowed into a lane and then stopped altogether. There was a wall of pine trees in front of us and marshy wetlands on our left. I hopped out, pulling on my jacket and putting up the hood. Solange landed lightly and rose out of her crouch, smiling. She was totally showing off now.

"Yeah, yeah," I grumbled at her good-naturedly. "Let's go already."

Pine needles crunched under my feet. The rain made everything sparkle but it was relatively dry under all the branches. The night glowed green and ferns swayed all around us. Gandhi trotted happily in front, stopping once to stick his entire head in a blackberry bush. Solange sniffed once, then frowned. She could probably smell moss growing now. An owl sang a soft, haunting song above us, brief and as old as the stars. It was a perfect autumn night.

You know, without the rotting severed blue hands dangling from the pines like deranged Christmas tree ornaments.

I gagged on the sudden waft of slimy mushrooms and stagnant pond water. I swallowed. "Okay, *gross.*"

Solange turned on her heel slowly, peering into the shadows. "I think we're alone." She sniffed once. "They don't smell fresh."

I tried not to throw up. "Seriously, who *does* that?" *Hel-Blar* were nasty, no question about it. They were even nastier dismembered. I backed away a few steps. "Helios-Ra?" I should reconsider my new self-defense classes.

Solange shook her head, decoding whatever it was she could see in the mud and the dried pine needles. "I don't think so. There are virtually no tracks. Only vampires can move so fast they practically float."

"Well, crap. Aren't we on Drake land?"

"Not here, no. I'll call it in." She sighed at her phone. "No signal out here. I forgot. They chose the most secluded glade they could for the Blood Moon."

"The Blood Moon?" I perked up, despite the macabre decorations around us. Humans were rare at a Blood Moon festival, and even then only when approved by a vampire tribe's ruler. I'd already been told there was no way the Drakes were bringing me. "Are you serious? I didn't think it was for another week at least."

"They've been prepping since the date was set," Solange said. "And some of the dignitaries have already begun to arrive from all over the world."

"Okay, that's freaking cool," I confirmed. "You're definitely forgiven. You can emo all you want." I grimaced at the hands. "You might want new decorations, though. These aren't exactly classy."

"Someone's killing *Hel-Blar*. They chop off their hands before they dust them so that everyone else knows about it," Solange said. "Mom would say they're a war trophy. And war trophies are a warning, especially when they're displayed so obviously like this."

"Also? Not very hygienic." I couldn't help but imagine them grabbing at me. "Can we get out of here?"

We hurried away while I tried to figure out how I was going to avoid nightmares tonight. I was really glad Christabel was safe at home, reading some boring book written two hundred years ago and hadn't gone out on one of her hikes. I did that shudder-dance you do when you think there's a spider crawling on you. I felt like there were about a hundred of them. Talk about having your Spidey sense tingle.

The rest of the walk was decidedly less picturesque. I couldn't get my shoulders to untense, and I kept expecting to find more *Hel-Blar* body parts.

"Lucy, I can hear you grinding your teeth from here," Solange whispered.

"I can't help it. That was totally disgusting."

"I know, but you'll alert the—" She stopped as a vampire dropped out of a tree in front of us. "Guards," she finished drily.

"Princess." He nodded smartly. There was a row of stakes on his belt and on a strap across his chest. "No humans," he said kindly to me.

I frowned. "That's racist. Or species-ist, whatever."

"No, just safer, little girl."

His hair was long and white and there were crinkles around his eyes. He looked like somebody's grandfather out of *Braveheart*.

Solange stepped close to him, closer than she usually stood near anyone.

"It's all right," Solange murmured. "You can rest for a while."

He suddenly looked sleepy. He struggled not to close his eyes. Even though I was mostly immune to vampire pheromones, I found myself yawning. I plugged my nose. Gandhi whined.

Solange hadn't been kidding when she said her pheromones were getting stronger. They weren't supposed to work on other vampires. That was why the new Helios-Ra Hypnos drug was in such hot demand—it offered a temporary hypnotic effect on vampires.

But Solange clearly didn't need any.

The guard sagged and Solange dragged him into a clump of cedars.

"Sol, doesn't he work for your family?" I asked, noticing the royal crest on his shirt before the brush swallowed him. My voice came out nasally because I was still pinching my nose closed.

"Yeah, but he never would have let us sneak in. And you wanted to spy, didn't you?" Solange shrugged. "Now we can."

I knew he wasn't hurt, but the way Solange was so cavalier about vamping him made my stomach feel like it were full of acid and insects.

"Let's go," she said impatiently.

I followed, trying to ignore the flutter of fear inside my chest.

But I knew she could hear it.

CHAPTER II

◆

Christabel

When I woke up, the man was still blue.

Which didn't make sense at all.

But neither did the way everything was smearing together like a wet oil painting, or the antique gold quality to the light, thick with dust motes. Even the floor underneath my palms was faded wood, like something you'd find in a pioneer cabin, especially with the iron woodstove and kettle in the corner.

Clearly I'd read so much historical fiction I'd made myself crazy.

Except I couldn't think of a single historical time period, or even a novel for that matter, with blue-skinned people.

And really, instead of running through the index of literary trivia in my head (*Jane Eyre*, red room; *Crime and Punishment*, yellow as an unlucky color . . .), I should have been focusing on the fact that someone had drugged me and kidnapped me. Nothing else explained the hallucinations or the weird white powder. I wondered again, horrified, if it were anthrax. Wasn't that supposed to be a white powder? But who the hell roamed tiny hick towns dosing unsuspecting girls with anthrax? And didn't it have something to do with cows?

I recited some of Alfred Noyes's "The Highwayman" to calm myself. "'They said no word to the landlord, they drank his ale instead, But they gagged his daughter and bound her to the foot of her narrow bed; Two of them knelt at her casement, with muskets at their side! There was death at every window—'"

Nope, definitely not calming right now.

I fumbled for my cell phone, dialing 911 before my eyes focused enough to see that I didn't have a signal. Of course.

I would have cried but my head hurt like the very devil. That line sounded vaguely familiar, like it was from an old book. *Pride and Prejudice*, maybe. That was comforting. Less comforting was that I couldn't remember *which* book it was from. I *always* remembered stuff like that. I was proud of my reserve of literary and historical details, even if it hadn't proven particularly useful so far. It certainly hadn't saved me from getting abducted.

I shut my eyes again, hearing movement. Fear made me feel fuzzy and blurry inside, as if I were filled with air instead of blood and bone. I clamped my jaws down on a mew of panic when footsteps sounded. My eyelids fluttered, trying to open even as I forced them to stay closed. It didn't make the fear any less acidic in my mouth; I hurt all over with the need to see. But I wanted to be left alone even more. I hoped, vainly, that if the blue man thought I was still unconscious, he'd leave. Then I could figure out how to escape.

"You needn't bother," he said softly, much closer than I'd thought he was. "I can hear your pulse, child, and I know you're awake."

I didn't know what to do. He might be testing me, just to see if I was conscious yet. I smelled something like wet earth. It was impossible not to think about dank, dark dungeons. My chest burned as I tried not to gasp or scream or give myself away.

"You'll want to breathe," he added calmly, as if he were offering me tea and crumpets. "If you don't want to swoon."

I opened my eyes, but only because he used the word "swoon." It was old-fashioned, out of a Victorian novel.

He wasn't.

He wore a cream-colored linen shirt, old jeans, and a wampum belt that he must have stolen from some museum. His hair was long and brown and tied back with a piece of rawhide. He might have been handsome, if he weren't a psychopath.

And very faintly *blue*.

Also, we were in a one-room cabin with wooden walls shrunken with age. There were shelves of old bottles and a layer of dust as thick as icing on a cake. I rubbed my eyes, even though moving my arms felt like lifting bricks and boulders wrapped in wet cement. No amount of retina friction changed the fact that he was blue. And his eyes were really bloodshot.

He crouched down in front of me. I scrabbled backward so fast I hit my head on the wall.

"What do you want?" I croaked, my throat so tight with fear it felt like I'd been eating knives.

"You're safe, Lucky. We're not planning to hurt you."

"I'm not Lucky."

He smiled a little. "We know your car."

I'd been right to hate Lucy's car. Her parents hadn't been paranoid with their curfew. Now it was too late to tell them I was glad they took me in. Too late to decide if I wanted to be a poet or a tattoo artist. If I wanted to go to college right away or travel and see London and France and Prague first. Too late to see my mother sober.

Like hell.

I didn't think; I just bolted into motion. My stomach went one way and my head felt like it went in the opposite direction. I wasn't about to let dizziness or fatigue stop me. I was going to reach that door and then I was going to run down the street, screaming at the top of my lungs until someone stopped to help me.

I didn't even make it halfway across the room.

The man was suddenly in front of me. I careened right into him, bruising the tip of my nose on his collarbone. I noticed a scar, long and old enough to look like puckered satin.

He sighed. "I wish you hadn't done that."

His hands were on my elbows, trying to steady me. I risked a glance. Bad idea. He had way too many teeth. And some of them seemed to be getting longer. And sharper. If they got any sharper I'd start hearing the *Jaws* theme song in my head. I blinked, telling myself not to panic and not to get distracted. I'd probably activated the last of the drug in my system by running, and that plus the adrenaline pumping suddenly through me was making me hallucinate. It sounded very scientific and logical.

It still felt like gibbering, mind-numbing terror, though.

I opened my mouth to scream and lifted my foot to kick.

"Don't."

Something about the way he spoke, about his strange smell, made my mouth snap shut. I felt light-headed again. I actually leaned toward him. That couldn't be a good thing. I knew I was terrified, but it didn't seem to bother me. I felt kind of sleepy and languid, like I'd just had a really long, hot bath.

"You should know not to run when faced with a vampire, Lucky."

Vampire. I giggled. Then I blinked, as shocked by that as by anything else that had happened to me tonight. I never giggled.

"Vampires don't exist," I told him. Even my tongue felt weird in my mouth, like it was swollen. "I feel funny."

"Pheromones. It will fade." He frowned. "There's no use pretending you don't know about us. We know about *you*."

My head felt too heavy and it lolled back, exposing my neck. He licked his lips.

"You're as reckless as they say." His voice was soft, hungry.

"Huh?" I sounded like my mother after too much gin. That thought alone cut through the peach-fuzz, overexposed feel of everything around me. It was like being dunked in cold water. I even shivered. Then I clenched my fists, digging my nails into the palms of my hands, clearing the pain in my head. The smell of wet earth intensified. I gagged.

His eyes weren't just bloodshot; they practically glowed. They were mesmerizing, like sunlight hitting rubies. I dug my nails harder into my palms with enough force that they drew blood. I felt the sting when sweat ran into the cuts. It pushed a little more of the fog away.

Which just left more room for the swamp smell.

The man didn't seem to notice. He just inhaled deeper, as if tantalizing cookies were coming right out of the oven. "You're bleeding."

Something about the way he said it made me jerk backward, but he was still holding me in place. His fingers didn't move at all, just encircled my arms like steel chains. I knew I'd have bruises later. Assuming there *was* a later.

"It smells . . . wait." He stopped and frowned. "You smell . . . wrong."

"That's not me, asshat, that's you." There. That was more like me. I clenched my hands tighter.

"Stop," he said, nearly as a plea. He sniffed again. "There's only the barest trace of the Drakes on you. That doesn't make sense."

"That's what doesn't make sense? Hello? You're blue! And a kidnapper! And dude, you should see a dentist."

"You keep to this deception?" He sounded mildly surprised. "Even now?"

"What deception? I *told* you, I'm not Lucy."

He stared at me for a long moment, then took my hand and forced my fingers to uncurl. My palm lay exposed, covered with tiny drops of blood like red glass beads. I tried to pull back but his hold tightened on my wrist.

"Stay still," he added, and his eyes were beautiful again. He was carved out of pale marble, mysterious and primal. He made me think of hunters and arrows and deer broken in the woods. When he lowered his head and lapped at my blood, I made only a small mew of protest. "You don't taste of them, either," he said softly, his dangerous teeth stained red. "And you are not immune to me."

"Why, are you sick? Or contagious or something?" I wondered out loud. Of course he was sick. He was tasting my blood. "Oh God," I said. In my head it sounded sharp and derisive but it came out dreamy and floaty. "Is this some weird vampire cult? Is that why you think I'm Lucy?" I concentrated on that instead of the fact that I was letting him run his tongue along my other palm. "Look, I know she's into those books and movies and stuff, but she's not nuts. She wouldn't fall for this, either. She knows vampires aren't real."

He actually blanched, which was weird considering his color. "You're really not her."

"I'm really not."

He dropped my hands so fast, I felt the muscles in my shoulders snap.

"That is a problem," he said darkly. He was still between me and the door, which suddenly opened. I hadn't heard anyone approaching and I barely heard anyone now. Her feet didn't make a sound. If I hadn't been looking at the door, I wouldn't have known she was even there. I stumbled back a step.

"Saga," he said, which I assumed was her name. She had long red hair, which should have clashed with her pale blue skin but somehow didn't. Her eyes were gray, almost glittering. She wore a black skirt with a ragged hem and a kind of silver breastplate-corset, molded to her chest and engraved with spirals and vine motifs. She looked like a pirate, except she was barefoot. And her teeth were just as sharp as the wooden stakes and jeweled daggers strapped all over her body. She even had a cutlass on her belt.

"Aidan, is this her?" Her voice belonged to a queen, but her eyes belonged to the forest, or a badger's den. In fact, a long hood hung down her back, edged with fur. I was starting to feel dizzy again. I was scared and confused and I just wanted to wake up from this drug-induced nightmare. I opened my mouth to let out the loudest, most bloodcurdling, glass-shattering shriek I could muster. I had barely begun when she spoke.

"Avast."

Her steely voice made the scream die painfully in my throat. Her silver eyes were like pins inserted into delicate butterfly wings; I might as well have been a specimen tacked to a velvet board for her collection.

"You have to know no one would hear you," she said. "You are most strange. I would expect someone under the protection of the Drakes to be quick-witted."

She'd just called me stupid. "Hey."

"That's the thing," Aidan interrupted. "She's not Lucky Hamilton."

Saga's pale, flower-fairy face burned with rage, but the fury came and went so fast it could have been a trick of the faint light from the single oil lamp. "Who are you then, lass?" she asked.

"Christabel."

"And what are you to the Drakes?" She was ominous, violent, like a sudden mudslide sweeping away half a town's oldest houses.

"Nothing." I thought of Connor and Nicholas and wondered just what the hell they were into.

"That is unfortunate."

It suddenly *felt* unfortunate. *Very* unfortunate.

"She knows Lucky. I think they're kin."

"Is this about drugs?" I asked lamely, remembering the jar in Lucy's hallway last night. I looked around, eyes uncomfortably wide as I fought an inexplicable surge of fatigue. I searched but couldn't see any drug paraphernalia, not that I actually knew what it would look like. My mother was strictly into liquor. But if this were a drug lab, surely I'd be able to tell?

"She was driving Lucy's car," Aidan explained apologetically.

"Son of a bitch."

While they stared at each other, I took the opportunity to dart out the open door. I nearly broke my ankle avoiding a rotten floorboard. When I leaped off the porch onto the dirt road, I should have kept running for my life—mountain lions, forest snows, and my utter lack of direction be damned. But I couldn't move. I could only stare as a creature shuffled out onto the deserted street.

He was a deeper, more vibrant blue than Aidan and Saga, and he had even more teeth. When the wind shifted I got a mouthful of his smell: not just mushrooms but rotting mushrooms, not just damp but stagnant swamp. I gagged. Something about the way he moved made my hands clench and sweat soak the back of my shirt.

He didn't say anything, just licked his lips. His eyes caught the faint light from the moon when the clouds parted. He inhaled deeply and snapped his jaws again, saliva dripping from his teeth.

Then he came at me, snarling.

And I knew I couldn't outrun him.

I tried anyway.

I whirled, trying to get back to the relative safety of the porch and the broken house and the slightly less crazy, less blue people inside.

I didn't make it.

He grabbed my hand, yanking me backward as I was running forward. My shoulder jerked painfully. I screamed. I was locked in place, twisted unnaturally, and he was trying to *lick* my hand.

Gross.

And weird.

I pulled harder, feeling sharp, sudden fear in every part of my body—my head, my knees, my spleen, and, most of all, my stinging hands.

And then Aidan was there, faster, stronger, and crazier. He grabbed the blue man's wrist and broke it, snapping it as easily as if it were a dry twig. The man howled. Something howled back in response from behind one of the buildings, and it wasn't a wolf. It wasn't animal or human. And it wasn't alone.

"One of the whelps got loose, did it?" Aidan said, his hands suddenly full of slender, sharpened sticks. No, not sticks. Stakes. One caught the man in the neck and, as he jerked back, another caught him in the chest. Aidan used the heel of his hand to shove the stake through skin and flesh and bone. My stomach threatened to turn inside out.

But it had to wait while my brain threatened the same thing, because the creature clutched at his chest, gurgling in pain before he crumbled into ashes. He looked like soot and crushed embers in the dirt. My vision wavered and my shoulder ached. I trembled all over. Aidan kept me in place, his hand on my wrist. I prayed he wouldn't break it, too.

The howling continued, louder, more high-pitched, as frantic as disembodied howling could get. Saga marched out to the edge of the porch and blew a wooden whistle.

The howling ceased, as sharp in its silence as it had been in its clamor.

CHAPTER 12

◆

Connor

Nicholas and I were patrolling in the forest near the road into town when my bike broke down. Computers I can handle, cars and bikes not so much. We were well off Drake land, miles away really, but there were so many *Hel-Blar* around and with the Blood Moon approaching, we couldn't afford to take chances. We hadn't made the *Hel-Blar*—they weren't technically our mess to clean up—but it would look bad if we didn't. Not to mention, people might get eaten.

"Could be the battery cables," Nicholas said. He lifted the seat and then shook his head. "They seem fine." He tightened them anyway and then dropped the seat back down and turned the key. It still didn't sound right. He looked irritated. Duncan was the mechanic of the family, but Nicholas was trying to catch up. He muttered to himself while I texted Duncan to meet us.

"I can fix it," Nicholas said, shooting me a glare when he caught me texting. He started poking at the innards of the bike. I leaned against a tree and checked my phone for messages while we waited for Duncan. I'd texted Christabel to see if she wanted to check out the bookstores in town.

"So . . . you and Christabel?" Nicholas asked.

I slipped my phone back into my pocket, shrugging. She hadn't texted me back. "We'll see."

"But you like her?"

When I just raised my eyebrows at him, he sighed. "Lucy wanted me to ask," he admitted.

"Tell her it's none of her business."

He snorted. "You tell her."

"Unless she'll put in a good word for me," I amended.

"So you do like her."

"What's not to like? She's hot and badass." Which made it sound as if I liked her just because she was pretty, which wasn't true. She was fierce in her combat boots but she read poetry. She didn't flirt but she was damn cute—and she smelled like cinnamon. She was also the first girl in a long time who was invading my thoughts like this.

But you didn't go off all sappy to one of your brothers. That never ended well.

Duncan pulled up, trailed by Quinn.

"I was visiting Hunter," Quinn explained, "and came across Duncan."

Duncan just grunted and went straight to my bike. His jeans

and white T-shirt were smeared with engine grease, as usual, and he was carrying his pack of tools. Nicholas made room for him and they both crouched, looking serious.

"I checked the battery cables already," Nicholas said. "But it's still bogging. Must be the carb again."

Duncan reached for a ratchet. "Good work, little brother."

They tinkered for a while. Black goo dripped onto the grass. Quinn tossed me a bottle of soda. "What are you doing patrolling when you could be flirting with Lucy's cousin?"

I groaned. "What, is there a bulletin out or something?"

"Dude, I'm your twin. And it's about a girl. I'm offended you'd think I wouldn't know."

"Doesn't matter," I said quietly. "I don't think she's interested."

Quinn just snorted. "She's interested."

I couldn't help but smile. "You've barely met her."

"Connor," he said. "We're pretty. The sooner you deal with that, the better."

I laughed. "I don't think she goes for pretty."

"What the hell's wrong with her?"

It took another half hour for Duncan and Nicholas to finish flushing the carburetor or whatever it was they were doing. Duncan explained it in great detail, but I was listening as well as *he* listened when I explained why his computer was freezing up. He smiled smugly when the engine finally purred. If it was a cat, it would have rubbed its head against Duncan's knee.

"You guys up for patrol?" Nicholas asked.

Duncan shook his head. "Can't," he said, grimacing. "Aunt Ruby's decided she wants her Mustang ready for the Blood Moon. You know, the Mustang that hasn't run since 1965?"

"How is she going to drive it to the camp? There isn't even a road."

Duncan shrugged. "Beats the hell out of me." He rode off without another word.

"I'm always up for patrol." Quinn grinned. "Let's hit the outskirts of town. *Hel-Blar* are running wild again. Hunter says the school now gets nightly bulletins from the Helios-Ra agents in town."

We rode around for a while but it was uneventful, until we were making our way back out among the farms nearest Violet Hill. There was a bright yellow car on the side of Cedar Road with the driver's door open. No one was inside.

"That's Lucy's car," Nicholas said, all but tossing his bike into the ditch when the kickstand didn't snap down fast enough.

"Shit," Quinn whispered as we ran after him. I already had my phone out. I wasn't sure if we were calling a tow truck or hunters. I called Lucy first while Nicholas raced around her car, shouting her name. She didn't answer.

"Her cell's out of range," I said when Nicholas stopped, hands braced on the hood, his expression painful to look at. Rain pattered around us.

"I smell mushrooms," Quinn said grimly, nostrils flaring. *Hel-Blar.* "Or wet earth?" Nicholas punched the car, denting the hood. "I don't smell any blood, though," Quinn added. "Nicholas."

Nicholas nodded, jaw clenched. "I heard you." He slid into the car's driver's seat. His fangs were out, his eyes faintly bloodshot. He was pale even through the window. "There's Hypnos on the steering wheel."

"Shit." I grabbed my laptop and monitored all the lines and signals going to any of the family phones or computers. Mom and Dad didn't know I'd set them up that way.

"Anything?" Quinn asked me quietly. "He doesn't look good, man. Hurry up."

"Nothing—wait, no." I hacked into Mom's private account. "Gotcha. Shit. Shit!"

"What?" Quinn read over my shoulder, going pale. "Shit."

Nicholas finally looked up from the section of the dirt road he was investigating. "What?"

"Message to Mom. From Saga."

"Saga? The one we thought shot at Solange?"

I nodded. "Nick."

"Spit it out already. What does she have to do with Lucy?"

"She kidnapped Lucy. She's holding her hostage in exchange for official recognition for the *Hel-Blar*."

Nicholas's eyes went wild, like lightning striking a moonlit lake.

Quinn looked at me. "You guys see if you can track her. I'll alert the others."

"They'll be out of range, too."

"I know," he said, jumping on his bike. "I'll send out texts and then hit the caves and the camp. Don't let him do anything stupid."

"I'll try," I said as he sped away. I approached Nicholas warily. "Find any tracks?"

"No." His voice was stark, cold as naked steel.

I inhaled deeply, cataloging the faint mushroom smell. "It's not the normal mushroom stink, more like wet earth and leaves," I said, frowning. "I don't smell swamp—do you?" He sniffed and shook his head. I froze. "But I smell cinnamon."

"Lucy doesn't smell like cinnamon," Nicholas said tightly. "She smells like cherry gum and pepper."

"I know," I replied just as tightly. "But Christabel smells like cinnamon."

"What the hell's going on?"

"I don't know." But I did know we were both remembering the *Hel-Blar* attacking us that night we went to the beach. "Lucy's prepared," I said. But Christabel didn't even know vampires existed. "Shit," I said as the rain started to fall harder. My nostrils flared. "That way toward the woods."

Nicholas turned on his heel. "I don't smell Lucy."

"Could Christabel have borrowed Lucy's car?" I asked.

"I guess so." He frowned. "I don't smell Lucy anywhere."

"And I definitely smell Christabel." I wiped water off my face, stepping off the road into the fields of goldenrod.

"Where are you going?" Nicholas called.

"I don't think they took Lucy," I said over my shoulder. Thunder growled and lightning hissed. "And I'll lose Christabel's scent if it keeps raining." Frustration simmered in my blood.

"Wait for me!"

"No, stay there. Just in case." Maybe I was wrong. Maybe they had Lucy, too, or maybe they'd separated the cousins. Either way, Nicholas was Lucy's best chance and I was Christabel's.

I didn't think. I just ran, trying to find my way through the smothering rain and the hundreds of smells in a forest during autumn: mud, leaves, apples. I concentrated on cinnamon, just cinnamon.

The faint trail took me through the deepest part of the oldest woods, where the canopy was so thick the rain barely came through. It was the only reason I didn't lose her scent completely. The spicy warmth of it tickling my nostrils goaded me forward, through the swelling river and the frost gathering at the foot of the mountain. There was a dirt road, overgrown with weeds but clearly some kind of man-made road. I heard howling and snarling and I wasn't sure if it was animal or vampire.

The road took me to the ruins of a frontier town, all rotting logs and sagging porches. Wooden signs creaked. The smell of mushrooms was thick, rancid. I gagged but took another breath anyway.

Because underneath the rot: cinnamon.

CHAPTER 13

♦

Lucy

I didn't know what to say.

And I *always* had something to say, to anyone, at any time. Especially Solange. She was crouched next to me in the ferns, delicate and pale as a pearl. The grizzled old guard was lying in the roots of a tree. I tried not to keep staring at him.

"He's fine," Solange muttered.

She was right. Technically he was fine. And I was going to ruin a perfectly good moment of intrigue. I pushed a frond out of my way, trying to peer into the shadows. There were a few torches in iron stands. The rain continued to patter listlessly, barely able to slide between the branches to the forest floor. The clearing was a narrow band of grass and wildflowers around the base of the mountain. Tents had been erected, like some kind of vampire circus or a production of Arabian Nights had come to town. There was a lot of silk, gold thread, carved mahogany, and a long wooden table roughly the length of the main street in town. Tin lanterns cast a warm pattern of light over its surface.

"Your aunt must love this." Solange's aunt Hyacinth still thought the only rightful queen was Queen Victoria, and she was in love with pomp and circumstance and a proper bustle. She'd also nearly been killed by rogue Helios-Ra agents, and the burns to her face hadn't healed as well as they should have. At least, that's what we assumed, since she still refused to lift her veils.

"She's in England."

"What? Since when?"

"She went on a pilgrimage to Uncle Edward's monument and to Queen Victoria's grave."

"Oh."

"She'll be back for the Blood Moon."

We watched two burly men muscle a huge clay amphora, like ones the ancient Romans used. I guessed it wasn't full of red wine like our history teacher told us. Well, not undoctored red wine, anyway.

"Hey." I frowned. "They're human."

Solange nodded. "Yeah."

"How come they're allowed and I'm not?"

"They belong to Bruno," she said. Bruno was head of the Drake family security detail. He'd skulked around our house more than once as well.

"What about her?" I pointed to a woman with large hips and a larger smile. "She's not a bodyguard."

"She's a . . . well, Kieran would call her a bloodslave."

My mouth dropped open. "Are you serious? He was right about that?" He'd once accused me of being a bloodslave and had looked for the telltale scars on my arms. I'd punched him in the nose, righteously indignant on behalf of my vampire family.

"She's not ours," Solange rushed to add. "She came with a European delegation. Apparently they think it's cute that we drink from blood banks and animals. One of them actually called us colonial." She didn't sound thrilled about that. "Only humans who are under a pheromone trance can attend the festival, and they're not allowed to speak."

"Seriously? That's medieval." I frowned. "I can't believe your dad would agree to that."

"He thinks it's too dangerous for humans to attend anyway. And you know what he says: one battle at a time."

I grinned. "As opposed to your mother, who says all battles, all the time."

"Exactly. Plus, it's tradition. Humans don't need to know how we govern ourselves."

"On behalf of humans, hey."

"You know what I mean."

I did know what she meant, and it only made it worse.

"Who's that?" I asked, mostly to distract myself. The girl looked in her early twenties and was wearing paint-splattered jean overalls. Her hair was a soft Afro decorated with a single pink flower.

"Sky," Solange replied. "And that's Sabrielle," she added, when another girl walked by wearing a beautiful blue sari stiff with silver-thread embroidery and glass beads.

"I totally want that dress for prom," I said.

"She serves with Constantine." Solange's voice changed.

I looked at her sharply. "Who's he?"

"He's a dignitary."

He was something more than that, I could tell by her tone—both guarded and nearly reverent.

"And?"

"And what?"

"You can vamp out until the cows come home, Solange, but you can't lie to me."

"It's noth—" She stopped and rose silently to her feet, pivoting to face behind us. Her knees bent slightly, and she had a long dagger in her hand. I didn't even see her reach for it. I thought of disembodied *Hel-Blar* body parts dangling from the trees and reached for a stake. Gandhi leaped in front of me, growling. His butt knocked me over.

Quinn was suddenly standing in front of Solange. His long hair hung in his eyes. "Sol."

Solange relaxed her stance. So did Gandhi. "Crap. You got me going." She sheathed her dagger and then shook her hands, as if they were full of adrenaline.

"Sol, oh God," he said. "They took Lucy. She's gone."

"I am?" I pushed out of the ferns, confused. "I'm right here." Quinn gaped at me, then plucked me up in a fierce hug. "Vampire strength," I squeaked.

He dropped me so fast I landed back on my butt in the mud. I shook my head. "What's *with* you guys?"

"You're okay!" he said, helping me up. He would have helped me brush the dirt off my backside but I slapped his hand away.

"What's going on?" Solange asked.

"Connor intercepted a message," he explained, "doing his computer voodoo. It said Lucy's a hostage."

I shivered, then scowled, hating the fear that scampered on insect feet over my spine. "Who sent it?"

"Saga."

"Okay, but they clearly don't have me. So what's the deal?"

Quinn jerked a hand through his dark hair. "Your car's dead on Cedar Road."

"What?" I thought about Christabel, borrowing my crappy car to get home after detention. "Oh shit. Shit!" I felt sick. "It's not me they have—it's my cousin."

Solange swore. "We have to get her out. Have you told Mom and Dad yet?"

"I sent texts, but they're bloody well out of signal range, too. I have to tell Nicholas you're okay," Quinn said. "He didn't look . . . right. I don't know if Connor can control him."

Solange swore again. "Okay, Quinn, you get to a signal spot and send out the call. I'll go with Lucy to find Nick."

"He was at your car, tracking for you. It's on Cedar, on the outskirts of town where it turns into a dirt road." Quinn was already running. He jumped over the prone guard. "What's with him?"

"He's fine." Solange waved her hand. "Just go."

"Call my parents!" I yelled after him. I was running too, but he was long gone. I leaped over an exposed tree root and got slapped in the face with a low-hanging pine bough, but I barely noticed.

Nicholas would do something monumentally stupid if he thought it would save me.

And Christabel wasn't with regular vampires. She was with the worst of the worst.

I ran faster even though I was getting a stitch in my side and spots danced through my vision. My lungs could explode later. I didn't have time. I did have time to be vaguely grateful for the Helios-Ra training—I wasn't able to run half this fast before. Gandhi loped beside me and Solange was a blur in front of us, barely disturbing the vegetation. She was waiting at the car with the doors open. Gandhi scrambled into the back, panting.

"Go," Solange yelled, shutting the door.

I fumbled, trying to jab my key into the ignition. "Where are you going?"

"I can't ride in the car with you," she said. "I'll try to keep up, but don't wait for me."

I planned to go way the hell over the speed limit, so I doubted very much she would keep up. A vampire couldn't sustain that kind of speed for long. She'd be okay over the rutted lane, but once I hit pavement, I'd stand on the gas pedal if I had to.

I rattled over the potholes and washed out divots in the muddy lane, rain spattering my windshield. Gandhi's breath fogged the side window. I couldn't even see Solange anymore. The transmission of my mom's car protested violently as I slammed into another rock, but I just kept going. I finally turned onto a paved road and floored it. The tires slid out a little with the smell of burning rubber, but luckily there were no other cars. I jerked into my lane.

"It'll be okay," I told Gandhi, mostly to reassure myself. "It has to be okay." He licked my ear. I cut across a deserted field and came out of a clump of yellow mullein stalks, perpendicular to my abandoned car. The passenger side door was still open.

Nicholas stood by the hood, looking stark and a little wild. I saw the pale gray of his eyes, like lightning, even from a distance. I went to throw myself out of the car but he was already there, yanking me out of my seat belt and crushing me up against his chest. His face was buried in my neck and his hands clutched me as if he were drowning in the rain. His lips were moving—I felt them against my wet skin but I couldn't decipher what he was saying.

And then his mouth was on mine and I knew his words; they were poetry, they were rain, lilies, sugar, chocolate. I drank them in. I forgot for one tiny moment that everything was falling apart and we didn't know how to put it back together again. He held me and I held him and I wasn't sure how the rain even managed to sneak between us. We kissed so deeply, everything in me ached and burned and stretched out like a cat in the sunlight.

"I thought . . ." He trailed off.

I touched his cheek. "I'm fine."

He nodded once, resting his forehead against mine so that we created a corner of the wet, angry world that was just ours. "There are traces of Hypnos powder in your car." His jaw clenched. "I couldn't find you."

My fingers tangled in his hair. "I'm right here." My throat constricted. "It's Christabel."

"We know that now," he said darkly.

I pulled away slightly, looking around. "Where's Connor?"

"He caught Christabel's trail," Nicholas said grimly. "He's gone."

"He went alone?"

"He wouldn't wait. And I don't know her scent, especially not with all this rain." He looked apologetic. "You're all I smell."

From anyone else, that would have sounded weird.

I wiped rain off my face. "What do we do now?" I whispered. "Poor Christa." She wouldn't know what was going on. Or how to defend herself. I bit my lip to stop from crying. It strangled the sob in my throat but a tear still leaked out, hot on my cold cheek.

"We'll find her," Nicholas promised. "Somehow, we'll find her."

"It's almost dawn."

"I know," he said grimly. "Let's get back to the farm. I'm sure your parents will be there by now."

Solange emerged from the field, soaked to the skin, her eyes the blue gray of polished abalone shell. Nicholas frowned at her.

"Are you okay?" he asked.

"Fine." She jerked her head. "Let's go."

She stepped onto the hood and then slid up to the roof, perched like a crow. Nicholas followed. I drove down the back roads of Violet Hill in the middle of the night with my best friend and my boyfriend sitting on the roof of my mom's car.

It was the most normal part of my night so far.

CHAPTER 14

•

Christabel

"What?" I squeaked. "What? What the hell?"

When they turned and those strange eyes were focused on me alone, I suddenly remembered that being ignored by drugged-up psychopaths was a *good* thing. "Uh," I stammered. "Never mind."

Saga sighed. Her hair was just red enough against her blue skin to be distracting, nearly the exact hues of sunset over the ocean. "I'll see to them."

She paused long enough for Aidan to kiss her so thoroughly and so hotly that I looked away. Old people making out. Hadn't I suffered enough?

She stalked away, trailing a ragged hem and the smell of wet earth and crushed leaves under a hint of lavender and rum. Aidan watched her go, smiling a little before turning his attention to me. I was casting wild glances around, trying to figure out how to escape.

"You'll never outrun us," Aidan said. "But you don't believe that, do you? Look around, Christabel. There's nowhere to go."

It was an old building, suited to candles and kettles. The walls were gray with age and there was a wooden sign hanging from a broken chain reading "Apothecary." The road was packed dirt, with more buildings across the way. There was a general store, a saloon, and a few houses with sagging fences around kitchen gardens. A post ran along the porches, to tie up horses. All that was missing was a stagecoach.

I'd been kidnapped, drugged, and dumped in an old western movie?

I grabbed my head. "Where am I?"

"Frontier town, been here for three centuries at least," Aidan answered. "It was abandoned after the Gold Rush. That was something to see, I don't mind telling you." He sounded oddly nostalgic, as if he really had been here over a hundred years ago.

"How long was I out?" I asked.

"Just an hour or so."

This was the weirdest kidnapping ever. I searched for hidden cameras. "Is this a TV show? Like, some historical practical joke thing?"

"No, Christabel."

I rubbed my arms for warmth. The rain was turning to snow. "Then what? Because I don't believe in vampires."

"You will," he said calmly. "But until then, take a good look. Nothing but mountains behind those buildings, and everywhere else is forest. If you make a run for it, you'll be lost for hours—days even. You're more likely to get eaten by a cougar than you are to find your way back to town." His lips twitched bleakly. "And there are other monsters out there, worse than us, as you've seen. You don't want to go up against a *Hel-Blar* alone. So do yourself a favor and stay put."

"Is that what that thing was?"

He nodded. "Aye, the worst of the worst."

"I don't understand," I said finally. "Are you waiting for a ransom?" I didn't know if I should tell him that my mother was in rehab and my uncle was far from rich. Unless they wanted a ransom of homemade pickles and free snow removal, Uncle Stuart wasn't solvent enough for a million dollars in unmarked bills, or whatever it was kidnappers in movies usually demanded.

"No. We don't want money."

"Then what?"

"It's politics. We want a seat on the council. We want to be recognized and buy safety for our kin."

I had no idea what any of that meant but I nodded anyway. "None of my family is in politics."

"No, but the Drakes are," he said. "Royalty, aren't they?"

If Nicholas was a prince, I guarantee Lucy would have teased him about it mercilessly. And I had a hard time picturing Connor wearing a crown. Carrying a ray gun, sure, but not a crown. But it was probably bad form to correct your abductor. I wondered whether he'd let me go if I threw up on him. I shivered, crossing my arms tighter over my chest. My jacket was barely keeping out the cold, but I felt better out here. Less like a prisoner. I'd take hypothermia over being locked up.

I should probably pretend he wasn't insane. Keep him talking. Isn't that what they did in stories? I was so going to have to read more spy novels when I got out of here; historical fiction and poetry just weren't helping me enough right now.

"Why are you kind of . . . blue?" I asked. Because obviously it wasn't a hallucination. Maybe it was some type of gang tattoo.

"*Hel-Blar* are different from the other vampires," he explained. He was wearing a beaded leather pouch around his neck. "Any vampire can become one of them, if they're starved long enough or are infected. The blue is a side effect of too much blood after not enough."

I swallowed. "Oh." I didn't ask about his teeth. Clearly he had an insane dentist in this insane ghost town.

He smiled, even though I hadn't mentioned it out loud. "The teeth help us feed. The deeper the starvation, the more teeth. Another side effect."

I so didn't want the details. I smiled weakly and edged away.

"This would've been much easier if you'd been Lucky."

I froze, narrowing my eyes. "You stay away from her."

He shrugged pragmatically. "Can't." He took a small cheroot cigar out of his pocket and lit the end. The smoke curled lazily into the cold air. He slanted me a glance. "You're getting nervous again. I can hear your heart flinging itself around in your chest."

I tried to take a deep breath.

"You're safe," he said. "The Drakes will buy you back, and eventually we'll let them."

My breath clogged in my throat. The Drakes barely knew me.

"Shame this place was left to rot," he said conversationally. "It sure was something, even before the gold diggers came and panned the streams. Fool's gold mostly, and some shiny stones, nothing worth all the fuss. But no one wanted to believe it." The tip of his cigar glowed red for a moment. "Even before the town, this place was beautiful. Reminds me of home."

"Home?" I asked. "Where's that?" That seemed like information a cop might want later.

"I was born in Upper Canada in 1633 as a Huron. We called ourselves Wendat. We were Attignawantan, the Bear People." He showed me the bear claw hanging next to the leather pouch. "I was turned one night in the woods, 1661 I think it was. Can't be sure now. Wasn't even sure then. I woke up in a bear cave past midwinter. Wouldn't have made it through the madness without that bear's blood." He held out his hand wryly, admiring his dusky blue veins and pale, moth-white skin. "Nearly didn't."

I was terrified, no doubt about it, but Aidan hadn't made a single threatening move, not since he'd dosed with me with that white powder. He was talking to me as if I were his little sister. Even my adrenaline was confused.

"I still follow the ways of my tribe as best I can—the feast songs and the proper way to build a longhouse and how to honor the dead. The same way we'd hoped Lucky would learn our ways and become a link between the tribes. She could have carried the wampum to the Blood Moon."

He was losing me again. But the talk of his life, like something out of a historical novel, was soothing to me. I actually wanted to ask him questions, which was probably ludicrous under the circumstances. But I couldn't help myself.

"What did you eat?" It was what I always wondered. What kinds of food did Henry the Eighth eat, or Joan of Arc, or Coleridge? Did they eat cucumber salads and drink lemonade? Did they put honey on their toast? I'd have driven my teachers to distraction with these questions if I'd ever let myself talk as much as I'd wanted to in class. But people remembered the girl who asked if Byron really drank vinegar to lose weight.

Aidan looked briefly taken aback before his brow furrowed, as if he was trying to remember. Crazy people who thought they were vampires freaked me out, but crazy people who thought it was 1661 I could gladly get along with. And after what I'd seen him do, I had no trouble picturing him running through the cedars with a musket.

"We ate mostly biscuits and venison when I was a lad, and boiled peas. Tea on Sundays when there was any, after the British came. Before that we grew corn and squash and hunted and fished the lakes." He licked his lips. "But now, blood."

Oops, shouldn't have asked about food.

"What about clothes?" I asked quickly, before he could go back to talking about vampires. "What did you wear?"

"The most beautifully beaded deerskin, soft as butter. And

moccasins. Later, after most of the Wendat fell, I lived near the towns for a while, but I never could get used to a roof over my head. And no one could get used to me," he added drily. "Some can pass for humans. Not the *Hel-Blar*, and not us. We have to give up everything. Saga sailed with Grace O'Malley," he said, the lines around his oddly pale eyes crinkling. "She was an Irish pirate, chatted with Queen Elizabeth," he explained when I looked confused. "But eventually the sun can reach anywhere on a ship—the brig is no exception."

Pirates and Bear People. Even captured, I was actually itching for pen and paper so I could take notes.

I was as crazy as he was.

He came back to the present with a sigh. He glanced at the sky. "You'd best get inside. We've things to do."

I went inside because I didn't know what else to do. The glass bottles on the shelves rattled as I crossed the room. How was I going to get out of here?

"Christabel."

I was standing in the middle of the room now, trying not to hyperventilate. And hearing voices. "Great," I muttered.

"Pssst, Christa, damn it, come *on*."

It took a good long minute for me to register the voice.

"Connor?" I turned, feeling unsteady. "Is it the drugs again? Or are you really there?"

He was crawling through the window, dust coating his hair and shirt. I'd never been so happy to see anyone in my entire life.

But then the door opened and Aidan was there, snarling.

"Run!" I yelled. "Connor, run!"

He ran, but idiotically he ran *toward* me not *away*. He was between Aidan and me before I could say anything else. They both had stakes in their hands.

Wait. *Connor* carried stakes, too? Was everyone in Violet Hill insane?

"Christa, get out of here," Connor said quietly. "I'll find you. Just run."

"No," Aidan said. "If she runs, she'll die."

"Mountain lions," I told Connor.

"He knows that's not what I mean," Aidan said. "If you run, we'll release the *Hel-Blar*. They obey us."

Connor went pale, even paler than he usually was. And now I was actually wondering if he was pale because he spent too much time at his computer or for entirely different reasons.

"And they have Christabel's scent."

"You bastard." Connor went for Aidan's throat. Aidan was faster. Which made sense if you believed he'd died in 1661 and had spent centuries roaming the continent.

Crap. Did I actually believe he'd died in 1661 and had spent centuries roaming the continent?

Never mind that. He was about to shove a piece of wood into the chest of a guy I kind of liked despite myself. But what the hell was I supposed to do about it? I didn't know how to fight. I knew iambic pentameter and all the verses of "The Highwayman." I did have good taste in shoes, though. The steel toes of my combat boots could splinter wood. And maybe bones.

I tried to kick Aidan, but it was surprisingly difficult to aim properly when two guys were fighting. Especially when they sometimes moved so fast that they blurred around the edges. I really wanted to believe that was a side effect of the drugs. I kicked again. Aidan grunted.

"Sorry," I muttered, since he hadn't tied me up in the trunk of my car or killed me horribly when he could have. "But stop trying to kill him."

Someone's elbow caught me in the sternum and I flew backward, crashing into a shelf. Dozens of bottles tumbled to the ground and rolled in every direction. A few broke into sharp pieces. I clutched my stomach. Connor ran to my side. He almost looked like he had fangs. His eyes were so blue, it hurt to look at them.

"Christabel, are you okay?" He was slurring his words. He glanced at the window and cursed. I looked, too, half expecting more of those blue creatures to be scrabbling through the window. All I saw was a lightening in the sky, a touch of gold in the east. It was comforting.

"What?" I asked. "What's wrong?"

He looked like he was in pain. "Dawn."

CHAPTER 15

◆

Lucy

It had been nearly a month since I'd been inside the Drake farm-house. It was the longest I'd ever gone without a slumber party of some sort, or just hanging out with Solange while she worked on her pottery wheel in the converted shed. The oak trees and the cedars were the same and the rosebushes were still as scraggly. Nicholas and Solange jumped down from the roof before I'd fully stopped the car.

I got out as the front door opened and the dogs barreled out, barking. They would have been intimidating if they hadn't both slept on my head when they were puppies. They danced around my legs and I crouched briefly to hug them, feeling the vise in my chest ease. Then I felt guilty for feeling better when Christabel was still missing.

My parents rushed out as various Drakes and Bruno cluttered the porch behind them. My mom was babbling and hugging me. Dad didn't say anything, only hugged me, the family tattoo on his arm standing out in stark relief. His eyes were shiny.

"Dad, don't," I whispered. If he cried, I'd cry, too. "I'm fine."

"You're grounded forever," he said into my hair. "In fact, I'm having you microchipped."

I laughed, the sound muffled in his shirt. "Dad, I'm not a dog."

"Why don't we all go inside?" Liam suggested. I would have hugged him, too, but my dad wasn't letting go of me. Mom ruffled Nicholas's hair, which he hated, but he never stopped her. Solange was quiet, drifting behind us into the house. I heard bats above the treetops. I ducked my head and ran up the stairs. A wolf howled somewhere in the forest. Gandhi howled back before squeezing himself through the dog door fitted into the gate to the backyard. Isabeau had put it in herself, insisting her animals weren't ever to be confined.

The lamps were lit inside the house and there was a fire in the fireplace, which I knew was for our benefit. Vampires didn't feel the cold, and now that Solange was fully turned, there wouldn't be much heat running through the rest of the house. The fridge would have only enough food for Bruno and his detail. No chocolate or ice cream since I hadn't visited in such a long time. I wondered if my candy stash was still in Solange's desk.

Liam stood next to the wingback chair where Helena perched, vibrating with the need to go out and break kneecaps. She was only sitting here because it was our family. Her fangs were out.

Even Liam's teeth were fully elongated, which was rare in what he would consider "polite company." Mom, Dad, and I shared a velvet couch, and Solange stood just out of the fire's light. She was wearing her sunglasses again. Quinn was pacing and scowling. He must have known already Connor was missing, too, and being twins would make it even worse for him.

Nicholas leaned against the wall nearest to me, like he didn't want me out of his reach, even in his own house. His jaw was still clenching spasmodically. There were a lot of humans sitting around being fragrantly anxious. We probably smelled like a banquet to the Drakes. I smelled only the faint lemon floor polish and the wilting lilies in a giant urn on the mantelpiece.

"I'm happy to see you're safe, Lucy," Liam said calmly. He looked at my dad. "We'll find your niece, Stuart. You have my word."

Dad just rubbed the spot where his ulcer must have been on fire. I half expected to see flames searing through his shirt. There was a jug of cranberry juice on the coffee table and a silver antique urn filled with tea. I poured him a cup.

"We've already got Bruno on it, and our three eldest are tracking," Helena said darkly. "And I plan to be out there as soon as possible." She looked at my mom. They'd known each other when they were girls, when Helena was still human. Mom nodded, just as severely.

"And Connor," Nicholas added. "He took off when he caught Christabel's scent."

"Since when do *Hel-Blar* hold hostages?" Quinn asked disgustedly. "And why the hell'd you let him go without me?"

"That's something I'd like to know as well," Helena said. Her black hair was like a braided whip down her back. "*Hel-Blar* have never organized."

"We don't know what the *Hel-Blar* are like among themselves," Liam said. "We see the ones most driven by madness. I've often wondered if there are others who survive. The Hounds rescue Montmartre's leftovers, but he wasn't the only one making *Hel-Blar*. We've always known that."

"The woman who shot the message arrow didn't look like regular *Hel-Blar*," Quinn said.

"Maybe they have other vampires working with them?" Liam asked, brow furrowed. "Though it seems unlikely."

"No, she wasn't like us, either. She was blue, just not *that* blue. And she didn't reek of decay. That's how she got so close."

Bruno cleared his throat from the doorway. He looked tired and grim, right down to the tattoos on his shaved head. "Message," he said bluntly.

Helena rose like smoke, trailing her husband, her sons, and her daughter. My parents rushed after them as well. Bruno stopped Quinn, Nicholas, and Solange. "You lot don't need to see this."

"They don't seriously think we're just going to wait here, do they?" I huffed. "That's my cousin and your brother."

Quinn tilted his head, raising his hand for silence. Nicholas was close behind me, close enough that every time I inhaled, my shoulder brushed his chest. Outside, the rain started again, like fingers tapping nervously on the roof.

"Hallway," Quinn mouthed.

Solange went to stand beside him. Nicholas and I went to the second doorway leading from the library to the kitchen. If I stood at just the right angle and cricked my neck to the point of near-permanent damage, I could see everyone in the reflection of an antique mirror. Hoping for an even better perspective, I went on my tiptoes and then nearly toppled over. Nicholas's cool, strong hand kept me from falling. I wondered how he could even hear their conversation over the pounding of my heart. He licked his lips and looked away. I wasn't worried. If I could resist chocolate cake—and I had, once—he could resist me.

"So they know they don't have Lucy. Does that make it better or worse?"

The sound of my name distracted me from the way Nicholas's hair fell over his forehead and the line of his jaw and his shirt, damp from the rain, clinging to his sleek muscles.

"Christabel is a political hostage," Liam said, skimming what must have been some sort of note. His mouth tightened. He was all about treaties and honor and this would push all of his buttons. "She'll be fine as long as we give them a seat at the council table during the Blood Moon."

"Bloody cheek," Bruno muttered. "For that lot."

"It doesn't fit what we know of the *Hel-Blar*," Liam agreed. "And Connor's there, too," he confirmed, nearly expressionless. That was never a good sign. "Unharmed."

Quinn's teeth were out so far, they poked into his lower lip. He clenched his fists, veins standing out on his arms.

"I'll kill them," Helena promised, almost pleasantly. Then she held up a decapitated blue hand. "Hell of a gesture of goodwill." She glanced at my mother. "It's not easy to cut off a vampire's body part, and once they're dust it's impossible," she explained. Mom swallowed. She didn't want to know any of this stuff.

"I want them, Liam," Helena continued with a cold smile, "on a stake." In so many ways she was more medieval than the actual medieval members of the Drake family. She belonged to a time of trials by fire and iron maidens. One of the dogs, Byron, heard something in her voice and whined, sticking his wet nose in my palm.

"After the Blood Moon," Liam said. "Not before. We have to accept this proposed treaty."

"Damn their treaty. Since when do we negotiate with kidnappers?"

"Since they have an innocent girl," he answered grimly. "And our son."

"It sets a bad precedent," she said, but she wasn't really arguing.

"You can't risk my niece," Dad said calmly, as if she weren't wearing a sword in her belt and couldn't snap his neck with a flick of her very delicate wrist.

"I know," she replied. "They have our son, too." She touched his shoulder, reminding him that she knew how he felt. Poor Connor. He really was the nicest of the brothers, and now he was at the mercy of vampires who hacked off body parts and used them as calling cards.

"They don't actually want a war," Liam continued to read, lips pursed in thought.

"Should've thought of that earlier," Helena said darkly, "before they touched my family."

"They say they sent delegates to request a private audience, but they were killed on sight." He rubbed his face. "That's on us, love."

"The Chandramaa shot that girl, not us." Helena stared at him. "And are we supposed to let *Hel-Blar* just waltz into the courts now, Liam? Are you forgetting what they're like?" She tossed the hand onto the narrow table against the wall. The faintly wet sound made my mom turn green. Liam moved a painted oil lamp to hide the stain of old vampire blood and decomposing flesh. Gag.

"They're attacking the secluded farmsteads now," Bruno added. "And taking livestock closer to town. Even the local papers are starting to grumble about gang violence."

"I know." Liam sighed, suddenly sounding a hundred years old though he barely looked thirty. "This Saga wants us to believe she's different and can control the others. She wants to prove herself to us."

Bruno read over his shoulder with the ease of someone who had worked with the family for more than two decades. "Claims she's behind the hands we've been finding in the forest. That's a hell of a way to clean up your backyard."

"The worst of it is, she's taken more *Hel-Blar* down than we have lately," Helena said, disgusted. "Even with our new alliance with the Helios-Ra."

"What's this got to do with my niece?" Dad interrupted. "Or *my* daughter for that matter."

Liam winced. "I suspect they meant to use Lucy as a liaison between the tribes." Nicholas made a sound that was suspiciously like a growl. I actually felt it rumble through his chest. "She's human-weak." Now I was the one growling. "And easier to abduct. But she's also like family to us, and as such, she has unusual influence."

I preened a little inside at that statement. It was nice that *someone* remembered me—even if it was some crazy vampire woman. At least Liam admitted I was like family. I was really starting to think they'd forgotten.

"They have something planned for just before dawn." Liam didn't need to glance at his watch. He felt the waning of night in his bones. Nicholas felt it even more, being so young. In fact, he was already getting paler. And I had a feeling Solange's eyes were very red behind her sunglasses. "We'd best get you and Lucy safely home now." He looked up and smiled right at me in the reflection of the mirror. I jumped. "So you can come out now, Lucy."

I poked my head out. "You know, it would be a lot easier if you just stopped trying to leave me out of stuff."

"Mm-hmm. We'll discuss it at a later date," Liam replied, faintly amused. "But I doubt your parents would agree."

I met Mom's eyes. Her bindi was lopsided now; she'd moved it while rubbing her face. She always did that when she was upset. I thought about the conversation we'd had on my bed. Had that been only last night? I would never believe that I was better off without the Drakes and they without me. Growing up, I'd seen them more often than my own grandparents. They were part of my landscape. And if that particular landscape suddenly included earthquakes and volcanoes and mudslides, then too bad; I already built a house there and dug the well and planted crops. It was an analogy my parents had to understand. They were homesteaders; they knew that once you found your home, you dug your roots. Period.

"I'm already part of this," I insisted softly. "You can't undo my whole life and pretend it didn't happen the way it did." I was tired of having decisions like that made for me. I was sixteen, not six.

Mom sighed, looking away.

"We'll take the truck and someone can drive Cass's car home later," Dad said, giving no indication that he'd even heard me.

Liam nodded. "Of course."

"I'll do it," Nicholas offered.

Dad just nudged me out the front door. He wouldn't even let me hug Nicholas good-bye. And Solange wasn't saying anything or standing up for me like she usually did.

I called for Gandhi and he lumbered into the backseat with me, taking up most of the space. He leaned so heavily against me, I soon lost feeling in my arm. The truck was ancient enough that it had a cassette player and nowhere to plug in an iPod. And in this part of the mountains, we were lucky to get any radio stations at all, never mind without a heavy film of static. Mom turned it off, fingering the mala beads around her wrist. Dad was driving a little fast but no one minded. I stared out the window at the pine trees and cedar woods.

I wanted to crawl into my bed and wake up to a lukewarm shower because Christabel had used up the last of the hot water. I wanted her to ignore me while she ate her breakfast granola and tried to finish her book before school. I wanted Connor rolling his eyes at my mom when her mere presence near a computer made it malfunction.

I wanted people to stop trying to kill my boyfriend, my best friend, and, frankly, me.

Something moved up ahead.

It could have been a deer, about to bound in front of the truck. It happened all the time out here.

Somehow, I doubted it.

Apparently Dad did, too. He frowned. "Now what?"

I had to shove Gandhi over to fit between the front seats so I could get a better look out the windshield. The high beams speared the road, gilded the edge of the bulrushes in the ditches, and showed the faintest glimmer of movement at the top of the hill. I knew that kind of shuffle—not really a crawl, not quite a walk. I swallowed.

"Dad."

"Yeah?"

"That's not good." I hit speed dial on my phone, calling Nicholas. Mom was already dialing, her eyes never leaving the shadows gathering on the hill.

"Helena," she snapped. "Now. Past the pear orchards."

"I know. We've already got the call." I heard her voice, tinny through the phone. I switched off my call to Nicholas. "How do you know?"

"We're surrounded," Mom said between her teeth.

The rain had stopped but the shadows gleamed wetly, and blue. Gandhi growled, ears pricked, shoulders quivering with the urge to launch himself outside.

"You're surrounded by *Hel-Blar?*" Helena shouted. "Go, go, go!" I didn't know if she was yelling at us or the others.

Dad swore and kicked the truck into reverse. The tires squealed. More *Hel-Blar* shuffled out of the woods on either side and a clump of them gathered in the road behind us. Dad didn't pause, just hit the gas harder.

"Hold on!" he yelled, and I grabbed Gandhi, who didn't have the benefit of a seat belt. We hit the first *Hel-Blar* with a harsh thump. The next two leaped into the back of the truck and walked toward the very small window between them and me.

"Shit." Dad jerked the wheel and we skidded sideways. One of the *Hel-Blar* flew off into the bushes. The other one didn't. I saw the gleam of his teeth. Gandhi was snarling and barking, spittle hitting the glass. Mom hit the door locks just as another one came at us from the side.

There were too many of them. I'd never seen so many. Usually there were two or three, just as busy snarling at each other as at their prey. Knowing an epidemic existed was different from being inside the maelstrom of it. Even through the thick glass, the car fumes, and dog breath, I smelled faint rot and mildew, like moldy dirt.

One of them had blood on her chin. And they all wore those copper collars.

"They've been feeding," I said slowly, peering into the shadows. Blood and hunger maddened them, turning them even more vicious. Sometimes, bloated with blood, they stayed in the woods and didn't bother anyone.

These weren't bloated.

Yet.

I'd thought about becoming a vampire before, of course. It might be cool.

You know, *later*.

But *not* a *Hel-Blar*. I had no intention of spending eternity smelling like *that*.

Time seemed to slow, and thanks to growing up with Helena and hanging out with Hunter, I found myself making an inventory of the weapons within reach. I had a stake in my coat pocket; there was a wire hanger under Mom's seat and a pen in the cup holder. The truck, Gandhi, sunrise. We could use any of those if we had to. I wished I had my crossbow. It was in Mom's car, useless in the Drakes' driveway. I really had to remember to keep everything in my knapsack from now on.

Mom reached back to grip my hand but I didn't need the comfort. I needed my hands free to fight.

"It's okay, Mom," I said. "We'll be all right."

Dad kept backing up and then going forward again, back and forth, back and forth, knocking as many down as he could. Every so often he would swing to one side to throw them off balance. A blue hand slapped the window near my face, then tumbled away. A *Hel-Blar* landed on the roof. The thump of his boots over our heads made Gandhi bark so loudly my ears rang. I gripped my stake tighter and reached for the sunroof.

Mom's hold tightened painfully. "Lucky Moon, sit back down."

"Mom, I can get him," I argued, balancing on the balls of my feet. "I know how."

"No! Stay here."

"Didn't I say you were grounded?" Dad snapped. "So ground. Sit. Now!"

The *Hel-Blar* scratched at the roof, making angry, hungry,

guttural sounds, like a rabid bear digging for grubs. I had no intention of sitting pale and plump under a rock.

"*Dad.*"

"*No.*"

Gandhi tried to bite at the roof. Mom yanked on my arm and I landed back on the seat, glowering. "The Drakes are on their way. Look."

Behind the blue faces gnashing their sharp teeth at us, in the very thickets of shadows, I saw a pale gleam. If I hadn't known what to look for, I would have thought it a trick of the light, the moon on water. Only vampires had skin that pale, and only vampires could move so fast, like paint colors smearing across a dark canvas. They were nearly as fast as Bruno and his detail roaring toward us in their trucks.

The *Hel-Blar* on the roof fell screaming into the road, a crossbow bolt in his chest. He writhed there for a moment before a second bolt joined the first, this one hitting his heart dead center. He went to ashes. The other *Hel-Blar* stopped, snarled, and backed away. They didn't flee, just hesitated. We were frozen in a strange, violent dance.

The Drakes only bothered fighting the ones that got in their way. Helena dispatched two with her sword; Quinn whipped a stake at one. The rest slipped between the *Hel-Blar* like deadly smoke until they ringed our truck protectively. I saw Isabeau with a small pack of dogs racing toward us between the trees. Nicholas landed by my window and shot me a glance, his eyes gray as a mountain storm. I reached for the handle.

"Lucky, if you roll down that window, I am sending you to a boarding school for delinquent girls," Dad said severely. I didn't know he could be that threatening—usually he was so laid back people accused him of being stoned.

I was pretty sure boarding school was an empty threat.

Still.

My hand dropped as Solange claimed the now-deserted roof, holding her favorite rapier. I could see her through the sunroof window, as graceful with her drawn sword as a demented ballerina. I envied her. She could fight for her family, next to her family. I was just supposed to sit here and be rescued.

The *Hel-Blar* with blood on her face licked her chin. Whether it was the smell of blood or something more subtle and intrinsic, it seemed to act as a signal. The rest of them shifted, ready to attack again.

"On the hill," Solange said suddenly.

On the hilltop, crowned by the last bit of fading moonlight and the truck's headlights, stood a woman. She was fairly short, her hair glowed red, and she was wearing a breastplate that looked as if it were carved from ice. She was tinted blue, like rare opals. She was utterly alone—no guards, no warriors, and certainly not Christabel or Connor.

She had to be Saga, from the ransom note.

Helena actually hissed, like a cobra kept too long in a basket.

Just as the *Hel-Blar* made to move toward us again, Saga lifted something to her lips and blew. A sharp, strange whistle shivered through the air. Nicholas and I looked at each other through the glass. It was the same whistle we'd heard on the beach.

And it had the same effect tonight as it had last night. The *Hel-Blar* jerked, screeching. They covered their ears, gnashed their teeth, and wailed. They didn't take a single step closer to us. Saga blew again, three short bursts, and they all turned, reluctantly dragging themselves in her direction, leaning as if they were fighting against a winter wind. That whistle was more powerful than Hypnos powder, though it didn't seem to affect anyone else, aside from being mildly unpleasant. Gandhi tilted his head curiously.

The *Hel-Blar* continued their forced march. These were particularly feral, barely able to speak. They were savage, furious, and wretched.

And enslaved.

We all watched, stunned and silent, as they climbed the hill, stopped in front of Saga, and then knelt at her feet. They twitched their heads and snapped their teeth, clawing at their collars as if she held them in iron chains. She whispered something.

They stood as one and bent their heads to show the sides of their vulnerable necks. It was a sign of submission among older vampires, something I'd never actually seen done. No one in the Drake family was very good at submitting or surrendering. Saga didn't smile or react; she just whispered another command. They dispersed, scurrying through the trees like beetles and badgers.

She'd just proven she could control them. But she hadn't killed them.

Because if they were dead, she couldn't use them as a weapon against us.

Lucy

I caught a glance of Isabeau. She looked angry and impressed but mostly sad. She wouldn't even put collars on her dogs. Solange looked enthralled.

Bruno was the first to speak, standing on the step of his truck. "Well, I'll be damned."

CHAPTER 16

•

Christabel

"I'm so sorry," Connor mumbled at me before he crumpled, falling onto the floorboards. Dawn lit the dust motes as they danced over him. I dropped to my knees, searching him for wounds. He didn't move at all. And he was cold to the touch, as if he'd been hiding all night in the snow-dusted forest.

"Did you kill him?" I gaped at Aidan.

Aidan shook his head. "He'll be fine come sunset. He's young, and daylight hits them hard."

I sat back on my heels, stunned. "What?" For someone so in love with words, I was repeating "What?" an awful lot.

"You called him Connor. He's one of the Drake brothers." Aidan crouched and lifted a trapdoor in the floor. "This may work to our advantage, actually."

He reached over to grab Connor's arm. I clutched his other arm. "Don't!" I wasn't sure what I was telling him not to do, but I felt strongly about it regardless.

"I'm not hurting him," Aidan said patiently. "I'm helping him. He'll be sick as a dog if he sits in the sun all day. And if anyone else comes across him like this, he'll be defenseless."

"Oh."

Aidan hadn't lied to me yet, unfortunately. I watched glumly as he rolled Connor over the floorboards and then dropped him into the cellar below. The trapdoor fell with a bang and a cloud of dust.

"You can try to run," Aidan said wearily. "But he won't move a muscle until sunset. You'd have to leave him behind. Are you willing to do that?"

Leave the guy who'd crawled into this broken old house to save me?

Of course not.

And Aidan knew it.

"Try to rest," he suggested, not unkindly. He looked tired but not tired enough to fall over like Connor. "There's water in that jug and food in the basket."

"Thank you." Was I thanking my kidnapper, as if he'd offered me chocolate? I suddenly felt like a Jane Austen heroine, proper in the face of adversity. Never mind, I still wore my combat boots. I must be tired, too—I wasn't making sense, even in my own head. But I knew I couldn't sleep, so I went out to the porch. Aidan was already gone. There was no one around except for Connor under the floorboards. The mountains were a hundred shades of gray and indigo as the sun rose.

I really was in a ghost town, full of weeds and muddy lanes and leaning houses that looked like they might fall right over if the wind changed direction too suddenly. The saloon doors creaked. The general store had no windows, but it did have faded gingham curtains. The wooden horse trough outside was filled with dead leaves and pine needles. I wouldn't have been entirely surprised to see a mail coach or a sheriff with a gun holster. The historical geek inside me bounced on her toes and wanted to skip into every deserted building. A very thin layer of frost coated the peeling shingles, already melting in the morning light. The sky was a field of red roses, pink tulips and lilacs.

It might have been beautiful if I wasn't suddenly afraid I was going to be stuck here. No hundred-year-old gingham curtains or pretty sunrises could make that okay.

I picked at the cuts on my palms, from where I'd dug my nails in. Vampires didn't exist.

Never mind the pile of blue gray ashes in the middle of the road from the *thing* Aidan had staked. Never mind Connor's cold, pale body in the cellar.

Just never mind.

I went down the stairs, avoiding the rotting step. The sun was higher now, shooting sparks off the dew and melting ice. I decided to explore the rest of the ghost town, which was really just one street, since my other option was to stand there and go quietly insane.

Luckily, anything antique, poetic, or just plain old always distracted me. I went into the saloon first, the red paint peeling off the creaking wooden doors. The floor was slanted, the bar polished wood. Behind it was a shelf full of old whiskey and sarsaparilla bottles. There was a staircase in one corner, missing most of its stairs, leading to a balcony where women in red corsets would have lounged. The tables tilted drunkenly, missing legs and covered in dust. I even found a bullet hole in one wall and couldn't resist sticking my finger in it.

I went into the general store next and poked about, lifting lids off glass jars dusted with sugar inside and lined with broken candies, finding a mouse-nibbled bonnet with moth-nibbled flowers, a barrel of flour full of insects, and rusted horseshoes. I explored a small house, the iron stove still filled with long-dead embers. There was a ladderback chair and clay jugs in one corner and hooks with pewter mugs. I could write poetry about all of this, once I was safely back at Uncle Stuart's house.

Outside, the sun was high now, warm enough to chase winter's breath off the mountain. Birds sang and squirrels rushed back and forth, carrying pinecones and acorns. I paused to listen for weird snorting or jaw clacking, anything that might herald one of those blue monsters. When I heard nothing but ordinary autumn sounds, I reminded myself that I was trying not to think about blue skin and ashes and fangs.

I was feeling tired, nearly drunk with fatigue, which made the not-thinking easier. I was actually shuffling my feet because it felt like too much work to lift them off the ground. Combat boots were heavy when you were exhausted. It must be an adrenaline crash—and the fact that I'd been awake for over twenty-four hours straight now. I just needed a nap and some food. And to be rescued, of course. I was pretty sure that would cure all my ills.

I stopped at the end of the road, the wind kicking up the dirt around my feet. I wanted to start running and not stop.

"'When the road is a ribbon of moonlight over the purple moor, a highwayman comes riding,'" I murmured to myself, but it didn't make me feel any better.

Sighing, I turned slowly back toward the crumbling ghost town.

"You don't leave a man behind," Saga said from the doorway of a crooked house. "Good girl." She was leaning on one shoulder, the light glinting off the tarnished silver buttons of her frock coat. She wore tight black rolled-up jeans underneath and a frilly white tank top.

I froze, then frowned. "Wait. Sunlight." I lifted my chin. "I knew you guys were insane. If you were a vampire, you'd burst into flames."

She extended one hand so that the light fell on her pale blue skin. It was like she'd been painted with watercolors, versus the man last night who looked as if he'd been smeared with rancid oil paint. She didn't burn or blister or smoke like charred meat. The scars on her hands and forearms went a little pink, but that was it. The vampire thing was a delusion. It was some sort of historical prank, or they were garden-variety crazy people.

Which didn't explain Connor's dead faint.

Or make me feel any better, actually.

"Sunlight won't kill me," she said, amused. "I'm too old. But too much will make me feel worse than I would the morning after a barrel of bad rum." She straightened. "Come in, girl. Aidan's snoring like a wildebeest and I'm in need of easy company."

I crossed the street hesitantly.

She smirked. "Not going to turn lily-livered on me, are you?"

I cleared my throat. "No." I stumbled when I noticed the blue hand nailed to the door.

Saga shrugged nonchalantly, as if everyone decorated with body parts. "It's a warning."

I swallowed. "To who?" And of what, exactly? Extreme grossness?

"To the *Hel-Blar*."

"The *Hel-Blar*? That sounds like a bad rock band."

She just waved me inside the old house. I went with a great deal of trepidation. I really didn't want anything cut off to be used as decoration, but someone who sawed off hands wasn't someone I wanted to defy. Not until I got my bearings, anyway.

The house was swept free of dust and there was a shelf covered in pewter mugs and a big harvest table. Several muskets hung on the wall along with a few curved daggers, but no body parts. A basket of stakes whittled to such a fine point you could have embroidered with them stood by the door. Huge clay jugs crowded one corner. It looked old-fashioned but normal.

She poured something amber colored out of a smaller pitcher and slid a mug over toward me. "Have a seat and have a drink."

I smelled it gingerly. It was like paint thinner. I wrinkled my nose and took the smallest sip possible, then choked violently when it burned down my throat and turned into fire.

"What is that?" I croaked, sitting on the bench with a thump. I wouldn't have been surprised if smoke came out of my mouth.

"Grog." Saga laughed loudly and drained her cup, slamming it down. "Finest moonshine rum there is. Makes me think of home." She refilled her cup and then leaned back, crossing her bare feet at the ankles and resting them on the edge of the table. She licked her lips. "Your heart's like cannon shot."

I cringed back, looking around for a weapon. There were dozens everywhere but none within reach. She ran a hand over her mouth. She scraped her chair closer to mine and all I could smell was wet soil. "Relax," she said. Against all odds, I did. My shoulders didn't feel like they were going to shatter.

She turned and drank from a narrow fluted bottle that looked as if it was once meant for perfume. There were tight lines around her gray eyes and her lips. I was pretty sure it wasn't alcohol in that bottle. For one thing, it was too red. "Never mind, lass. I've fought harder battles than this. I was born in Tortuga, and I sailed with the best of them. Grace O'Malley, Anne Bonny, Mary Read." She smiled with what I could only term as nostalgia. "Once a pirate, always a pirate."

"Is that why you took me? So I could be a pirate?" This was making less and less sense.

"I stole you because *I'm* a pirate. It's what we do." She leaned in, whispering conspiratorially. I jerked back, but her eyes gleamed with laughter, not hunger. Whatever was in that bottle had sated her. "We like to steal things."

I nearly smiled. She was scary, with the daggers and muskets hanging all over the place, not to mention the needle-sharp teeth, but she was kind of fun, too. It didn't make sense. She didn't act like a kidnapper or a monster, or even like someone who claimed to be hundreds of years old.

Maybe I really had been kidnapped by a pirate.

That was so bizarre, it was almost cool.

And the smell of mushrooms and dirt, when they weren't rotten, wasn't so bad.

"Doesn't matter how old I get," she said. "I still miss the sea and the deck of a fine ship. As soon as the Blood Moon's done, I'm getting out of this cursed place. I wasn't meant to be a landlubber."

"What's a Blood Moon?"

"A gathering of the vampire tribes. Very rare. It's my chance to prove myself, to steal back a little respect for my people and my bloodkin. We're tired of being shot on sight. We deserve better."

"You and the pirates?" I asked, confused. "You know this is the twenty-first century, right? There are no pirates." Not like Johnny Depp, anyway.

"For us," she corrected me, her expression as grim as hardtack. "Worst of the worst, or so they'd have you believe. No one can control us." She sounded more than a little proud of that. "Except me and mine. We're not like the *Hel-Blar*, despite what we look like." She admired her skin. "The blue puts the fear in them, sure as flying the pirate colors used to. I like to think it's the color of the ocean. The others will tell you it's the color of death." She sighed, tilting her head back lazily. "You'll have to make up your own mind, I guess.

Regardless, you're our warning shot across the bow. And what's done is done." She yawned. "Go on back to your prince now."

I stood up, weaving slightly on my feet. The fatigue came back, all at once. Before I closed the door behind me she spoke again.

"Christabel." When I turned around, she tossed me a silver flask. "Grog. You might need it. I hope you make it through the next few nights. I truly do."

It took me too long to get back to the apothecary. I was stumbling, as if I'd had a jug full of Saga's awful rum instead of the barest taste. I briefly contemplated eating an apple or the bread Aidan had left in a basket. Chewing seemed like a monumental task, though, so instead I drank some of the water from the jug, sniffing it first to make sure it wasn't grog.

Even though daylight burned at the windows, I lit one of the oil lamps with the matches I found in an iron box shaped like a bird. I didn't want to wake up in the dark, if I did manage to fall asleep. I stretched out on the floor on my belly, peering through the wide gap between the boards. Connor's face was as pale as a consumptive Romantic poet. Shelley might have envied that kind of translucence. His eyes were closed and he looked restful, as if it were an ordinary kind of sleep, except he wasn't snoring and he didn't move at all, not even when a spider crawled across his cheek. I shuddered on his behalf.

Even lying there all creepy and corpselike, he was comforting. So I stayed there in the dust, staring down at him until my eyelids finally lost the battle with my fear.

Of course, I dreamed of vampires.

I was walking down a deserted road, the same one where I'd been taken. It was raining but the stars were still out, about a million of them, whirling white, like cream in coffee. I was soaked through and shivering. I was running but I didn't know if it was away from someone or toward someone. And then suddenly I was in the middle of a field of tall goldenrod and roses, in the shadow of a gray castle crumbling into an ocean that shouldn't be there.

And I wasn't alone.

A man in a dark suit, with brown hair and a brown beard, stood leaning on a walking stick. He was decidedly Victorian.

Bram Stoker.

Another man came toward us, through the grass. He wore a white cravat and had wild hair, strewn with red poppies. Two women trailed behind him, one in a silk dress with a cold smile, the other younger, in a dress and bonnet. I'd know her anywhere. Christabel. The one from the poem—so that made the man the poet Samuel Taylor Coleridge. His was the first poem I'd ever memorized, about a girl named Christabel who is hunted by the vampiric Geraldine.

They were closing in and my only escape was suddenly blocked by who I assumed was Lord Byron himself, limping toward me, corsets creaking. He held a bleached skull filled with red wine, from which he drank and then grinned at me, teeth stained red.

I whirled, trying to find a way out, but they tightened around me like a poisonous flower closing its petals for the night.

Ordinarily this would have been a great dream, full of poets and lace cravats.

But it felt wrong.

And my neck hurt.

When I lifted my hand away from my neck, it was covered in blood.

I wiped it frantically on my jeans but the blood kept pooling, dripping between my knuckles. And then it sparked and burned like embers before catching fire, as if my palms were filled with gasoline instead of blood. I smelled scorched flesh, smoke, spilled wine.

I woke up choking on a scream, my hair damp with sweat.

I couldn't immediately figure out why everything hurt and there was dust up my nose. I was just glad I wasn't really on fire. I lay there, cataloging my pains: the bruised hipbone from lying on the ground, the aching arm from where Aidan had grabbed me. No burns.

I knew the sun had gone down because I was in near darkness, except for a sliver of honey-tinted light from the lamp. If I moved my head slightly, the light fell between the floorboards and onto Connor's face. He really was beautiful, crazy or not. He'd risked himself to find me even though we barely knew each other. And for a computer geek, he had all sorts of interesting muscles. His eyes were impossible, mesmerizing.

Open.

They opened so abruptly, I started. Before I could say anything, his blue gaze caught mine, held it, trapped it. His lips lifted off his teeth; fangs lengthened and gleamed violently. I didn't see him lunge, but the trapdoor by my head suddenly snapped open, showering me with splinters and dirt. I scrambled backward as Connor landed in a crouch, still watching me hungrily.

Hungrily.

"Not good," I muttered, straightening. "Not good, not good." I swallowed, tried to smile, tried to make my tone soothing and not shrill. "Connor."

He rose slowly, so slowly I couldn't help but stay where I was, enthralled. I felt like a deer freezing in the shadow of a predator, hoping not to be noticed.

It was *not* a nice feeling.

Especially when he'd made me feel safe not a handful of hours ago. But whoever this Connor was, he wasn't human. Even I could see that, unbeliever that I was. He wasn't playacting or deluded. He was dangerous. And struggling for control.

I put my hands up, as if that would stop him. He just kept moving, stalking toward me, backing me into a corner until I had nowhere else to go. I remembered Lucy, when I assumed she was drunk, telling me to move slowly, and Aidan telling me I could never outrun them. It wasn't a theory I wanted to test. But just standing there didn't seem like a good idea, either. And I was getting annoyed. I was used to people being scared of me or not seeing me at all. This wasn't a pleasant alternative.

"Connor, stop it."

He half smiled. It was more of a smirk, and it made him look like his twin. "I just want a little taste, Christabel."

"What?" I scowled. "And *ew.*" He took a step closer. I slapped a hand on his chest. "Hey! Back off."

He stopped but was still close enough that all he had to do was bend his head to run his mouth along the side of my neck. I shivered despite myself. His fingers clamped around my wrist, lifting my hand off his chest. His very still chest. I frowned over that while he lifted my hand to his nose, sniffing me as if I were a rose. There was a dangerous edge to him that he hadn't possessed before.

It shouldn't have made him more attractive.

Damn that bad-boy thing.

I should have been furious. I should not have been feeling ticklish. I tried to jerk my palm away from his gentle nuzzling. His nostrils flared. Something moved across his face, something angry and cold.

"Connor?"

"No. Can't," he muttered to himself, as if I were a bottle of wine turned to vinegar. He tilted his head. "But . . ."

And then he was pressed against me and I was pressed against the wall and there was nothing but his mouth on mine. His palms were flat against the wooden boards on either side of my head. I couldn't have moved if I'd wanted.

I didn't want to.

Instead I kissed him back.

A lot.

His kisses were the opposite of his laid-back, friendly personality. They were wild and burned all the way down to my knees. I barely had time to catch my breath between kisses. His tongue touched mine, I gently bit his lower lip, he made a sound in the back of his throat that made me feel faint.

And then he pulled away, still leaning on the wall, head next to mine. His hair tickled my cheek and his hands were clenched into fists. His eyes sparked like embers.

"Connor?"

He didn't say anything but I knew he was fighting some kind of battle. He wanted to advance, wanted to retreat, wanted something I couldn't recognize and didn't know how to give him.

"Are you okay?"

When he finally spoke, it was like his voice hurt. "No," he forced out. "Get out of here."

Where exactly was I supposed to go? Not only was he blocking me, but I was kind of kidnapped in the mountains. Not a lot of options.

"I'm not . . . safe," he said. "Need blood."

"Gross."

"I'm serious," he ground out. He lifted his head, fangs poking out of his gums, expression both hot and cold.

Before I could react, the door swung open and Aidan barreled through it. "Christabel, behind me!" he ordered.

But Aidan was technically my kidnapper, even though he'd already saved my life once. To say I was confused was an understatement.

"Christa, listen to him," Connor said, shifting to give me an exit. His jaw clenched. "*Please.*"

It was the "please" that galvanized me into moving. I darted under his arm. Aidan shifted, meeting me halfway. I saw Connor twitch at the movement, like a cat suddenly focused on a fly, getting ready to swat it out of the air and eat its wings. Aidan shoved a jug toward him. It looked heavy but neither of them seemed to notice. Connor started to drink from it and I eased around Aidan's shoulder to look at him, then frowned. Was that *blood?*

It was getting really hard not to believe in vampires.

Connor looked at me, made a strange sound, and then turned around so I couldn't see him drinking. He tilted his head back to get the last drops.

"He's a young'un," Aidan explained. "Sunset makes them a mite ornery. It can take years, decades even, before a vampire can wake easily. He's already done better than most. Give him a minute."

Connor finally turned around, wiping his mouth. He looked partly chagrined and partly defiant. And mostly human again. I fought a small sigh of relief. Aidan looming next to me made it hard to feel true relief.

"Let's go," Aidan said.

Yup, no relief at all.

CHAPTER 17

◆

Lucy

I snuck out after my parents went to sleep.

I felt bad about it, but not bad enough to stay home.

I'd slept until noon and went to my afternoon classes, where Nathan informed me I was cranky and distracted. I had to walk to Mom's work and wait for her shift to end so I could get a ride home. My car was languishing in a garage somewhere with little hope of resurrection. I would have to get a part-time job soon to replace it, but there were no want ads for vampire sympathizers. I wasn't entirely sure I was qualified to do anything else.

When the sun set, my day didn't exactly get better. There were more *Hel-Blar* roaming the edges of town and almost everyone was out hunting them down. Solange wouldn't answer my texts again, and even Nicholas was in the caves and out of range.

Christabel was still gone, though apparently the Drakes had received a photo of her to prove she was unharmed. That was something, at least.

But I couldn't possibly be expected just to go to sleep and hope someone else figured it all out.

So when Hunter texted me and asked if I wanted to join them on patrol, I actually did a victory dance, scaring one of our cats under my desk. Finally, someone who didn't think I was useless because I was human or because I was sixteen. I made a lump of clothes into a person-shape under my blanket and then pinned a note underneath to my pillow just in case my mom figured it out. If my parents found my bed empty with no note, they'd have twin heart attacks and die on the spot. Dad's ulcer might actually explode. I tucked a chamomile tea bag next to the note, just in case.

Hunter pulled up to the end of my driveway and turned her lights out at precisely one thirty a.m., as planned. I snuck out of my window, landing in the bushes. If my parents caught me, they'd probably move my bedroom up to the attic and invest in a set of iron bars for the windows. I ran along the side of the driveway, staying close to the cedars and the lilac bushes. I had a vial of Hypnos up my sleeve, secured in an old tear-gas pen Hunter had given me, stakes in my shoulder bag, my cell phone, and a knapsack full of water, food, and a hand crossbow I'd "liberated" from the Drakes. I was prepared. Despite what everyone seemed to think about my supposed recklessness, I wasn't an idiot.

I slid into the backseat next to a duffel bag bristling with more stakes, crossbows, and throwing daggers. Hunter's friend Chloe was in the front seat, frowning at her laptop.

"Don't you have wireless out here?" she asked in lieu of a greeting.

I snorted. "Please, we're on dial-up."

Chloe looked horrified. "How do you live like that?"

"We're just lucky we have actual power lines. The farm down the road has to use oil for heating and solar panels and a generator for electricity."

Chloe just blinked at me like I was a particularly strange science project. Hunter eased the standard-issue Helios-Ra Jeep down the road before switching the headlights back on. Her long blond hair was caught in a tight braid and she was wearing her school cargo pants. I was wearing black jeans and a black hoodie, which was about as military as I got.

"Did you hear?" Hunter glanced in the rearview mirror at me. "Hope killed herself."

"Seriously?" Hope had run the Helios-Ra with Kieran's uncle before the truth came out that she'd murdered the old director, Kieran's father. She'd also secretly sent out rogue units to kill Solange. And she'd allied herself with Lady Natasha. The Helios-Ra had not been impressed.

"Apparently she didn't want to deal with League justice."

"Dare I ask what that even is?"

"You don't want to know."

I really did, actually. But I knew she wasn't allowed to tell me, since I was an outsider and an outsider with vampire connections on top of it. She was starting to have those same connections, through Quinn. I wondered how the other students were dealing with that. Hunter had a way of making you think she could handle anything. I made a note to ask Chloe later.

"So where are we going?" I asked for now.

"Pretty much point to a map of the wilds around Violet Hill, and it's crawling with *Hel-Blar*," Hunter answered. "We're still cleaning up from Montmartre and Greyhaven, and now this new thing with your cousin. Are you holding up okay after last night? We hear you got ambushed."

"It was bizarre," I admitted. "Saga had them controlled like she fed them Hypnos or something, but she just had that whistle. And they wore those copper collars."

"We don't know anything about her," Hunter said, sounding both apologetic and frustrated. "We didn't even know *Hel-Blar* could stand one another enough to go after some sort of political goal."

"I know," I grumbled in agreement. "It's annoying."

"It really is," Hunter grumbled back. "Any word on your cousin?"

"All signs point to her being alive," I said. I'd reminded myself of that about a thousand times today.

"I hear they were trying to get you," Chloe said. "Bummer."

"Yeah. How'd you hear about that, anyway? Quinn?"

Hunter nodded. "And word's out through the League."

"The League," I teased, wanting to stop the burning in the back of my eyes and the way my throat was suddenly feeling tight. "I'm surprised you guys don't go out in Wonder Woman Underoos."

"Hunter had a pair when she was a kid." Chloe grinned. "I've seen pictures."

Hunter narrowed her eyes. "Are we sharing embarrassing kid stories? Because I'll remind you of—"

Chloe winced. "Sorry! I take it back!"

Hunter smiled smugly.

"I have a photo of Quinn dressed up like Batman, tights and all," I offered.

Hunter's smile widened. "I'll remember that."

"Do the Drakes sit around wearing crowns?" Chloe asked dreamily. "I'd love to be royalty."

Hunter and I exchanged a glance.

"The Drakes aren't like that," I said. "Well, mostly. The brothers kind of act like princes, but that's nothing new. They've always been bossy."

Chloe sighed. "Can you imagine being a princess? It must be awesome."

I knew Solange would much prefer to be a girl sitting in a car with her friends, like Chloe. Well, the old Solange would have preferred that. I really couldn't tell with her now.

"So, anything else weird going on?" I asked. Hunter and I had taken to sharing strange intel with each other when we could.

"Besides the *Hel-Blar*, not really." She turned onto a road that narrowed almost immediately to a dirt lane. Tree branches scraped at the windows. "There are a bunch of cabins down by the end of the lake," she explained, interrupting herself. "*Hel-Blar* were spotted here last night." She stopped the Jeep, parking it under a huge pine tree. "So we're supposed to do a sweep. You?"

"My mom told me one of the New Age shops was broken into this week."

"Why's that weird?" Hunter wondered as we climbed out of the vehicle.

"The only thing missing was a basket of bloodstone." Bloodstone wasn't red as expected, more of a dark green with rust-colored veins. It was used for healing in New Age circles. But because of the name, it held some interest for the vampire tribes as well. I'd have to ask Isabeau if she ever used it for anything magical.

"Bloodstone?" Hunter repeated quizzically, adjusting the stakes on her belt.

"Yup." I was a little proud. It wasn't easy getting the scoop on something Hunter didn't already know, especially if it wasn't about the Drakes. "Not even a penny out of the till."

"Huh. That is kinda weird."

"I know, right?"

Chloe checked her weapons and tied back the enormous weight of her long black curls, pulling them out of her face. "Ready?"

I loaded my miniature crossbow with a bolt, keeping the rest in my pocket. My aim was my best weapon by far, and it kept me out of easy reach of any attacking vampires. "Ready."

"Stay in visual range," Hunter whispered, nodding at Chloe. "You take rear, I'll take point."

We crept through the trees, toward the faint glimmer of the lake. One of the cabins had a motion sensor light that flicked on as we passed. Hunter was on the edge of the light, out of range. Chloe and I had tripped it. Chloe looked as irritated by that as I was.

We patrolled the area, scaring a racoon, a porcupine, and two bunnies but no vampires. We eventually found claw marks in the mud on the edge of a garden and a thin trail of blood leading from there to the woods.

"It's dry," Hunter said. "Not tonight's, maybe not even last night's."

But it ended at a pile of bones and fur.

"That better not have been someone's pet," I said ominously.

Hunter shook her head. "Looks like a badger."

"I'm not even going to ask how you know that."

"Definitely not an animal kill," Chloe added, pointing to the dirt. "That's a footprint."

We did another sweep, ending back at the main lane leading out of the forest, away from the lake. The wind rained autumn leaves over us. Hunter frowned, holding up her hand and pausing. Chloe frowned as well, squinting to see what Hunter saw. I didn't catch anything out of the ordinary either, just a bear-proof box for residents' garbage and the glint of a soda can.

"Hear that?" Hunter asked so softly I had to strain to hear her. She pointed in the direction of a clump of cedars. It was very faint, like a pig snuffing the ground for truffles. I nodded, eyes widening. The snuffing sounded more ferocious now that I suspected it was *Hel-Blar* and not someone's escaped pig. "We need to flush them out," Hunter mouthed.

I nodded, pulling a hunting knife off my belt and jabbing the tip into my thumb. I swore under my breath. It hurt way more than it looked like it did in the movies. I squeezed the small puncture, letting blood drop onto the ground.

Chloe's eyes widened. "You're nuts!" she exclaimed, impressed, and fumbled for her weapons.

I shrugged one shoulder and wiped my thumb off so the blood wouldn't make my grip on the crossbow slippery. Hunter raised a wickedly pointed stake. The snuffing got louder and turned to snarling. We could hear the clicking of jaws before we could see them. I lifted my crossbow, taking aim. The sound stopped abruptly. It was just as creepy as the snarling.

Hel-Blar exploded out of the trees. A wave of rotten-mushroom stench made me gag. There were four of them, wearing muddy rags of clothing, probably the same ones they were wearing when they'd pulled themselves out of their graves. I released the crossbow bolt. The faint whistle of the arrow in the air made one of them stiffen and pause so that it caught him under the collar bone. Not my best work. I reloaded and fired again, this time piercing his heart. He fell to ashes and torn clothing. He wasn't wearing a copper collar.

Hunter was fighting two of them and I couldn't shoot without the risk of hitting her. Chloe had one screeching, thick blood spouting from a deep gash in her side. Even her blood smelled full of decay.

"Chloe!" I yelled. "Down!"

She dropped, used to obeying orders. I aimed and fired, the bolt flying true. The *Hel-Blar* crumbled, still clutching her wound, saliva dripping from her many fangs before she turned to dust.

Chloe threw herself into a roll, coming up next to Hunter. Another *Hel-Blar* fell to a combination of Hunter's legendary roundhouse kick and a stake. There was only one left.

He whirled and ran and there was no catching him. I barely saw the blue smudge of his skin in the darkness until he reached the edge of the drop into the lake. His silhouette was clear enough that I fired again. I missed. He leaped over the edge and we heard the splash of his body hitting the water. We ran to the hilltop and Hunter flicked on her flashlight, scouring the inky water. He could stay under water for hours since he didn't need to breathe. Or he might already be swimming for the far shore.

"He's gone," she finally said, turning off the light. "Damn it."

"Still," Chloe said, wiping mud off her hands. "Three out of four is pretty good."

"I guess."

"Let's get out of here," Chloe nudged her. "It's late."

We piled back into the Jeep. I checked my phone as Hunter pulled out from under the tree but there were still no messages from Solange. Twenty minutes later Hunter turned onto my road and stopped several houses away from my driveway.

"Thanks," I said, stifling a yawn. "I needed that."

Hunter grinned. "Which proves you're as weird as we are."

"True. Night."

There were no lights on, so I assumed my parents were sleeping, blissfully ignorant. Still, I circled around to the back, keeping on the grass so my footsteps were muffled. I wasn't about to give myself away at the very end like this. I felt better, like I'd accomplished something. I should probably have worried that my version of accomplishing something included killing monsters, but I had enough to worry about.

Like the fact that someone was standing at my bedroom window, leaning inside.

CHAPTER 18

◆

Connor

"We must go," Aidan said. "Saga is waiting," Aidan insisted when neither of us moved. "We had to steal *children*," he muttered. "Young'uns still wet behind the ears."

I straightened.

Aidan sighed. "Just come on, before you make things worse."

"Worse?" Christabel squeaked. I reached to take her hand. I couldn't imagine what she was feeling right now. "How can it get worse? Wait. You're not going to call up one of those blue things, are you? A vampire's one thing, but that . . ." She shuddered.

I frowned. "You saw a normal *Hel-Blar*?"

"That was *normal*?"

"As far as we knew," I said. "I've never known a *Hel-Blar* to act like this one does."

Aidan's face was implacable and ever so faintly ironic. "The colonials used to say that about us when they landed. Savages and all that."

"I didn't mean it like that."

"Mmm."

"Aidan saved me," Christabel admitted.

I blinked at her. "From a *Hel-Blar?*"

She nodded.

"War between the tribes." Aidan pushed the door open. "You asked what would be worse than the *Hel-Blar*," he elaborated.

"What tribes?" Christabel asked. "Is this about that Blood Moon thing?"

"I'll explain later," I whispered.

"*We'll* explain," Aidan corrected him. "Your lot don't see us as real vampires, and you certainly don't know anything about how hard we've fought to survive."

"You're not . . . like the others," I agreed.

"No. And neither will either of you be, if you play your cards right and keep your mouths shut. Saga is easily insulted for all she might seem otherwise. Took war trophies from her own kind, didn't she? Imagine what she'd do to her enemies if there was war."

We followed Aidan onto the porch. Night had settled over the crooked roofs and the dandelion-thick road. A howl shivered through the air, not a wolf or a dog. Sounded like *Hel-Blar*.

Christabel's hand tightened around mine. She dug her heels into the dirt. "Can we make a run for it?" she asked softly.

"No," Aidan interrupted drily. "You can't."

Christabel scowled. She had no idea how well we could hear. "I actually thought I liked Saga earlier today," she whispered. "She was slightly insane, granted, but kinda *fun* in a weird way. You know, for a monster who has girls stolen from their cars for kicks."

Yeah, Saga was going to pay for that. Out loud, because I knew exactly how well Aidan could hear, I just said, "She thinks she's saving her people or getting political power or whatever. Like Princess Leia."

"You're not seriously comparing her to your precious Princess Leia?"

"I guess not. She's got more Xena in her."

She smirked a little. "I just bet you used to have Xena posters all over your wall."

"Hell, no."

"Why not? I thought that'd totally be your thing."

"She's way too much like my mom."

"Oh. Ew."

"Yeah. Gabrielle's cute though," I admitted. "And Callisto."

"Wasn't Callisto psychotic?"

"I have a thing for blondes." I didn't quite look at her but I knew she was running a hand through her tangled, dusty red-blond hair.

"You must have loved Buffy then."

"Not really. She's hot, don't get me wrong, but we're not exactly portrayed well. And what, the only good vampires are Angel and then Spike? I heard Lucy go on about Spike until we all threatened to gag her. Believe me, I know I can't compare."

"You'd be surprised."

That would have been my moment to kiss her properly, without being all fangy and tortured. But we were kinda still kidnapped. Another reason to hate Aidan and Saga.

Saga was waiting for us in a field near the last house on the road. She was perched on the new wooden farm fencing stretched out behind her. The wind toyed gently with the ragged hem of her dress, lifting it to reveal her bare feet. The sword strapped to her side was curved, the kind of cutlass a pirate would have been proud to carry.

"So we've gained ourselves a prince in the bargain." She shook her head. "Can't say that's a help." She sighed at me as if it were my fault. She slid off the fence. "Now we'll have your parents putting the Black Spot on us, marking us for vengeance. There's a reason we went for a human." She shrugged one shoulder prosaically. "Ah well."

"I'm sure my parents have agreed to your demands," I said steadily. Christabel shot me a look, as if surprised at how calm I was. She really didn't take me for a tough guy. I might be annoyed at that later. "So are you going to keep your word and let us go?"

Saga lifted an eyebrow. "Take after your father, don't you, boy? All that talk of honor and treaties." It was easy to picture her balanced on the prow of a ship. She had the rolling gait to her walk, even after centuries, and that gleam in her eye told you she'd rather fight than talk any day. "First we have something to show you." She climbed up a pile of rocks, casting an impatient look over her shoulder. "Tally-ho, children."

I blinked and looked at Christabel, who just blinked back.

Saga sighed. "Honestly, what do they teach you in school?"

"Not pirate vocab if that's what you're asking," Christabel muttered. "The *weirdest* kidnapping *ever*."

We climbed the rocks, Aidan behind us. "High ground's best," he murmured.

Something my mother had drilled into us.

Which meant this was going nowhere good.

"Stay close." I kept a grip on Christabel's hand.

"Losing feeling in my fingers," she said.

"Sorry." I loosened my hold. I hadn't held a lot of hands since I turned into a vampire.

Snarling and the clacking of jaws skittered out of the darkness. Saga and Aidan were proof there were *Hel-Blar* who could speak well enough, but these weren't them.

Then the smell hit, thick and recognizable.

Christabel wrinkled her nose. "What's with all the rotten mushrooms?"

I swore, tensing. I didn't have any stakes or weapons inside my coat anymore. Aidan must have cleaned me out yesterday when the sunrise dropped me. But he didn't know about the dagger in my left boot and the stake in my right one. I was reaching for one when Saga blew her whistle.

The cacophony of feral vampires turned off as if she'd flipped a switch. She stood by more fencing, metal and lined with wire, both barbed and electric. Behind her, *Hel-Blar* clawed and snapped, copper collars gleaming around their throats.

"Get behind me," I told Christabel, stepping in front of her when she didn't move fast enough.

Saga flicked a hand. "If I meant to feed her to the *Hel-Blar*, boy, I'd have done it by now."

I bristled.

"We only want to show you what we've done, and what we *can* do," Aidan said. He was holding a video camera now.

Saga grinned. "So pay attention."

The *Hel-Blar* scrabbled to get away from her when she stepped closer to the gate. One of them howled. Christabel winced. I swallowed thickly, keeping my mouth closed. The proximity to so much anger and adrenaline made my fangs poke out of my gums, and I didn't want to scare her.

There was enough of that going on.

"She doesn't need to be here," I said tightly. "Let Christabel go and I'll be your witness."

Saga laughed and shook her head. "She's stronger than you think. And I like her."

"I'm fine," Christabel said to me. "And I'm not leaving you alone, either. I broke Peter's balls at school. I can break vampire balls if I have to." I didn't point out that neither Aidan nor Saga were as easy to take down as a high school jock. She knew it already. She lifted her chin.

Aidan smiled gently, which was incongruous behind the creepy camera. "Good girl," he approved. Christabel clenched her back teeth together. He probably didn't mean to sound condescending; he was nearly five hundred years old after all.

Saga took a wineskin off her belt and popped the top off. The smell of blood tingled through my nostrils. The *Hel-Blar* pressed frantically at the fence, drooling and snarling.

"Don't get any of their saliva on you," I told Christabel.

"Aidan already licked the cuts on my hand!" She paused, wild-eyed.

I froze, and if my heart still beat, it would have shattered with the violence of the cold inside my chest.

Aidan had infected Christabel and she didn't know.

He'd kept it a secret.

That's how *Hel-Blar* were made—infected through blood or saliva and then left to go wild through the bloodchange. Few survived.

I went for Aidan's throat.

He was older, stronger, and faster.

I knew it and I didn't care.

I barely reached him, for all my mother's training. And I'd broken my dad's cardinal rule: don't act out of anger.

I only managed to shove Aidan, since he bent out of my way long before I could put any real force into the movement. Saga whipped one of her knives at me, catching me in the back of my right shoulder. The hit propelled me away from Aidan and face-first into the dirt. Pain flared, the steel slicing through muscle and sinew. I might heal fast, but that didn't mean wounds didn't hurt like a son of a bitch. The *Hel-Blar* howled and one of them laughed.

"Connor!" Christabel scrambled to get to me. She landed hard on her knees. "Connor, shit, don't die."

"I'm not dying," I said, disgusted, blood dripping from my nose. I cracked it back into place with a hiss. "Ow." My shoulder was on fire. "Damn it. Can you pull the knife out?"

As a gesture to defend Christabel's honor, my attack clearly left something to be desired.

Saga was there before Christabel could move. She yanked the dagger out and I bit back a scream. Warm blood pooled at the wound and stuck to my shirt. A *Hel-Blar* actually wept with hunger. I clenched my jaw against the pain.

I would *not* scream like the sissy comic geek Christabel seemed to think I was. If I was ever going to get out of the friend zone with her, I had to demolish her expectations. I was used to it. People always assumed I was weak and socially awkward because I liked comics and computers. I used it against them all the time.

"That was a warning, princeling. I could have had your heart. And if you ever attack my mate again, I will."

Aidan looked down at me. "I'm not contagious," he said. "I'm not *Hel-Blar*, not like them."

Hope trickled through me. "But you're blue, and you have all those fangs."

"Less blue, fewer fangs. It makes a difference. You know the ones the Hounds save aren't contagious." He was right. Logan's girlfriend had more fangs than us (but still fewer than Solange) and she wasn't blue or insane, and she should have been *Hel-Blar*. She'd been left in a coffin for two hundred years or so, after all.

Christabel stared at Aidan. "Your spit could have turned me?" She ran her palms over her jeans until they chafed. The tiny cuts opened up again. "Like that whole licking thing wasn't gross enough."

"Don't do that," I said tightly. The smell of blood when we were wounded was even sweeter. Even that tiny drop smeared on her knee made me push back a little so she was out of my reach.

"I'm going to throw up," she added, sounding strangely calm.

"You're fine," Saga said nonchalantly.

Christabel eyed her with an impressive glint of steel. "You stabbed him."

"He's fine, too."

I rose to my feet, then helped Christabel up as well. "She's right," I said. "I'm fine. It's already stopped bleeding."

"She *stabbed* you."

"We heal from almost anything, so you'd be surprised how often that kind of thing happens," I explained wryly. "And I have six brothers," I added.

"If we're done with the mollycoddling?" Saga inquired. "We have business to be getting on to, lad." At least she hadn't called me "boy" again. It was hard to impress a girl when a crazy vampire pirate kept treating you like a child.

Saga reached for the lock on the gate.

"Shit." I leaped in front of Christabel, wondering how I was going to get us out of this. The cut on my shoulder would be a beacon. I stepped away from Christabel again. She'd be safest the hell away from me.

Saga poured the blood from the wineskin on the ground and then sprinkled the last drops like rose petals.

She opened the lock and stepped back.

The *Hel-Blar* bottlenecked at the gate, fighting one another to get through, diving for the blood, eating the dirt it had soaked. Three of them got free before Saga shut the gate again to the frustrated, enraged howls of the rest of the nest. The last one out sniffed the air, clapped his angry red eyes on me, then jumped over his companions, smelling fresher blood. They were the only kind of vampire who drank from other vampires. My blood wouldn't feed him, wouldn't help him survive—only human or animal blood did that. Human blood worked best of all. Vampire blood only worked if it was passed from an older vampire onto someone younger in the same lineage.

All that to say he wasn't after me for survival—just the pleasure of the kill.

He was in midair, fangs flashing, hands curled into claws, when Saga blew her whistle.

The sound stopped him. He paused there, like a cartoon character about to realize he was falling off a cliff, then he hit the ground, screaming.

"I was wrong." Christabel's voice was strangled, scared, and pissed off. "I don't like her *at all*."

I might not admit it to her, but my throat was clogged with panic, too. If I breathed, I'd have been gasping. The *Hel-Blar* writhed on the ground at my feet, alternating between clutching his head and his copper collar. The stench of burned mushrooms and green water made me gag.

The others in the cage dropped to their knees, waiting.

Saga was one scary-ass woman.

"Go." She ordered the three *Hel-Blar* back into the cage. They whimpered and hissed. The gate clanged shut. "Seen enough?"

Christabel and I both nodded jerkily.

"Then come with me." She was smiling again, proud and helpful, as if we were on a school field trip. We climbed past the

Hel-Blar enclosure while they paced along the perimeter, snarling at us. I tried not to feel sick. They'd been people once. And Isabeau could have turned into one of them, if she'd been any less strong. I hoped Logan never saw this.

A complicated maze filled the plateau in front of us, reaching nearly to the foot of the mountain. Torchlight gleamed here and there, like eyes. The cedar hedges were thick as walls and reinforced in weaker points with barbed wire and thorny vines.

"You made a maze?" I asked, startled. It was the last thing I'd expected. For one thing, it was totally cool and out of a movie.

"We didn't." Saga shrugged. "Someone meant to turn this place into a kind of carnival amusement park in the twenties, but then the stock market crashed and the whole thing was abandoned."

There was a small fire belching pine smoke. There were benches set around it with three more faintly blue vampires waiting for us.

"Crap," I said.

CHAPTER 19

•

Christabel

Connor lifted his chin. I knew he was picturing himself as a space captain to her ship's captain. He looked older, more certain.

I just felt like an idiot.

"We're going to tell you about our bloodchange," Aidan explained. "And what we mean to do as a tribe. The council needs to know." He set up the camera again and glanced at Connor. "We'll send this to your mother."

"I doubt my mother will do what you want," Connor said evenly. "Unless eating your own spleen is what you had in mind."

"Yes, I've heard the stories," Saga approved. "It's what gives me hope. There was no sense in talking to Lady Natasha; she was all vanity. Do you know how the *Hel-Blar* got their name?"

Connor nodded. I had no idea.

"It's some old Viking word, meaning 'blue as death,'" Connor explained for my benefit. I noticed he kept a wary eye on the other vampires.

"Aye," Saga confirmed, tossing her red hair over her shoulders. "The Norse word for vampire is *Draugur*. And there are two types, the *Hel-Blar* and the *Na-Foir*."

"*Na-Foir?*" Connor frowned. "I've never heard that word."

"Of course you haven't," she returned. "We've lived in secret for centuries."

"Your note said you represented the *Hel-Blar*."

"A small ruse to buy us time. For too long we've been confused with the *Hel-Blar*, been hunted or used as scapegoats. But we're not like them." She lifted her arm, the firelight making it look almost healthy. "*Na-Foir* means 'corpse-pale.'" She grimaced. "Not entirely flattering, I'll grant you. But we've been lost in folktale and legend long enough that it hardly matters.

"We're not contagious," she continued. "And some of us used to look more *Hel-Blar* than we do at present. But in reality we're more like the Hounds or Montmartre's Host, though we've never served him. We survived the bloodchange as they did, through will and luck and strength—only we have more scars to prove it."

Connor looked faintly stunned, as if he couldn't process all the information we'd been given. For me, it was just another chapter in the fantasy novel my life had turned into; he looked like he was about to descend into a full-blown existential crisis.

"This color"—Aidan pushed up his sleeve, showing off blue-tinted muscles—"is not the color of madness. It's the color of survival." His eyes glittered. "The hunger that makes the *Hel-Blar* so vicious would do the same to anyone, prince and pauper alike. They turn blue because they're bloated with blood and still not sated. We're as pale as any other vampire now because we found a way through that starvation, but our veins remember." He flexed, those blue veins as ropey as snakes under his skin. "The fangs are a side effect of the hunger." He'd said that before. The fact that it was starting to make a little sense was not actually comforting.

"We had a scientist," he said to the camera. "And she spent years working in her labs, testing *Hel-Blar* and finding out what makes us different. We're willing to share those discoveries with the council and with Geoffrey Drake."

"My uncle. He's a scientist," Connor said to me. "Are you their scientist?" he asked the only other female vampire at the fire.

She shook her head.

"Gretchen was eaten."

I gulped. "Eaten?"

"By one of her test subjects."

I had to remember to stop asking questions. I hadn't yet gotten an answer I liked.

"We've spent centuries hiding from other vampires, from *our own kind*," Saga said quietly. "But no more. I've bloodkin to protect. We might never pass for humans, but we'll damn well pass for vampires now that a new Blood Moon's been called."

"And the *Hel-Blar* you're keeping in the backyard?" Connor asked.

Saga shrugged one shoulder. "I might need them. An army's an army, and we can't afford to be picky."

"That's enslavement."

"Or pragmatism. It's certainly not any worse than what you do to us."

"We're trying to save people from being hurt!"

"So are we, little boy."

He bristled at that. So did I.

"You think we're all the same," Aidan interjected smoothly, looking at the camera again. "It's time you heard our stories. They could just as easily become your own. This is our court, who'll be attending the Blood Moon. We expect them to be allowed past your guards, Liam Drake, if your talk of peace treaties all these years has been honest." The *Hel-Blar* were shrieking in their pen, rattling the fences. He lifted his wampum belt.

"This is a record of my people, the Wendat, and of myself, Aidan Hawkfeather. After I was turned I was too ill to notice the bear hibernating at the back of the cave I'd dragged myself to. By the time I was desperate enough to think of drinking his blood, I'd already changed color and grown more fangs than I might have otherwise. But I've never been feral." He quirked a smile. "I might have been, if I'd been saved by a porcupine spirit instead of the Great Bear."

I tried to imagine drinking all the blood from a giant brown bear and gagged.

"And Emma," Saga said.

"I was turned just three years ago," Emma said softly. She was a plump woman in her thirties. She looked quiet and calm, except for the silver stakes glittering on a strap between her breasts and the scar bisecting her eyebrow. "My family thought I was dead.

I heard them weeping and then I heard the embalmers discussing chemicals. I could smell them, sharp and poisonous, but I was too weak to open my eyes." She was marbled with blue and gray and pale, pale white. "The poisons didn't kill me, but they stopped me from waking before I was buried, kept me too weak to claw my way out for months." She pointed to the scar, tilting her head so we could see where it ran in a jagged line down to her chin and past her collarbone, toward her heart. "Another vampire did this to me. When Saga found me, I couldn't even speak. "

The man next to her was wearing an expensive suit and a ring set with an emerald on his pinky. He could have been a lawyer or a wealthy businessman, except for the faded tribal tattoos on his neck and hands.

"Max." Saga nodded to him.

"Maxixcatzin, as my mother named me," he said smoothly. "The hunger had me for nearly a hundred years. I lived in the rain forest, and when I knew myself enough to know I needed blood, not sugarcane or papayas, I drank from jaguars and panthers—and it was enough to survive. Barely. I never drank from a human because I never came across one. My tribe's shaman had me banned before I was turned. I don't know what I would have become if I'd lived in a city or been buried under concrete. By the time Saga found me, I was more panther than vampire."

"And I was born on Tortuga," Saga said with a bloodthirsty grin. "I was turned at port but I didn't know what the sickness was until we were at sea and too far from land to feed properly. I knew I was ill, knew something was wrong, so I locked myself in the brig and swallowed the key. It was months before we made it to shore.

I nearly didn't survive." Snow was falling, settling in her hair, and the last of the fire gilded her hard expression, her pale, red-veined eyes like maple leaves in autumn. "But I was lucky, strong. So I spent centuries chasing legends, chasing witches, doctors, and scientists. It took me that long to find a way to train the *Hel-Blar*, to have them heel to me so we might prove to others that we are different. The whistle I use was taken from a snake charmer in India, made three hundred years ago and since blessed by a shaman. The collars have magic in them—old magic and old blood." Her smile went wolfish. "But you don't need to know all of our secrets.

"We meant to take your Lucy so she could be a link between our families. But I think Christabel is a better choice. She doesn't come with your prejudices and she comes with your son. So we'll take our council seat by your promise," she threatened darkly, "or we'll steal it. I have enough *Hel-Blar* trained to the whistle to carry out my plans, whichever choice you make."

The snarling was close.

Too close.

The vampires around the fire rose to their feet, smooth and soft as the smoke. Light glinted on fangs and stakes. Snarls and the clacking of teeth made all the hair on my body stand up straight. Goosebumps tightened my skin. I was so tense I wondered how I didn't break into pieces, like porcelain hitting the ground.

Hel-Blar scrabbled toward us.

"You haven't trained them all," Connor said, whipping a stake out of his boot as the smell of wet mushrooms hit the back of my throat. I retched.

Saga lifted her whistle and blew it hard. Her eyebrows met, making her look like a stern teacher. I'd hate to know the kind of detention she'd give out.

Connor took a knife from his other boot and handed it to me. "Trust me—if you need it, you'll know how to use it. But try not to jab yourself with it in the meantime."

I clutched it and made a few jabbing motions.

"You're not chopping onions," Connor said, the corner of his mouth lifting despite our circumstances. "Here, hold it like this." He adjusted it so that it was lying along my forearm, point toward my elbow.

"It's backward. And when did you get all tough?"

"It's easier to stab this way," he said, ignoring my question. "Lift your arm." I did. "See? It's already facing out and you haven't had to move your hand at all."

"Oh. Cool."

"And if you get surprised from behind, it's easier to stab backward."

I felt the need to defend my lack of fighting skills. "I'm used to pepper spray."

"Can you run?" he asked.

"Of course I can."

"You might have to," he said grimly when Saga blew her whistle for a third time and still the *Hel-Blar* ran at us.

"Mangy, scurvy-rotten dogs," she spat, trading her whistle for a cutlass. Emma was already flinging silver-tipped stakes. The *Hel-Blar* descended like cannibalistic beetles. They weren't wearing collars. The sounds they made and the way they moved, shuffling and creeping, made me shiver all over. Even my toes were trembling.

Connor grabbed my arm and hauled me out of the way. We jumped over a bench and he half carried, half dragged me toward the maze. The battle continued behind us, jaws snapping, stakes flying, Saga laughing.

"Into the maze," Connor said. "Before they realize we've gone."

Okay, I take it back. Geeky nice boys are way hotter than bad boys.

Especially when they were taking off their shirts.

"What are you doing?" I asked. I was thinking, "Whoa. Hello."

"There's blood on this." He contorted to wipe the last bit of blood off his wound, then threw the shirt in the direction opposite of where we were going. "Might buy us a few minutes."

The entrance to the maze was narrow, cedar catching at my hair. White flowers glowed in the darkness, tendrils climbing the odd labyrinth. The ground was weedy underfoot. I was already lost and we hadn't even stepped inside yet. I hated puzzles. I wasn't any good at them, despite the hundred times Lucy had made me watch the movie *Labyrinth* to swoon over David Bowie in tight pants.

"I really hate everyone right now," I announced, running to keep up with his long strides. "I just want to be reading *Pride and Prejudice* for the hundredth time and eating ice cream."

"I know," Connor said, still holding my hand, cool fingertips grazing the inside of my wrist.

An owl called from somewhere in the forest, but all we could see was the path through green darkness and the barest hint of light from the moon hitting the snow on the mountaintop. I wondered if my mom felt like this right now, lost in her own battle. If she could defeat her illness, I could defeat this. I was just going to have to pretend it was that simple.

We ran, skidding on weeds and pine needles and old leaves. I smelled mushrooms faintly. The *Hel-Blar* were on our heels, despite the battle.

"Hold on," I said when we had to double back a second time and retrace our steps. My breath was burning in my throat. "In the story of Theseus and the Minotaur, Ariadne gives Theseus a red thread to carry through the labyrinth. So he doesn't get lost."

"I don't have thread," Connor said doubtfully. "You?"

"Well, no," I admitted. "And she holds it at one end so he can find his way back from the center. But we want to go straight through."

"Still, it's a good idea. We have to find a way to mark where we've been so we don't end up back at the beginning." His fists clenched. If he thought any harder he'd hurt himself. "I know! My mom told us about something like this. A military trick to help you not get lost."

"Your mom knows weird stuff."

"You have no idea." He put his hand on the cedars. "Apparently, if we always stay to our left, we won't get lost. And one of us has to touch the wall at all times."

I followed behind him, ducking under a stray flower. "Not all the turns are left, though," I pointed out when we came to a dead end three turns later.

"But it's easier to backtrack," he said, even going so far as to walk backward to the last left we'd taken. He went right, then went back to staying to the left of the path and taking all left turns. It might take us forever, but hopefully we'd find our way out. "We need weapons." He looked at the ground. "If you see any good stones, fill your pockets."

I jogged to keep up with him. We passed a statue of a woman draped in a toga and moss. Her head was at her feet, staring blankly at us.

"Uh, Christa?"

"Yeah?"

"Run faster!"

CHAPTER 20

◆

Lucy

I was reaching for a stake before I recognized him.

I knew that dark hair, the pale skin, and the very fine muscles as he bent over farther into my bedroom.

Nicholas.

"Lucy," he whispered. "Lucy, wake up!"

I would probably never get another chance to surprise him again. He normally had all the advantages: speed, strength, and a preternatural nose. But right now I was downwind, and he wasn't expecting me. I smiled, taking out my cell phone.

"Boo!"

He jumped so fast and so hard, the window rattled. He also made a weird sound, like a choked scream, followed by a stream of curses. Then he whirled, stake in hand. It all happened in the space of a single heartbeat. I hit the camera button and took a photo of his shocked face, gray eyes wide as plates.

Then I laughed so hard I doubled over, gasping for breath.

"You know, some people are scared of vampires," he informed me drily, sauntering over to my side. I just snorted, still laughing. It wasn't very attractive to snort like a pig in front of your boyfriend, but I couldn't help it. I dropped onto the cold grass, chortling. He looked down at me. "Are you done?"

I wiped my eyes, shaking my head. I might just laugh until the sun came up. It felt good, normal—if I ignored the faint edge of hysteria to my wheezing. My stomach muscles ached. He sat next to me, smelling like wood smoke and rain.

And between one chuckle and the next, he pressed me back into the grass, his mouth closing over mine.

He swallowed my laughter and kissed me fiercely, deeply, as if I were delicious. I kissed him back, feeling powerful and yet weak in all the right places. My knees went soft, my belly was as warm as if I'd drunk a pot of hot chocolate. I didn't care that the ground was cold and there was a rock digging into my left ankle. He covered me and, though he should have felt heavy, he just felt right. His hand traveled lightly along my side, tickling, until his fingers closed tightly over my hipbone. He kissed my collarbone, the side of my neck, under my ear. He nipped at my lower lip and I nipped back, touching the tip of his tongue with mine. I could have stayed there for hours, but he pulled back slightly, his eyes the translucent gray of a seashell.

I couldn't remember why I'd been laughing so hard, or why he was here.

"Hey," he said softly.

"Hey," I said back. "What are you doing here?"

"I came to show you something," he rolled over, sitting up.

I wrinkled my nose and sat up as well, pretending I was interested in the bag he was dragging from under my window. I just wanted to keep kissing.

He pulled out a blanket.

I blinked at him. "You brought me a blanket?"

"Just wait." He spread it out and then nudged me onto it. The thick wool cut the damp cold of the grass. He pulled out a second blanket and a pillow. "Okay, now lie back."

I shot him a look.

He rolled his eyes. "Just do it. God, you're stubborn."

I grudgingly lay back and turned my head to look at him as he did the same. "Now what?"

"Look up."

I glanced up, expecting stars and tree branches. It wasn't just the stars, though there were millions of them, thick as spilled salt, or that the Milky Way looked close enough to touch, pouring out across the sky. It was the clear crystal of the light, the velvet of the sky arching over us in a way that made me feel tiny. I exhaled. "Whoa."

He pointed to the left. "There."

The sky was washed with colors—green, red, and blue—all wavering and dancing. They flickered like torchlight, moved like water. It was beautiful.

"The northern lights," I whispered.

He nodded. "Isabeau said it's a sign."

"Uh-oh. Good sign or bad sign?"

"She didn't say. She rushed out to do some kind of magic thing. Solange and Logan went with her."

"Oh."

He slanted me a glance. "But I wanted to come here instead."

"Oh," I said again, more cheerfully. I shifted and hugged his arm. "You're a good boyfriend."

"You have no idea," he teased. I kissed the side of his mouth, hugging him tighter. I was an idiot if I let the weirdness with Solange interfere with the most romantic night ever. And since I was so determined to prove to everyone that I wasn't an idiot, I should start now. I kissed him again and tilted my head back to watch the northern lights dancing. It was like a kaleidoscope of smoke and crystals, forming and reforming into different shapes.

"Does that look like a two-headed cow to you?" I asked.

"I see a phoenix."

"How is that a phoenix?"

"The red part there."

"Oh, I meant the green." The green shifted into a dragon and then a rowboat. "That blue part looks like a cat sitting on Bruno's head."

Nicholas chuckled. "I'm sure he'd be thrilled. There, lion on top of a pyramid."

I snuggled closer. "This is nice."

"Wait, I forgot the best part." He shifted and I heard rustling. He triumphantly held up a bag.

"Chocolate!" I grinned, popping one in my mouth. "*Real* chocolate, not carob. I totally love you right now."

I paused as the words echoed around us. I swallowed chocolate and nougat and tried not to blush. We'd known each other forever. We made out on a regular basis. I shouldn't feel embarrassed to be the first one to say "I love you." Even if he didn't say it back. We'd saved each other's lives a bunch of times. Words were just words. Right? I ate another chocolate before I said something really stupid.

He turned over onto his elbow, his gaze intense. I looked away. His finger touched my chin gently, lifted it so I had to look at him.

"If you make fun of me, I'll stake you," I muttered.

He raised an eyebrow. "Way to ruin the moment there, Lucky."

Oops.

The way he was looking at me made me feel suddenly shy. That was definitely new for me. I never felt shy. And now I actually had to stop myself from squirming awkwardly. It was probably just the sugar. Or an allergy to nougat.

He leaned in, his lips stopping just short of touching mine. He was so close, if I took a deep breath we'd be kissing. Something warm tingled through me. He didn't even need vampire pheromones, he was that hot.

"I love you, too," he whispered, one corner of his mouth lifting into a smile. I grinned back, then kissed him until I felt light-headed and breathless.

My phone vibrated in my pocket just as things were starting to get interesting. Nicholas pulled away. I sighed. Stupid phone.

"What?" I answered it crossly. I frowned. "Kieran? Is that you?" I checked the call display, then nodded at Nicholas. We both sat up. "What's going on?" I held the phone away from my ear slightly so Nicholas could hear.

"It's Solange," Kieran said.

"Is she okay? What happened?"

"She's okay," he assured me. Nicholas stood up, hauling me by my elbow so fast I got a little dizzy. "I think."

"What's happening?"

"We were supposed to meet up in the woods, near the swamp before you get to the Blood Moon fields we're not supposed to know about." Nicholas's mouth thinned at that. "By the time I got here, she was already . . . um . . ."

"*What?*" I nearly shouted, then lowered my voice, glancing up at my parents' bedroom window.

"She's feeding." His voice went even tighter. "On a bloodslave." Nicholas and I stared at each other.

"Are you sure?" I asked.

"I'm looking at her, aren't I?" He sounded freaked out and definitely not like the usual arrogant vampire hunter with all the answers.

Nicholas took the phone from me. "I'm coming. Stay there. *Don't* call my parents!"

He tossed the phone back to me and took off across the lawn toward the lilac bushes. I chased after him.

"Like hell you're going without me, Drake," I called after him. I shoved through the lilac branches. Nicholas was already tossing a motorcycle helmet at me. It nearly hit me in the nose. I pulled it onto my head, fiddling with the straps as Nicholas walked the bike out onto the road, away from the house so the noise wouldn't wake my parents.

"Get on," he said, already straddling the bike.

The fact that he wasn't trying to leave me behind made me want to kiss him even more. I climbed on and wrapped my arms around his waist, holding on as tightly as I could. He'd barely notice anyway; it's not like he needed to breathe. We hurtled down the street, past the pumpkin patches and the apple orchards and the struggling vineyard, toward the mountains and the forest. Violet Hill was a small collection of lights behind us.

I couldn't believe Solange was drinking from a human. It was one thing to drink from blood banks and willing donors, but feasting in the woods off some bloodslave was . . . disconcerting.

"Can you go faster?" I shouted over the roaring wind.

"Hang on," he shouted back.

The night was a blur of shadows and asphalt and cold wind. I was losing feeling in my fingers and my arms were cramping. We finally turned off the road and cut through a field. Purple loosestrife brushed my knees.

In the woods, the ground was even more treacherous. Nicholas did his best to maneuver around tree branches and rocks and fallen birch trunks bursting with moss and lichen. A pine bough slapped him in the face. It smelled like Christmas all of a sudden. He went over a bump and my helmet bounced off the back of his. The next bump made my teeth rattle. The next two made him stop altogether.

"We'll have to go on foot from here," he said, tossing his helmet aside. I clambered off, legs stiff. I hung mine on the backseat and jogged after him. We soon passed Kieran's motorcycle under a hemlock. The trees this far into the forest grew taller, so tall I wouldn't have been able to see their tops even in the daylight. Ferns feathered at our feet.

By the time we reached Solange, I was sweating and panting. She looked worse than me, sitting in a nest of mossy roots and leaning against an aspen, its yellowing leaves quivering above her. There was blood on her face and her shirt was torn. Nicholas swore and blurred, reaching her side in one blink. He crouched next to her and she smiled wearily at him.

"I'm good," she said, sounding drunk.

Kieran was standing in the path, over the prone body of the bloodslave woman Solange and I had seen in the Blood Moon camp. She was nearly as pale as Solange but smiling. There was blood and teeth marks on the inside of her elbow. They weren't as elegant as the scars on her neck.

"Is she sleeping?" I asked.

Kieran nodded. "Solange told her to go to sleep. So she did." We exchanged a grim glance. I stepped over her hand, flung out like a fallen calla lily.

Solange had blood on the side of her mouth. Her tongue darted out to lick it. There was a deep gash on her arm and scratches on her face. Her sunglasses were broken, lying in a clump of primrose.

"Oh, Sol." I reached out to brush her hair off her face where it was stuck to a cut already scabbing over. She jerked back, moaning.

"No! Get away!"

I snatched my hand back, stunned. "What? Sol, it's me."

Her eyes went wild, veined with red all around irises the delicate blue of Wedgwood china. All three sets of her fangs were extended, but that wasn't a shock anymore. The way she was looking at me was—as if I was hurting her, as if I was food. I could have been naked, with blood pouring out of my wrists, and Nicholas still wouldn't have looked at me like that. I froze, confused.

Nicholas swore and tilted Solange's head back so he could see into her eyes. "How much did you drink?"

She smiled lazily. "Don't know. She was nice." She ran her tongue over her teeth. "Like chocolate-covered strawberries."

"Great," I muttered. "I'll never be able to eat those again now."

Nicholas glanced at me. He hadn't looked this worried since Solange's bloodchange, when we weren't even sure if she'd survive. His gaze shifted to Kieran. "What the hell happened?"

"I don't know. I just found her like this. She was wounded."

"I got ambushed," she told us, closing her eyes. "I got him, though."

"Hel-Blar?"

She nodded. "Nasty one, all stinky. I really hate mushrooms," she added, suddenly serious before bursting into laughter for no apparent reason.

I rubbed a hand over my face. "At least she's a cheerful drunk," I said.

"Is Constantine here?" she asked suddenly.

Kieran's eyes narrowed.

So did mine. "Why?" I asked.

"And who the hell's Constantine?" Kieran added.

"He told me Penelope was nice. He was right."

"Okay, I'm so punching Constantine in the nose," I said brightly. "And who's Penelope?" I pointed to the woman curled in the ferns. "Her?"

"She's used to it," Solange informed us, slightly slurring. She was acting like Penelope had veins full of wine. I hoped she'd have a hell of a hangover in the morning. She clearly needed something to wake her up. "Kieran's just mad because I wasn't drinking from him." She sat up, tilting her head. She smiled at him. "Come here."

Kieran took a bewildered step forward. I knocked him back with a hard shove, then whirled on Solange. "What the hell are you doing?"

She shrugged. "I was just asking," she said, pouting.

"That's not asking," I told her through my teeth. "That's force. What's wrong with you?"

"Penelope doesn't judge. She said so." Solange eyed me. "But you're judging."

"You're damn right I am."

Nicholas hoisted Solange to her feet. "I need to get her home."

I went to help him but she snarled at me. Nicholas's jaw clenched, then he held up a hand. "I have her."

"Is she going to be okay?"

"She'll be fine," he assured me, but I could tell he wasn't sure. And the fact that he didn't want his parents to know didn't bode well. "I'll take her home, and Kieran, you take Lucy back."

"What do we do with her?" Kieran asked, standing over Penelope.

"We need to wake her up and send her back to the camp," Nicholas said. "I can call someone to meet her once she's on her feet."

I crouched next to her and shook her shoulder. Her cleavage was impressive, even lying on her back. "Hey, wake up!" There were scars along her collarbone, too, like tiny stars. I couldn't stop staring at them. "Penelope!" I slapped her cheek lightly. Nothing happened. I jerked back suddenly, landing on my butt. My tailbone hit a rock and pain tingled up my spine. "She's not dead, is she?"

"No." Solange sighed dramatically. "You're overreacting."

"Solange's pheromones should wake her up." Nicholas turned Solange, nudging her toward Penelope. I got out of the way. "We can't wait for her to do it on her own."

"But she needs to rest," Solange said, sounding almost like her old self.

"She needs to rest in her own bed."

"Oh." She sat down next to Penelope, leaning in close. With her black hair she looked lethal and beautiful, like an obsidian blade some ancient tribes used for human sacrifices. "Penelope? You have to wake up now."

Penelope stirred.

"Wake up right now!" Solange commanded.

Penelope's eyes opened abruptly. She blinked, then smiled.

"There," Solange said, pleased. Nicholas pulled her back up. "See? No problem."

Penelope sat up slowly.

"Send her back home," Nicholas bit out.

Penelope smiled. "There's no need," she said, perfectly at ease.

As if she wasn't wearing bite marks like jewelry. "I can find my way without a blood command."

We stared at her. Kieran was the first to speak. "Someone will meet you."

She nodded, then curtsied to Solange. "Thank you, Your Highness."

"Your Highness?" I echoed, disgusted. I was even more disgusted when Solange didn't look uncomfortable being curtsied to. "Seriously?"

Solange shrugged as Penelope turned and made her way between the tall pines. Nicholas texted one of the guards to collect her.

"Constantine said I shouldn't fight being a princess. It's not like it's a crime."

"I hate Constantine," I muttered. "He's an ass."

Solange turned on me so fast, her hair actually lifted in the breeze. Her eyes went even more red, her lips lifting off her teeth.

"Don't say that about him!" Her voice felt like a thousand needles bristling in my skin, like a sunburn, like broken glass.

I was too shocked even to make a fist. If one of the Drake brothers pulled that on me, I would have punched them.

Nicholas yanked Solange away from me. "Shit, Lucy. Get out of here," he told me, struggling to hold Solange back. She was furious.

Kieran grabbed my arm. "Come on."

"Kieran, that's not her," I said through the tears in the back of my throat.

"I know."

I thought of Penelope's scars. "You thought I was like her," I said quietly, remembering the first time I'd met Kieran. I hadn't heard the term "bloodslave" before. The Drakes were more interested in seclusion than power. And they had other methods of feeding. It hadn't really occurred to me that other vampires might not have the same scruples. It wasn't the blood I minded so much. I mean, if Nicholas or Solange or any of the Drakes needed a mouthful of my blood to survive, I wouldn't begrudge them. And even Kieran had given Solange his blood on the night of her sixteenth birthday to save her. It was the slightly cultlike joy on Penelope's face that made me queasy.

"But I guess it's her choice," I said, mostly to myself.

"Maybe," Kieran replied. "Maybe not."

I glanced over my shoulder, watching Nicholas lead Solange away. Everything felt wrong. I should be going with them, not back home with a vampire hunter. And I shouldn't be trusting that vampire hunter more than my best friend. I didn't know how to help her.

She looked back at me once, then drooped, as if she were wilting.

CHAPTER 21

◆

Christabel

Hel-Blar stampeded through the field above us, and when the wind shifted it was full of rotten mushrooms and slimy pond water. I heard them shoving to get through the narrow opening to the maze.

I ran faster, clutching the back of Connor's belt. He was moving so quickly that I was like those cars using the wind drag behind transport trucks on the highway. We went left, left, came up against another dead end, doubled back, went right, then left again. I felt the *Hel-Blar* closing in. Fear made my heart feel like it was too big for my chest. My stomach hurt, my lungs tightened, my legs tingled. I could almost feel their decayed breath on the back of my neck. I tried but I couldn't run any faster.

And then Connor suddenly stopped and whirled around me, as if we were dancing, blurring around the edges as if he was smoke. Later I'd be impressed by that. He ended up behind me just as a *Hel-Blar* leaped to clamp its jaws on me. Connor pushed me back with one arm and threw the *Hel-Blar* with his other. I stumbled and tried not to stab myself with my dagger. I turned just in time to see a billow of ashes.

"They're coming," he said. "How's your aim?"

"How the hell should I know?"

"Well, we're about to find out. We'll have to make our stand here." He nodded at the torchlight. "That way you can see better than they can. These *Hel-Blar* don't like light. When we've got a chance, we can make our way to the next torch. Stay back behind the barbed wire there; it'll narrow their way in to us."

"Connor?" My palms were sweating around the knife hilt and the stones from my pocket.

"Yeah?"

"Thanks for coming to get me."

"You're welcome."

"And I'm sorry you're going to die horribly."

He actually grinned. "We're not going to die, Christa."

"We're not? Maybe you're not paying attention. The monsters are about to eat our brains."

"They're not zombies."

I actually reached out and pinched him. "No geek semantics. I'm trying to say I'm sorry I got you into this."

"You didn't." He turned and dragged me forward, his hand closing around the back of my neck. He kissed me hard and quick. "Are you ready?"

"Hell, no!"

And then there was no time left to talk.

We were seriously outnumbered.

The *Hel-Blar* bottlenecked between the two hedge walls with the barbed wire. Blood dripped onto the ground from their cuts, from their mouths.

"Don't get any on you!" Connor warned me. He caught one under the jaw with his elbow and then used his stake when the *Hel-Blar* reared back. Ash made me gag and cough. Another came through the opening. He snarled at Connor and threw a stake at him. It whistled as it whirled toward Connor's heart.

Wait, they had stakes, too? Not just teeth and contagious bites? That was totally unfair.

I choked on a warning yell. Time was soaked in honey, slow and sticky. Connor leaned sideways and the wood grazed his arm, like a bullet. That's how fast it was traveling and how strong the *Hel-Blar* was who'd thrown it. Connor was faster, though. Even as he leaned away, he used his foot to kick at my knee, knocking me out of the way. The stake went by me, so close that I could see the grooves from the knife that had whittled it in the torchlight.

"Christa, don't freeze on me!" Connor yelled, jumping back into the fight.

Right. Standing there waiting to be eaten was bad.

And Connor was tiring. I'd always scoffed at those girls who waited around to be rescued. I hated that in books. So I should do something. *Anything.*

I tried to pretend I was back at home, maybe riding the subway alone too late at night, or crossing through a dark parking lot. I'd dealt with scary people before and I never froze. I'd kicked Peter when he tried to grab me, didn't I? I could do this.

I threw stones like they were grenades. I think I was even yelling. My aim wasn't great, but I was persistent and annoying. It distracted them just enough for Connor to get the upper hand. And when they got close enough that I saw saliva gleaming on their creepy teeth, I kicked out with my combat boots. I heard a shin bone snap when I caught a leg at a particularly good angle. It was mostly luck, but I wasn't going to get picky about it.

Luck damn well owed me.

One of the rocks bounced off a *Hel-Blar*'s shoulder and caught Connor in the cheekbone, drawing blood.

"Sorry!" I threw another stone, more carefully this time. Connor staked another one, and I grabbed the torch and waved it threateningly. The two closing in on us hissed.

That gave me an idea.

I patted my coat, frantically searching for the flask Saga had given me. It was full of that nasty grog, and I was pretty sure only rubbing alcohol had a higher alcohol content.

"Behind me!" I told Connor. "Now!"

I took a big mouthful.

It always worked in books.

Not that I could think of one right now, but I was sure I'd read about it somewhere.

I tried to blow the rum out in a wide spray over the flame, hoping fervently I wasn't about to set fire to my own face.

There was a horrible moment when nothing happened.

And then, the fire spread. It rained over the encroaching *Hel-Blar* and they screamed. It wasn't much, just enough to make them pause. Connor took the flask from me and poured it over the cedars, then threw arcs of the amber liquid over the *Hel-Blar*. He added the fuel from a lighter in his pocket. The fire swelled and crackled, eating through the hedges and licking at the frantic *Hel-Blar*. The next scraggly hedge caught fire.

"Whoa. You're even better than Princess Leia," Connor told me as the snow sizzled and evaporated over the flames.

"Yeah, yeah. Don't get any ideas about that gold bikini." I grinned. "Now come on, this way."

"What way? That's a wall."

"It's cedar," I scoffed, "not concrete. We shove through it and aim that way and just keep going through the branches until we get out of here."

"Yup, hotter than Leia."

We pushed through the branches, getting scratched and mauled by needles and thorns from the vines. Flower petals scattered with the snow, making everything cold and slippery. The fire crackled. There was a pulse of light glowing over the maze. Burning evergreen masked the thick slime of mushrooms. It was trickier than it seemed, contorting yourself to fit between branches that wouldn't break off or bend easily. Marble statues of Roman goddesses missing various body parts watched us coldly.

"Barbed wire," he said, stopping me before I ripped my face open.

My hair curled around a metal thorn and turned into an instant knot. I yanked at it, my scalp stinging. "Ouch."

"I've got it." He bent the lengths of barbed wire apart, making an opening. He wiped his hands on his jeans, leaving bloody streaks. "Go."

He glanced behind us to make sure nothing was sneaking up on us while I climbed through the rusted iron tangle of wire and thorns.

"Think we're almost out of this thing?" I asked, hacking away at another hedge.

"I don't think that's what we have to worry about right now." He sounded tense and he was sniffing the air.

I groaned. "What now?"

"The fire's coming this way."

"Already?"

"It's been a dry season." He pushed me along faster. "The trees are like tinder right now, and the wind just shifted."

He was right. Cold air whirled around us and then pushed from the other direction.

The smell of smoke stung my nostrils. I coughed. "Shit."

We tried to run as we broke through woven branches and the odd clump of barbed wire. Fire snapped its own jaws at us. It couldn't be contained or predicted, and there wasn't nearly enough snow to put it out. The flames licked the sky. It was easy to see where we were going now—angry orange light closed in enough to give us long, frantic shadows, which darted through the cedars ahead of us.

Maddened, the *Hel-Blar* who'd managed to find their way around the fire before it spread out of control followed. They crashed through after us, some even vaulting the hedges altogether. Which is how two of them ended up in front of us and then turned back, drawn by the scent of the blood smeared on Connor's jeans and beading all over my hands and face from scratches. The fire was behind us, just as hungry and deadly. We couldn't turn back, and the maze was too complicated—as likely to lead us into the belly of the fire as out of it. A *Hel-Blar* woman made a grab for me. Trying to avoid her smell and the smoke, I was breathing shallowly through my mouth. It was making me feel light-headed.

Connor was grappling with the second *Hel-Blar*, who was built like an angry wrestler. I couldn't help him and he couldn't help me.

I jabbed my dagger out viciously, blindly. She leaned back, grinned her ghoulish grin, and didn't seem particularly concerned. Damn it. Someone was going to have to teach me how to use one of these things properly. And to think, I used to worry about social workers getting me.

It soon became apparent that there was no way I could win in combat against a creature crazed with both hunger and an animal's terror of fire. I just wasn't properly equipped for this kind of fight.

So I'd just have to use the only weapon I could actually do damage with.

Fire.

A wall of heat was starting to make my nose and cheeks feel

sunburned. The metal buttons on my jacket were already too hot to touch, scalding me when I brushed against them. The wind played with the flames, flinging them around like a dancer's skirt. A thin pine tree wobbled precariously. Now or never.

I grabbed for a smoldering branch near my foot, ignoring the heat that singed my palm. The other end burned like one of the torches, so I threw it as hard as I could at the feral woman. She instinctively stumbled back a step, embers scattering over her. The pine tree groaned, creaked, and then gave in to the fire eating its roots. It fell in a plume of smoke and fire right on top of her. She shrieked, batting at her singed hair and the blisters on her face, pinned under the burning trunk. Pine sap flared.

I jumped in the other direction, yelling at Connor, "Watch out!"

Connor and the wrestler tumbled in the dirt, Connor falling flat on his back. He looked winded and in pain. I was pretty sure I'd heard something crack. The wrestler grinned and reached out to grab Connor's shirt to haul him back up within reach of his dripping teeth. Connor rolled over and scissor-kicked back, catching him across the back of the knees. He fell and he fell hard. Connor flipped over and drove his stake through the *Hel-Blar's* back and into his heart. There was a howl and then ashes mixing with the embers of the cedars toppling around us.

The fire was everywhere now, and I could barely hear myself think though the crackle and hiss of flames eating their way through the evergreens. I felt sick. I'd burned that woman alive. Even if she'd been trying to maul and kill me, I couldn't feel good about it. But I didn't really have time to feel bad, either.

"Go." Connor crowded behind me, trying to take the blast of heat for both of us.

We crashed through the hedges and finally fell into cold, sharp air, snow, and a view of the mountains. We crawled to a safe distance and collapsed. There was enough bare dirt between the maze and the fields stretching to the forest at the base of the mountain that the fire wouldn't spread. Still, birds filled the sky above us, squawking in panic. I heaved air into my lungs. My chest felt like an ashtray.

Connor crouched next to me, but I had no intention of trying to stand up again until my legs felt more like legs and less like Popsicles left in the sun. Snow dusted the weeds and the flowers, pretty as a cupcake.

"Are you okay?" Connor whispered in my ear. He was cold, colder than regular body temperature should be, but I felt too hot. He was like cool water on a humid day. I edged closer to him.

"I have no idea," I answered. At this point I might have recited "The Highwayman" to myself, but I couldn't even remember the first line. That scared me more than anything.

But it wasn't over.

There were shadows on the burning edges of the maze and more coming down the mountainside.

"Now what?"

"More *Hel-Blar*."

"How many of those things are there?" I asked, scrambling to my feet beside him.

"Kind of an epidemic right now," Connor admitted.

"I hate this town."

Someone erupted out of the fire-licked darkness. I threw my knife. It went a foot wide, and Aidan watched it mildly as it flew past him. "You'll need to get better at that."

"You scared the crap out of me."

He retrieved my dagger and handed it back to me. "Learn fast."

"Where's Saga?"

"Busy."

And then we were fighting again.

I'd love to say that I was a natural. That my attitude and my ability to scare bullies made me fierce in the face of battle.

But the truth was, my aim sucked and I was too slow.

I was outgunned and outmaneuvered. The only reason I was still standing was because Aidan and Connor kept me between them. And then it just wasn't possible anymore. The *Hel-Blar* were persistent and vicious. Connor had only the one stake, and Aidan was covered in blood and mud. He was the best fighter I'd ever seen, but he couldn't be everywhere at once. And some of the *Hel-Blar* had stakes. Well, whittled sticks, but it amounted to the same thing. They pelted us like sharp, deadly rain. One caught Aidan in the left arm and he hissed. The blood maddened the *Hel-Blar* further, which I wouldn't have thought possible. The battle was nearly too fast for my human eyes to see.

I didn't need to see the stake to feel it pierce my skin, to feel it bite through flesh and muscle and slide past my ribs.

There was numb shock. I gurgled a sound.

Pain flared like electrical shocks. I fell to my knees. Connor and Aidan whirled to look at me. I closed my hand around the makeshift stake and yanked it out of my chest just as Connor paled and began to shout.

"Christabel, no! Don't pull it out!"

"I'm okay," I said, then I fell right over. Throbbing lances of fire burned through me. Blood spurted, soaking through my jacket. I was cold and confused. Connor was fighting to get to me but he was too far away. His lips were moving. He was saying something but I couldn't hear him. Why couldn't I hear him?

Aidan reached me first. "Stake hit an artery," he said grimly. "She's losing too much blood, too fast." He pushed his sleeves up as Connor dispatched another *Hel-Blar*. There were two more between us. He kept fighting.

"Turn her!" he yelled, and I could finally hear him, though my vision was graying. "Turn her now!"

Aidan used the tips of his fangs to slice through the skin of his inner wrist. Blood trickled, the color of raspberries. He pressed the wound against my mouth.

"Drink."

I struggled, gagging.

"Drink or die, Christabel."

My mouth was open because I was screaming. Blood slid down my throat, coppery and thick. I gagged again but I was too weak to do anything but swallow. My eyelids closed as Connor finally reached us, covered in ash and blood. He plucked me away from Aidan, cradling me against his chest. He was cold. Or was I cold?

"Go," Aidan said. "Run. I'll keep the rest of the *Hel-Blar* off your trail. You have to get her back to your farm. She needs blood and it's not safe here." He made a sound, as if he were throwing a weapon. I didn't have the strength to open my eyes to see. I didn't even have the strength to care if there were a hundred *Hel-Blar*. "She's my bloodkin," he added. "And I'll claim her as my daughter.

"Now, run!"

CHAPTER 22

◆

Lucy

I was crawling in through my window when I heard the creak of the floorboards outside my room. I jumped into my bed, messing up the body-shaped pillows and crumpling the note into a little ball, just as my mom knocked and pushed open the door. She paused, eyeing me blearily.

"What are you doing?"

"Nothing!"

She swung the door open wider and marched in, flipping the corner of my comforter over. "Lucky Moon, why are you dressed? Where have you been?"

"Nicholas came by to show me the northern lights," I explained hastily. It wasn't technically a lie. And it worked. She looked distracted.

"Really, the aurora borealis is out?" Usually that meant she'd be out in the yard, naked, singing old songs. "Finally, a good omen." She tucked me back into bed. "We just got word from the Drakes."

"About Christabel?"

She nodded, looking sad. "Yes."

I felt cold all over. "She's okay, right? Right? And Connor?"

Mom forced a smile. "She's okay. They both are. And they should be at the Drakes' before dawn."

I frowned. "Why's she going over there instead of back here?"

Mom sighed. "She was turned."

My mouth dropped open. "*What?* Christabel's going to be a *vampire?*" I thought of Solange and all the Drake brothers and what they'd gone through, and I shivered. There was a chance Christabel might not survive. I suddenly felt heavy, as if I were wearing clothes made out of stone. "Can I go see her?"

"Soon," Mom assured me. "They're taking care of her. Try not to worry." She ran a hand over my hair, as if to prove to herself that I was all right. It was supposed to be me, after all. I was supposed to be turning into a vampire, if Saga's plan had gone as expected. "It's late. You should sleep. You're not a vampire, honey, and you shouldn't be keeping their hours. It's not healthy."

"Mom, I'm fine."

"Promise me you'll try." Her voice was strained and the lines at the corners of her eyes more pronounced. "It could've been you."

"But it wasn't." I didn't say it, but it might have been better if it *had* been me. At least I was prepared; I knew what was going on. Poor Christabel.

I couldn't sleep, not until I got a text from Nicholas telling me he was home safely and Christabel was tucked into one of their guest beds.

The next day I tried to follow my mom's advice and act like a normal teenage girl, one who didn't know anything about vampires and whose life wasn't constantly in danger.

If only because Christabel couldn't anymore.

I sat in the sunshine at lunchtime with Nathan and Linnet.

"Where's your cousin?" Nathan asked. "I haven't seen her around since she kicked Peter in the balls."

"She has the flu," I said. "She's all sweaty and gross." If you embellished a lie with just the right details, people generally didn't want to know more.

Linnet wrinkled her nose. "Is your mom making her drink that herbal thing?"

I nodded. "And anyone else who comes by the house, just in case." Both Linnet and Nathan knew my mom's herbal concoctions intimately. She made them for colds and headaches and allergies. You had to strain big lumps of valerian or hyssop through your teeth. Nathan shuddered.

"Tell her we say hi," he said. "And thanks."

"Sure."

We talked about school and skipping gym class and whether or not we could sneak off campus for a latte before our next class. I tried not to think about Christabel or Connor or tainted blood being delivered to the Drakes.

After school we wandered down Main Street with mochaccinos and chocolate-chip muffins. We threw crumbs for the seagulls and I stopped to buy soothing incense for my dad. We had another latte and Linnet started talking really fast. Nathan and I grinned at each other.

"We need to give you extralarge lattes before your presentation next week," Nathan decided. Linnet was deathly afraid of public speaking. She made a face at us and licked more milk foam off the lid of her cup.

We were crossing through the parking lot toward Linnet's car when it happened.

We'd had a nice afternoon and I wasn't even feeling particularly jumpy. Plus, the sun was still out, so there was no need to worry.

But when the guy came up behind us on his bicycle, I heard the squeak of his wheels, the soft scrape of rubber against the pavement, and everything in me went on high alert. Especially when a quick glance revealed he was wearing blue.

I gave a battle cry Xena would have been proud of and spun around, throwing my cup in the air with one hand and a stake at him with the other. The stake bounced off his wheel well and veered him off course. He went one way and his bike went the other. He landed awkwardly and rolled up against a garbage can.

"Oh my God!" I yelled. "I'm so sorry!"

"Oh my God!" Nathan yelled too. "What's the matter with you?" I knew he was only saying that because the guy was cute. He rushed over to see if he needed help. I grabbed the stake before anyone got a good look at it and started to wonder why I carried sharp sticks in my bag. The biker got to his feet, his jeans torn at one knee and dirt clinging to shirt. He pulled off his helmet and stared at his bike, then at me.

"I'm so sorry," I said again. "Really."

"Shit," he muttered. "Are you crazy?" He rode away before I could apologize again.

I'd almost maimed a guy because he was wearing a blue shirt.

In my defense, I associated that particular shade with *Hel-Blar* determined to tear my head off my shoulders.

Still.

"You need to lay off the caffeine, too," Nathan told me, his eyes wide. "There aren't so many cute guys in this town that you can just throw shit at them like that."

I groaned and shook my head. "I know. He just spooked me."

Aside from my spazzing out, the day had been nice. And I really did try.

But it was clear that this girl just wasn't me.

Like being a girl who hung out only with the Drakes and never with Nathan and Linnet wasn't me either, and neither was being monitored like a criminal by my own parents.

Besides, I had a better idea.

I just had to make one stop first.

"He spooked you?" Nathan snorted, oblivious to the conclusions I was making in my head. "It's Violet Hill. Nothing ever happens here."

◆

Nathan dropped me off at my house around sunset. I didn't go inside, just hopped right into my mom's car and took off before she could stop me. I texted her to tell her where I was going and that I wouldn't be long. When she called me back, the phone ringing insistently, I switched off the sound.

The drive to the Drakes' was uneventful. I passed three guards on my way into the farmhouse. Solange's uncle Geoffrey's barn-slash-laboratory had all the lights on and the door shut tight, which meant he was hard at work on something scientific. The dogs raced up to greet me when I reached the house and got out of the car. They chased me up the porch steps, drooling on my knees. I knocked hard.

Nicholas answered the door. He still looked sleepy, his dark hair mussed, his shirt unbuttoned.

Yum.

I launched myself at him and he caught me with one arm, burying his head in my hair. "'Morning," he mumbled. I clung to him for a long wonderful moment before reluctantly stepping back.

"Hey, where're you going?" he asked. His serious smile had a wicked glint. "I wasn't done."

I smiled back, despite all the anxiety churning in my stomach. "Is Christabel okay?"

He shoved his hair back. "Too early to tell," he said gently.

"Can I see her?"

"She's unconscious," he said. "What's going on? You've got a weird look on your face."

"You're so romantic." I snorted.

"And you're being sneaky."

"I don't know what you're talking about." I kissed him.

"Misdirection," he said against my lips, smiling again. I kissed him deeply, slowly. He dug his hand into my hair. "Hey, what's wrong? There's something else."

He'd known me long enough to read the brittle edge to my movements. I nodded. "First, how's Solange?"

"Okay." He lowered his voice, touching his finger to my lips. "Shh."

"You know I still want to track that Constantine down, right?"

"I know."

"What are you doing here?" Solange asked suddenly, coming down the hall toward us from the kitchen. She didn't look drunk anymore, or even hungover. Just angry. At me.

I glowered back. "What do you think?"

"I want you to stop threatening Constantine."

I blinked at her. "That's seriously all you have to say to me?"

"Until you promise, yes." She folded her arms.

"Solange, do you even remember what happened last night?"

"I don't want to talk about it," she said frostily.

I laughed bitterly. "Too bad."

Nicholas cringed and looked deathly afraid. He'd faced down crazy Lady Natasha with less fear than he had right now for his girlfriend and his baby sister. Not that I blamed him. I was as mad as Solange looked.

Well, almost.

She pointed to the door. "Go home, Lucy."

I just crossed my arms, too. "Make me." We hadn't had a fight this immature since we were eight.

"Fine, I will."

She leaned in closer. "Go. Home. *Lucky*."

I leaned in just as close, until we were like two prizefighters, practically nose to nose. "Your pheromones don't work on me, *princess*," I taunted, even though the soles of my feet were actually itchy with the need to move. That had never happened before.

"But they work on him," she said haughtily, angling her head in Nicholas's direction.

"Hey!" He held up his hands. "Leave me out of this."

She stared at him. "Nicholas, make her leave."

He jerked as if he'd been stuck with a pin. "Solange, *don't*."

She was getting stronger for her pheromones to work not only on other vampires but on a member of her own family. Nicholas was struggling, the muscles of his forearms and across his chest rippled as if he were lifting weights. He was in pain.

I suddenly wanted to punch Solange right in the nose, and she was one of the few people I *never* wanted to punch.

"Leave him alone!" I tried to go around him to reach her, to get her out of his personal space.

She just lifted her chin. "Now, Nicholas."

His hands closed around my arms and he walked me backward toward the door, forcing me when my feet dragged. His eyes were wild. He was still struggling but she was stronger.

"Nicholas," I whispered, leaning into him, trying to unbalance him. "Please."

"I'm sorry," he whispered back, his jaw clenched.

His gray eyes were still on mine when he closed the door in my face, leaving me alone on the porch.

◆

I cursed all the way home.

I hadn't even had a chance to tell Nicholas what I'd decided.

Solange and I were going to have it out—just see if we didn't.

I tried to act normal around my parents. Mom gave me *the look* for sneaking out to the Drakes'. I waited until we were drinking tea and eating mango slices at the table, the candles still burning at the windowsill. Dad wasn't rubbing his chest. Mom was playing Ravi Shankar on the CD player. Even Gandhi and Van Helsing were content, gnawing on massive rawhides.

Now or never.

"Um, Mom? Dad?"

"Yes, honey?" Mom added honey to her cup.

"I need to ask you something."

Dad closed his eyes. "Please let it be about a new car."

I was briefly distracted. "Well, that—no," I said sternly, telling myself to stay focused. "That's not it. It's about . . . you know."

Dad actually blanched, like curdled almond milk. "Sex? Is it about sex?"

"No! It's about vampires."

"Oh. Thank God." For the first time in months he sounded thrilled to be discussing vampires. I guess it was all a matter of perspective.

"I want to go to Helios-Ra Academy," I blurted. It sounded weird coming out of my mouth, even to me.

They stared at me.

"Seriously," I added, a little disgruntled when they didn't otherwise react. I pulled the application Hunter had given me from my bag and slid it across the table. It was already mostly filled out. I'd even used blue ink instead of my signature purple glitter ink so it looked grown-up.

"Oh, Lucky," Mom said, touching the papers and looking concerned. "I don't know. Have you really thought about this?"

I nodded, biting my lip. "Yes."

"You know how I feel about cultivating a culture of violence. And that kind of environment is so restrictive. You're not exactly good with rules, honey." Mom pointed out, smiling. "We raised you that way on purpose. We wanted you to question the establishment."

"I know. And it's not that I don't want to be here," I rushed to explain. "But I can't have a sunset curfew all through winter. I'll be trapped inside by four-thirty every night. I can't handle that. And I don't want Dad to get another ulcer. And I can still come home on weekends."

"But . . . boarding school?" Dad said.

I knew it was a lot for them to take in. Frankly, I was still dealing with the idea myself. They were hippie homesteaders at heart, and to them family lived together. You didn't send your children away. And I was a vampire lover. To me, you didn't run away to join a league devoted to killing them.

But I needed a place to call my own and people who understood me. Right now, I felt lost.

And I'd nearly killed a guy in a blue shirt.

Not that I'd tell my parents that.

And I needed to find a way to help Solange.

Not that I'd tell my parents that, either.

"I was kidding when I said that earlier, Luce," Dad said.

"I know, but it got me thinking."

"I thought you didn't like the Helios-Ra?" Mom asked, perplexed.

"I didn't," I admitted. "I really didn't. And I still kind of think they're silly with all that macho ritual and their lame code words. But Kieran and Hunter are cool. We share the same language." I shrugged. "And, I guess, I see another side to them. You know, as long as it's only *Hel-Blar* they go after. The minute they break the treaty with the Drakes, I'm out of there." I fiddled with my chamomile tea. "Mom, I know you think I'm obsessed with this vampire stuff, but they're family, too. I can't help being the way I am. This way, you don't have to worry so much and I can learn to take care of myself. I mean, Dad, think about it. There's nowhere safer than on the Helios-Ra campus, surrounded twenty-four-seven by vampire killers."

Wait. When, exactly, had that become a good thing?

Dad rubbed his face. "I can't deny I like the thought of you being surrounded by people who know what to do when a vampire attacks."

"Dad, not all vampires attack," I felt forced to say, even though my best friend had just temporarily turned my own boyfriend against me, proving me wrong.

"I know. But the Drakes are in the center of the storm right now. And you're known to their enemies." His expression was stark, angry. "Look what happened to your cousin. That was supposed to be you, Lucky. *You.*"

"All the more reason to send me to school there. I could start next week. I'm pretty sure Liam could get Hart to put in a good word for me. And Kieran and Hunter already said they'd vouch for me. I've been going there anyway."

"I suppose."

"Please?"

They exchanged a glance. Mom sighed. "Maybe. We'll think about it."

That meant yes.

Everything really was changing.

CHAPTER 23

◆

Christabel

I felt horrible.

Too horrible to move or even to open my eyes. I wanted water. I was so thirsty that my lips were peeling and cracked, but I didn't have the energy to swallow. There were people moving around my room, standing by my bed, talking in the kind of hushed whispers that are laced with fear.

I was lying on a bed. Was I lying on a bed? Hadn't Connor and I been running through the woods? When did we stop?

"If she doesn't get better by sundown, I'll have to call her mother," Uncle Stuart said. He smelled funny. Not like mushrooms, but like sweat and worry and the coffee he'd been drinking. I shouldn't be able to smell the coffee on his breath, should I? "She'll want to know. She'll want to be here."

I tried to move, but I felt like spikes were pinning me to the soft mattress. I didn't want anyone to call my mom. She was busy getting better. If she knew I was sick, she'd leave rehab. And if I didn't get better, she might slide back into her addictions. I didn't want that. I struggled again but nothing happened.

"I was supposed to take care of her," Uncle Stuart said roughly. "Damn it, Liam!"

"I know," Liam murmured. "So were we." He sounded like he was pacing.

"I'm not a violent man, Liam," my uncle said. His tone said something else entirely.

Liam nodded. I could actually hear his head move, his hair brush against his collar, his lips tighten. Was that normal? I couldn't remember.

"Helena's counting swords even as we speak."

"Is my niece going to turn into one of those things? And how the hell am I going to explain that to her mother?"

"Christabel won't be *Hel-Blar*," Liam assured him. "But she will turn, Stuart. We can't stop it. If we try to, she'll die."

Uncle Stuart swore and wiped my forehead with a cold, wet cloth. It hurt. I practically felt the sizzle of the water hitting my hot skin and evaporating. I whimpered in my head. No sound came out.

"Are you sure we shouldn't call a doctor? She's burning up. And her veins are so blue."

"Geoffrey's been here," Liam reminded him. "He's seen this sort of thing before. And Connor told him everything he knew about Aidan. He's her sire now. We'll have to deal with the implications of that later."

"You did this eight times?" Uncle Stuart must have buried his face in his hands because his voice was muffled. Or my hearing was blurry. Could hearing go blurry?

"Yes," Liam said grimly. "It's a little different in our family, but essentially yes."

I wanted to cringe away from the hot sunlight falling across my pillow, nearly stabbing me. I felt it there, as threatening as the fire that tore through the maze.

Is the night chilly and dark? The night is chilly, but not dark. . . .

I tried to say it out loud, but I couldn't. Still, the rhythm of a poem I knew so well was soothing. I could only remember snippets, though. The stanzas didn't make sense out of order. *He did not come in the dawning; he did not come at noon; And out o' the tawny sunset, before the rise o' the moon, When the road was a gypsy's ribbon, looping the purple moor, A red-coat troop came marching— Marching—marching—*

That wasn't even Coleridge. It was someone else and not the poem with my name. But who? Why couldn't I remember?

"She's got Aidan's blood in her veins," Liam said. "All we can do now is wait."

◆

I floated in and out of consciousness, as if I were being tossed about on a dark ocean. It was all poetry and fatigue and blood. Bram Stoker was there again, but Saga ran him through with a cutlass and buried his head in a wooden chest on a sandy beach. It was confusing.

Just when I felt so feverish I might burn up like a human

candle, the sun set. I could feel it, between the parched dreams. I sighed with relief, barely.

"Did you hear that?" It was Connor. "She made a sound."

I tried to lift my eyelids and managed only a small slit, not enough really to see. Everything was washed out in red.

"She's weak," Geoffrey said sometime later. "Her veins are so prominent that she looks as blue as any *Hel-Blar* I've ever seen."

"She'll be fine," Connor protested fiercely. "She can do this. Christabel," he whispered to me. "You have to fight."

Four for the quarters, and twelve for the hour; Ever and aye, by shine and shower, Sixteen short howls, not over loud; Some say, she sees my lady's shroud.

I didn't realize I was muttering aloud until Uncle Stuart spoke. "What's she saying? What does that mean?"

Connor answered, because I couldn't. "I think it's a poem. She does that." He sounded close. I thought I might be able to feel his hand holding mine. Only it wasn't as cold as before. Or maybe I was cold now, too?

"Coleridge," I answered. My lips moved, I was sure of it. There was barely any sound, but Connor had vampire hearing.

"Coleridge?" he repeated. "You're quoting Coleridge *now*?"

I tried to smile. I must have faded away again because the next person I heard was Liam.

"She's past the worst of it," he said. "Stuart, you can put the phone down."

"She'll want to know."

"She won't believe you over the phone. Best to let Christabel tell her. After."

I felt a glass vial at my lips. I recognized the smell, coppery and strange.

"Drink it, Christa." Connor was holding the vial. I recognized his smell right away, all licorice and soap. Blood trickled between my lips. I could barely swallow. He angled my head back so that my throat opened. The blood was vile tasting and it tingled as it traveled throughout my body.

I didn't have a heartbeat. I thumped my chest, panicking. It didn't help.

"It's okay," Connor said as I thrashed in the bed, dislodging pillows and blankets. A glass of water on the table fell to the floor and shattered. The sound elongated and scratched along my nerves. I wasn't breathing. I wasn't *breathing*.

"She needs more blood," Geoffrey said, and suddenly there was a bottle where the vial had been. Unrelenting rivulets of thick blood filled my mouth. I gagged. It was like chewing pennies. It coated my teeth and tongue.

At least it was distracting me from the terror of not having a heartbeat.

Which didn't seem to be holding me back, actually.

The revolting taste of blood was more immediate. Nausea flooded me. I made some kind of recognizable gesture, or else I'd turned green instead of blue because a plastic garbage pail was suddenly at hand. I pushed the bottle away and threw up. I didn't feel like I was dying anymore. I felt worse.

"You need to drink more," someone insisted.

I threw up again.

I really hoped Connor was somewhere else.

I felt a little stronger; the blood was healing me but I just couldn't swallow any more. My throat closed up at the thought. I felt sick again. But I was aware of so many other layers to the world. I could hear a dog snuffling at the door, footsteps in the hall. I could smell blood and sweat and the rosemary in the garden outside the window. I heard a mouse in the wall behind my head.

"You haven't had enough blood," Liam said.

"Can't," I croaked.

"You have to. You'll starve otherwise. That's the first step to turning into a *Hel-Blar*."

"I've got my kit." Geoffrey burst into the room, carrying his old-fashioned black leather doctor's case just as I was wondering how blue I'd turned. "If you can't drink it," Geoffrey said to me, pulling out a long needle, tubing, and a plastic bag of blood, "you'll need a transfusion. Several, in fact."

I turned away as he swabbed my arm at the crease of my elbow. The needle bit into my skin, sudden and sharp and as irritating as a hornet's sting.

Still better than the alternative.

When I woke up again, the needle was gone and I was alone for the first time in what felt like days. The window was still open, letting in the garden and night-scented air and washing out the miasma of illness. Tree branches scraped the glass, rustling red and yellow leaves. The bed was an antique, piled with quilts and my salt-stained pillowcase. A small fridge hummed quietly, clashing with the faded, elegant decor. The wallpaper was silk; the fringe on the damask chair was threaded with what might have been real pearls.

I sat up tentatively, expecting to feel weak and queasy.

I felt good.

Well, better.

I went to the antique washstand and stood in front of the mirror. I was scared to look. It was an actual test of courage just to open my eyes. Which were now a light hazel, when before they'd been plain old brown. They were nearly the same shade as Saga's grog. My hair was lank with dust and sweat, and the scratches from the cedar maze were scabbed over, nearly healed. There was mud under my fingernails. I was haggard and gross, traced with prominent veins.

But I wasn't entirely blue and I didn't smell like I was rotting from the inside out. I smiled.

And nearly sliced my lip open on my fangs.

I had fangs now.

I was going to kill my mother for naming me after a poem about a girl who falls under the spell of a vampire.

I poked at my teeth, which were as sharp as the needle Geoffrey had stuck in my arm. I poked them harder, trying to get them to retract into my gums, which were swollen and tender. They didn't move. There must be a trick to it. I'd ask someone, just as soon as I'd had a shower. My stomach grumbled as I went toward the door. I was starving, but I didn't know for what.

Well, I *knew*, but I was sure there must be some mistake, despite everything.

I should be craving pizza and ice-cream sundaes and grilled-cheese sandwiches. Normal stuff. But my body insisted on craving blood, even though my brain recoiled and shut down at the idea. Not to mention the empty cavern of my chest. I pressed my hand over my heart, but when I felt nothing I stopped. I could easily give myself a panic attack. How long would it take to get used to this? Would I ever? Had I really ever noticed my heartbeat when I had one?

And what happened now? I couldn't go to school anymore, obviously. I'd have to take classes online. And did I have to stay here with the Drakes? And did I have to hang out with just vampires now? What about my family? How could I see my mother only at night? Wouldn't she get suspicious? Especially since no face powder in the world could cover the blue veins. If I told her the truth, would she believe me? Would she start drinking again? My head whirled.

Shower now, deep thoughts later.

The bathroom was next door, with a huge shower tiled in painted ceramic. There were fluffy towels and pretty soaps. I stood under the hot water for nearly half an hour, washing away the dust of the ghost town, the dirt from the maze, the ashes from the fire, the sweat of my bloodchange. The water was brown as it circled the drain. I washed my hair again. My fingertips were wrinkly when I finally stepped out in a cloud of steam, wrapped in a towel.

I eyed the toilet speculatively. Did vampires pee? I didn't have to go right now, but was that because I'd been dehydrated and feverish for so long?

I shook my head. I had to stop all this thinking or I'd freak myself right out. The point was, I was relatively okay, for a dead girl anyway, and I wasn't alone. It could have been much, much worse. I could have been left to starve horribly and turned into a *Hel-Blar.*

When I went back into my room to get dressed, it smelled differently, like licorice. I glanced around for Connor but no one was there. There was a book on the dresser, however, and a note with his handwriting. *For you, Christabel. Happy Birthday. Connor.*

The book was old and lined with fabric the color of green opals. The pages were as thin as moth wings and full of poetry. I recognized Shelley and Coleridge right away. It smelled like libraries and dust. It was an antique. I sat on the edge of the bed and smiled stupidly at it until my damp towel dried and began to itch.

Just because I was a vampire now didn't mean I wasn't still me. And I didn't sit around thinking dreamy thoughts about cute boys.

I made myself get dressed in the clothes and some of my stuff Uncle Stuart must have brought me. The jeans were torn and soft, the tight T-shirt had a faded Ramones album cover. I put on my combat boots, like armor, even though I was in a friendly house. Connor's mom was scary. I remembered her from evening barbecues at the lake when I was little.

I clutched my new poetry book as if it were a shield.

CHAPTER 24

◆

Connor

When I checked on Christabel, she was sitting on the edge of the bed, holding the book of poetry I'd given her. She dropped it when she saw me, looking embarrassed.

I hoped that was a good sign.

"Hey," I said quietly, leaning on the doorframe. "You okay?"

She nodded. "I guess so." She held out her arm, traced with blue veins. "It's just weird. Really, really weird."

"I know," I said. "I'm sorry I couldn't save you," I added. The knowledge of it burned.

She frowned. "But you did save me. You got me out of there. You ran all the way home carrying me."

"I didn't save you from the stake."

She made a face, her fangs poking out slightly. It was cute as hell. "This isn't a comic book, Connor. You can't be everywhere at once." She still looked befuddled and probably would for a while. "It doesn't feel real." She winced when the wind slammed one of her bedroom shutters against the outside wall. "Even if my ears are wicked sensitive."

"You'll get used to it," I promised. "We all did."

"My mom is going to freak right out."

"Have you called her?" I asked, stepping into the room and shutting the door behind me. She raised an eyebrow. "Six nosy brothers who eavesdrop," I explained, sitting next to her.

"Oh." She flicked on her MP3 player. Music flooded over us.

"So?" I pressed. "Your mom?"

She shook her head. "No way. How do you even begin to explain something like this over the phone? Plus, she's in rehab for at least three months. I'll tell her when she's been out for a while and I can actually see her." She swallowed. "What do I do now?"

"Whatever you want."

She leaned in closer to me. She felt different now. Her skin was cooler, her eyes were lighter, and she was less fragile.

"You're still Christabel," I whispered, lifting a long reddish blond curl off her shoulder. "You're still *you*."

"I wonder."

"Quick—first three lines of 'The Highwayman'?" I asked.

She answered like it was a pop quiz. "'The wind was a torrent of darkness among the gusty trees, The moon was a ghostly galleon tossed upon cloudy seas, The road was a ribbon of moonlight over the purple moor.'"

"See?" I grinned. "Still you."

Some of the tension left her shoulders. "You're pretty smart, Connor," she said. "And you're nice, too."

I was *nice*.

Otherwise known as the Kiss of Death.

If she called me "cute," my humiliation would be complete.

I eased back, sighing. I could actually feel the rusty bite of disappointment in my chest. I wasn't surprised, though. Lucy had already told me the kind of guy Christabel went for. It was just my luck that I was falling for her—and falling hard.

"And you like bad boys," I said evenly. I wasn't going to beg or weep or gnash my teeth.

At least, not in front of her.

I got up to leave before I made an ass of myself.

"I like *you*," she corrected me softly, catching my hand in hers before I could move away. She tugged once and I sat back down, staring at her.

I must have heard that wrong.

"What?"

Apparently Quinn got all the suave in the genetic lottery and the bastard didn't leave any for me.

"I like you," she repeated.

Maybe I didn't need the suave after all.

Which was good because I knew my grin was decidedly goofy.

"Yeah?"

"Yeah."

"Well, all right, then." I hauled her over to sit in my lap, curving my hand around her waist. Her hair draped over my arm. The heel of her combat boot bumped my shin. "Why didn't you say so?"

"I've always gone for bad boys before," she said. "We had heat. Lots of heat."

"Not loving this," I pointed out drily.

She grinned. "Just listen. We had nothing but heat. They didn't know about me and I didn't know about them. I liked it that way. There was no risk that one of them would drop by and find my mother passed out at the kitchen table." She ran a hand through my hair. It was really hard to concentrate on what she was saying. She smelled like cinnamon and she was running her fingers through my hair. "I thought it had to be one or the other   hot or nice. But maybe it doesn't. Maybe there are other options worth exploring."

I closed the small space between us with every intention of kissing her until she forgot she'd ever liked bad boys in the first place.

"But am I under the influence of the infamous Drake pheromones?" she asked just before my lips touched hers. "I mean, is this just biology or chemistry?"

"Maybe I'm under the influence of your pheromones," I pointed out.

She blinked. "Is that possible?"

I shook my head. "No. Vampire pheromones don't work on other vampires," I told her. Except for Solange's, but she didn't need to know that yet. "Christa?"

"Yeah?"

"Shut up now."

She was laughing when I finally closed my mouth over hers. The kiss caught like a spark in a dry field. I'd thought I was feeling ordinary bloodlust that first night in the ghost town, but I wasn't. It was her. Just her. Our tongues met and I could taste her, drink her, practically breathe her. I couldn't get close enough. Her hand tightened in my hair and we melted back onto the bed. There were lips and hands and the burn of want in my veins, sweeter than blood. When she lifted her head, her lips were slightly swollen, her eyes heavy lidded.

"Worth exploring?" I asked hoarsely.

She smiled in a way that made me forget my own name.

"Definitely worth exploring."

CHAPTER 25

◆

Lucy

I was officially a student of Helios-Ra Academy.

Weird.

Christabel was okay. I'd wanted to visit her myself, but I didn't have a car anymore and Mom needed to get to work. I had to trust everyone's assurances that Christabel really was fine, especially since she wasn't ready for the temptation of humans yet. She was at the Drakes', recovering and learning about her new life. Or death. Whatever.

And I was learning to be a vampire hunter.

My mom pulled away from the school only after making me promise for the third time that I would double my sun salutations, meditate at least once a week, and come home to visit as much as possible. She was a little teary. It was nothing compared to the guilt trip I'd gotten from Nathan. And I still hadn't talked to Solange, but Nicholas swore she was sorry. He also swore we'd find a way to see each other. Vampires weren't exactly a regular occurrence on campus, even if they were treaty vampires. But Quinn and Hunter managed, so we would, too.

It was late afternoon and the sun was already behind the mountain, making the crisp autumn day crisper and filling it with blue shadows. Students jogged around the track and poured in a steady stream between the dorm and the library and gym. According to my schedule, this was a break between classes, which would resume at eight o'clock and go on until midnight. I was already on a similar schedule, staying up late to hang out with Nicholas.

I had a map and my room assignment and a belly full of butterflies. I wasn't nervous around vampires, even when they were cranky. But this school was already making my palms sweat. I was behind and I sided with the vampires—most of the time.

This should be interesting.

I forced myself to ignore two girls who stared at me and then started whispering the moment I passed them. I heard "Drakes" and "princess." The path was lined with birch trees and led me to the dorm's front doors, which looked like something out of a medieval cathedral. They were solid oak with metal hinges and narrow pointed windows on either side.

Inside, it looked like the old house it had once been over a hundred years ago, before modern additions and stampeding students. The staircase looked original, polished wood with a carved banister. I dragged my stuff toward it. There were doors everywhere, leading to bedrooms and common areas. A guy in a baseball cap ran past me, yelling something back to his roommate and nearly knocking me over. He stumbled to a stop, dropping his Frisbee.

"Sorry! Hey, you're the new girl."

"Yeah," I admitted. "Is it that obvious?"

He shrugged. "Not a lot of us here. And you scream hippie."

"Guilty," I said, unoffended. I was wearing my mom's favorite crystal, after all, and wraparound sandals with my patched jeans. Plus, my parents were legendary in Violet Hill.

"I'm Malcolm," he introduced himself. "You must be the famous Lucky Hamilton."

I winced. "It's Lucy and, oh God," I groaned. "What are they saying about me?"

"That you were there when Hope tried to take down the Drakes."

"She's was a bitch." I paused. "Please tell me she's not your aunt or something?"

"Dude, no." He looked curious. "I heard your boyfriend's a vampire. Is that true?"

"Um, yeah. It is." I lifted my chin, prepared to fight for Nicholas's honor.

"Too bad." Malcolm said, teeth flashing white in his dark face when he shot me a grin that looked almost disappointed.

"Malcolm!" one of his friends yelled through the open window. "Let's go!"

"They want this." He lifted the Frisbee. "See ya around, hippie."

I started up the stairs feeling a little better. He seemed nice. And with Hunter and Chloe, I now knew a total of three people. I could do this.

And then a cluster of girls sneered at me.

"Your *boyfriend's* really a vampire?" one of them asked. "God, this place used to have standards."

I looked her up and down doubtfully. "If you say so."

Then I marched up the stairs while they whispered to each other. My room was on the second floor, down the hall and wedged into the back corner. Number 207. I knocked before going in.

I'd kind of hoped my roommate would be out so I could acclimate on my own. No such luck. She was sitting at her desk, wearing an ironed school T-shirt and the regulation cargo pants. There was an identical outfit folded neatly on the bare bed. Gah. School uniforms. I'd forgotten about that part.

"Hi," I said cheerfully, determined not to let the end of the freedom to dress myself bring me down. "Are you Sarita?"

"Hi." She smiled back at me. "Lucky?"

"Just Lucy."

She frowned, checking a list in an uncreased folder next to her keyboard. "It says Lucky Moon Hamilton."

"They even put my middle name in there? Were they *trying* to mortify me?" I dropped my knapsack.

"It's school policy," Sarita replied, puzzled.

She was scarily organized, between that folder and the perfectly sharpened pencils in a cup with the school logo on the side. Her bed was neatly made with military precision, and her shoes were lined up at the foot. There was no music playing and no posters on her side of the room at all. I was planning on plastering the wall over my desk with Jensen Ackles and Johnny Depp. My mom had already put together a box of Nag Champa incense for me, and I'd glued rhinestones on all my boring black binders.

Sarita was going to hate me.

I ripped open the garbage bag serving as the suitcase for my sheets and dumped them on the bed. My fleece blanket was printed with Jack Sparrow's face. He stared at Sarita rakishly. She smiled weakly. I pulled out my laptop and set up my Ganesha statue on my desk next to it for good luck.

She blinked at his elephant head. "What's that?"

"My dad gave it to me. He's an Indian god."

"Oh."

"He likes candy."

"Oh."

Silence pulsed between us. My roommate thought I was a freak. I was just scared she was going to force me to make my bed every morning.

This was going to be even harder than I'd thought.

"That dresser over there is yours," Sarita offered finally, politely. It was pine and dented all over. "And the closet there. There's a kitchenette around the corner, and the common room is by the stairs. That's where the TV is."

"Okay, thanks."

The room was small. Between the two beds, two dressers, and two desks, there wasn't a lot of room left. I liked to dance around when I studied. That might prove difficult.

"There's a study curfew from four thirty to six thirty, when everyone's supposed to be quiet," she felt compelled to add. "And lights out by one thirty a.m."

"Are there a lot of school rules?" I asked cautiously. I had a feeling she'd know.

"They're all for our benefit," she said. "And you get demerits or detention if you break them."

"What's standard detention?" I asked, laughing. "Because I have a feeling I'm going to need to know."

She actually looked scandalized. I didn't know sixteen-year-old girls who were learning to stab pointy sticks into undead creatures of the night could even *be* scandalized.

"It's usually kitchen duty," she finally answered. "I've never actually had a detention."

Of course not. I shrugged. "Well, I'll let you know what it's like."

She swallowed. "Um . . ." She trailed off uncomfortably. "Vampires aren't allowed on campus."

Clearly my reputation preceded me here, too. All I needed was for her to find the condoms my mother had undoubtedly snuck into all of my bags.

"That's fine. I don't think my boyfriend would like it much here, anyway."

Her eyes went so wide they nearly bulged. It was probably wrong of me to find that amusing. Or to want to take a photo of Nicholas with his fangs out and wearing a black cape lined with red satin and then hang it over my pillow in a heart-shaped frame.

Before my warped sense of humor could alienate her completely, there was a knock at the door. Hunter poked her head in. "Hey, guys."

Sarita straightened in her chair, as if Hunter were a teacher. And as if she hadn't already been sitting sword-straight before. "Hi, Hunter. Can I help you with something?"

Hunter smiled. "Just want to borrow your roommate." She met my gaze pointedly. She looked serious. Vampire serious. I knew the expression intimately. "I need her help. Right away."

"Sure." I leaped to my feet, probably a little too eagerly. It was definitely a bad sign that whatever crisis was brewing seemed like more fun than sitting here in an awkward silence with my straight-laced roommate. One minute down, eight more months to go.

"You know Lucky?" Sarita asked.

"Sure, we train together."

"Malcolm said there was a hippie in the building." Chloe grinned over Hunter's shoulder. "I wanted to call an exterminator."

I grinned back. "We're like cockroaches. You can't even spray." I grabbed my bag. "Bye, Sarita." I closed the door behind me. "What's going on? Also, good timing."

"Come down to our room," Hunter said quietly. "It's more private."

When my phone vibrated I expected it to be Nathan with another guilt trip, but the text was from Hunter.

Cameras and bugs in the halls. Act normal.

Hidden cameras and microphones? What the hell had I gotten myself into?

"Shit, they roomed you with Sarita?" Chloe said conversationally as I slipped my phone back into my pocket. "Classic Helios-Ra room assignment." She shook her head. "They do it on purpose."

"They do? Why?"

"To teach us how to get along with people and to see how we do under stress," Hunter explained.

"Please." Chloe snorted. "It's because they're just plain mean."

"Sarita's not so bad," Hunter said. "She's just . . . organized."

"Anal," Chloe corrected. She shot me a pitying look. "And I'm pretty sure she'll tattle. For your own good, of course."

Hunter wrinkled her nose. "You're probably right about that."

"But hanging out with Hunter will give you a buffer," Chloe assured me. "Sarita has a serious case of hero worship for her."

"She does not." Hunter rolled her eyes.

"She does so."

"Even though you have a vampire boyfriend?" I raised my eyebrows. "She seemed pretty strict about that. And I've only known her for about five minutes."

"She thinks they're just ugly rumors," Chloe said. "The saintly Hunter would never defile herself that way." She smiled slowly. "Then again, Sarita's never seen Quinn."

Hunter poked her.

"What? He's pretty."

The hallway seemed deserted, the dorm more quiet than it had been when I arrived. Even the lawns were empty. "Where's everyone?"

"At dinner." Hunter waited for Chloe and me to step into the room before shutting the door and pressing her ear against it. Chloe was already at one of her laptops, entering in a password.

"Okay, so what's up?" I asked when Hunter crossed the carpet, satisfied that no one had followed us. She flipped on their stereo anyway to muffle our voices. Solange and I used that trick all the time after Logan and Nicholas turned and we wanted to make sure they weren't eavesdropping on us.

"Chloe intercepted messages between some of the hunters who hide out in the mountains," Hunter told me in undertones. "One of them was flying his bush plane and found the burned remains of a maze near an abandoned ghost town."

I exhaled suddenly. "That's where they kept Christabel."

"I know," Hunter said grimly. "There's at least six of them going in pretty much now. They want to take out all the *Hel-Blar* and anything that moves."

"Shit, they don't know about Saga and the council treaty thing," I exclaimed. "If they go in looking for a fight, they could start a civil war between the tribes. No one would believe the Drakes weren't involved!"

"What do you want to do?"

"We have to tell Christabel." I fumbled for my phone. "When she was sick, she muttered about Aidan. He saved her life, ironically. We can't just let him get ambushed!"

"I already texted Quinn and Kieran," Hunter said while I copied my message to Christabel to Nicholas and Connor. I didn't copy Solange. Usually she'd be a lethal sword in the fight, but right now she was a live grenade. She might blow us all up.

Plus, I was holding a grudge.

I could admit it to myself, if to no one else.

"Can you get ahold of Hart? Have him call it off?"

"He can't be officially involved in vampire politics, treaty or no, any more than Liam could be involved in League business," Hunter said. "Besides, it's a hunter's right and duty to take out *Hel-Blar*. Not to mention, Aidan essentially killed your cousin."

"Turned her. There's a difference."

"She wouldn't have been in danger if he hadn't kidnapped her. Anyway, they're out of range by now," Chloe said.

"It's a different world," Hunter said apologetically. "We're not trained to save vampires from themselves."

"If there's a civil war, everyone will be involved," I argued.

"I know," she agreed calmly.

"And the Drakes won't be up and out for another hour at least," I said, frustrated.

"It'll take us that long to drive to the maze," Hunter said, reaching for her knapsack. I knew it was full of weapons and hiking supplies. She was prepared like that. "They can meet us there."

Chloe unplugged her laptop. "Ready."

I blinked. "You're going? Both of you?"

"Of course. We're all going," Hunter said. "Don't be stupid."

CHAPTER 26

◆

Christabel

Connor grabbed me in the hall and pressed his mouth to mine.

"Shhh," he murmured against my lips.

"I didn't say anything," I murmured back, baffled. But as usual, the feel of his lips on mine was distracting.

He jerked his head toward the window. "Come on," he mouthed. I followed him, peering down into the gardens. The tops of thorny rosebushes waved at me. Light from the conservatory spilled out onto the lawn in perfect yellow squares.

"That's a two-story drop," I whispered when Connor flung his leg over the sill and waited for me to do the same. "Last I checked, vampires didn't sprout wings." I stared at him. "We don't, do we?"

He chuckled despite the solemn cast to his eyes. "No."

"What the hell, then?"

"Keep your voice down," he said. "We need to go. Now."

"There are these new things called stairs," I whispered back.

He shook his head. "You really are Lucy's cousin. All of a sudden I can see the family resemblance. Will you please just come on?"

"Connor," I said patiently. "I can't jump out of the window and I'm a lousy climber. Just let me sneak out the back."

He sighed. "Fine. But hurry. Meet me behind those cedars."

"More cedars," I muttered. "That can't be good."

Connor didn't answer, just dropped out of view. I didn't even hear him land. I heard some of the brothers walking around on the third floor. I went quietly down the stairs, peeking into the living room. It was empty. I snuck down the hall toward the garden conservatory. I felt like I was back home, creeping around so I wouldn't wake my mother when she was in one of her weepy moods.

"Hey, Christa."

I hollered, jumping a foot off the ground. Apparently, I'd lost my stealth entirely when I died. "Solange!"

She tilted her head, smiling. She looked less scruffy than she used to, wearing a flowing shirt and with her hair in a neat braid. But her irises were delicately ringed with blood. My eyes were bloodshot but I'd been assured that would fade. Solange's were getting more pronounced.

"You're sneaking out," she declared knowingly.

Crap.

"Um. No?"

"Are so." She waved her hand. "Doesn't matter. I'm sneaking out, too."

"You are? Where?"

"It's not exactly sneaking out if I tell you," she said, grinning. "You go that way." She pointed toward the back rooms. "I'll go out the front." She leaned in and the smell of her, wood smoke and roses, made me feel fuzzy. "Don't tell anyone you saw me."

She was gone before I could reply. I hurried through the glass-walled room, around potted orange and lemon trees with glossy leaves and banks of red lilies. Ivy trailed around the door.

The flagstones were littered with rose petals and acorns. I stepped onto the lawn instead and ran toward the cedars. Connor was shifting impatiently from foot to foot.

"This way." He turned and darted away. I chased after him through the field. The grass was tall and damp. Birds lifted out of secret weedy nooks when we passed by. I was briefly distracted by my new ability to run fast and not lose my breath. I was grinning when we stopped on the outskirts of the forest. Moonlight percolated through the pine boughs.

"Do you know about the Helios-Ra?" Connor asked.

"Only that Lucy's going to school at their academy outside town. Why?"

"They're vampire hunters."

"Yeah, I know that."

"Well, sometimes they go all survivalist wackjob in the mountains. Some of those guys found the ghost town, and they're going in to take everyone out—not just the *Hel-Blar* but Saga, Aidan, and their people, too."

"How'd you find all this out?" I asked.

"Lucy called me," he replied. "She's been at that school for less than a day." He sounded impressed despite the worry in his shoulders.

"That's Lucy," I agreed. "Shouldn't we tell your parents or something?"

Quinn emerged from the trees. "No. Mom will charge in, and Dad will be caught in some diplomatic trap. Meanwhile, the hunters will take out the *Hel-Blar*, we'll get blamed somehow, Saga's undead pets will be let loose, and then who knows what will happen? It's bad enough the royal court had to negotiate with kidnappers. But we'll send the parents a message when we get there."

"That's why we're going in," Connor explained. "But you don't have to. Aidan kidnapped you, after all. You're allowed to hate him a little."

"But he saved my life, too," I said. "Twice. And if he dies, I'll never find out about myself. My new self," I corrected.

"We could use you," Quinn admitted. "You might have negotiating power. You're Aidan's bloodkin now."

My blood ran cold. Aidan wasn't my father, but he was the closest thing to it in my new world. The *Na-Foir* were basically an unknown, according to Connor and his family—according to Aidan and Saga, too. I wouldn't get answers about my bloodchange from anyone else. "I'm coming."

"I figured," Connor said, rifling through the pack his brother handed him. He pulled out a handful of stakes and gave them to me. "Here. But stay behind us when we get there. You barely know how to use these."

"Let's go," Quinn urged. "Lucy and Hunter might already be there by now. The hunters were trying to go in before sunset to ambush them at their weakest. We might be too late. Nicholas already left."

"Do you know the way back?" I asked Connor.

"I left a trail," he answered, zipping up his hoodie. "Between that and the GPS coordinates I got from the hunters' bush plane, we're fine."

"Are we running all the way there?" I asked. I might not have to worry about wheezing myself into an asthmatic fit, but running would take too long. I remembered that much about finding our way back.

"We've got a motorcycle trail that will take us most of the way," Connor said as we skirted the edge of the forest, leaping over ferns and fallen trunks. Startled and sleepy squirrels chittered angrily over our heads. We ducked into the woods proper, on the other side of a copse of birch trees. It was another few minutes to the bushes where Quinn had stashed two motorcycles. The engines shattered the forest quiet, rolling out plumes of exhaust. I clutched the back of Connor's jacket with two hands and we rattled and bumped over the uneven ground. It wasn't a trail so much as a way in unencumbered by broken trees or large boulders. When the thick undergrowth gave way to sparse red pine, we stopped the bikes and hopped off.

I could smell the faint taint of smoke even before we came out of the trees. We stayed in the shadows, circling around the crooked street of the ghost town to assess the situation from a safe distance.

The charred remains of the maze were sad lumps of blackened tree trunks and burned barbed wire. The pen where Saga had kept some of her *Hel-Blar* was empty. There was movement, a shifting of shadows by the wooden houses. A window broke and there was a shout. Footsteps scraped the dirt. A door slammed shut repeatedly, caught by the wind.

Quinn's phone vibrated in his inside coat pocket. I wouldn't have heard it if I'd still had regular human hearing. He skimmed the text, then motioned for us to follow him. We went around back, aiming for a narrow alley between two houses. We met Nicholas along the way.

"What's the word?" Quinn asked.

"Just got here," Nicholas said. "Had some trouble with a *Hel-Blar*."

"I'll go this way." Quinn nodded toward one of the alleys. He and Connor exchanged a look before he raced off. We joined Lucy, Hunter, and another girl at the end near the street. They were armed with so many stakes, they looked like porcupines. Nicholas rushed forward.

Behind us, a *Hel-Blar* jumped out from a pile of firewood. He clacked his jaws, grabbing Connor's shoulder. Connor whirled, dislodging his hold. Nicholas turned back to help but Connor had already staked the *Hel-Blar*. Mushroom-colored ash drifted to our feet.

"You made it." Lucy breathed. She was incongruous in her peasant blouse and crystals next to her friends' military-style cargos. She hugged me tightly. "Are you okay?"

I thought about it. Not long ago I hadn't even been able to recite my favorite poem. That had been the scariest part.

"'One kiss, my bonny sweetheart, I'm after a prize tonight,'" I quoted. "'But I shall be back with the yellow gold before the morning light.'"

Lucy rolled her eyes. "Back to normal."

"Whoa," Chloe said. "You're kinda blue."

"Not *Hel-Blar*," Connor explained. "*Na-Foir*."

"*Na-Foir*? What the hell's that?"

"A new breed of vampire," he said. "Well, old breed."

Chloe groaned. "Seriously? Like we don't have enough weird names of vampire tribes to memorize for exams already?"

"The hunters had staked half the *Hel-Blar* by the time we got here," Hunter said. "A whole bunch more were released after that. They're everywhere, and the fight called the others hiding in the mountains."

"And the hunters?" Nicholas asked, flattening himself against the wall and sneaking a peek down the road.

"Mostly on the rooftops now," Hunter replied. "Where's Quinn?"

"He went around the other side," Connor replied. "Stealth mode."

A war whoop and a mocking laugh belied that comment.

Hunter sighed. "He's across the street, being a lunatic, you mean."

"That's stealth mode for him." Connor threw us a grin before rushing out to help his twin. I watched him disappear into the saloon. It sounded like a bar brawl was going on in there, between the splintering of furniture and the breaking of bottles.

Hunter looked at Nicholas. "He's not following any plan I've ever heard of."

"Does Quinn ever?"

"We were going to do a quiet sweep."

A *Hel-Blar* flew out of the saloon doors, rolled off the porch, and exploded into ashes.

"That's Quinn's version of a sweep," Nicholas replied.

"The *Hel-Blar* are running loose, one of the hunters is dead, and the others are talking about setting the whole town on fire," Lucy updated us.

"I nearly did that," I said. "It could work, unfortunately."

"They have the gasoline for it," Hunter said. "There are jerricans down by what's left of the maze there, and a big guy with a lighter."

"Anyone seen Aidan or Saga?" I asked. Saga was more like Quinn; she'd have been shooting her way through the hunters with her blunderbuss. That she *wasn't* meant she *couldn't*.

Lucy shook her head. "Every time we move from this spot, the *Hel-Blar* think it's dinnertime."

"I was about to go out there and be the distraction," Chloe said, "until Quinn decided it was playtime."

"Aidan might be with Saga in that house on the right. The one with the blue hand nailed to the door." I stepped out of the alley toward it.

Nicholas and Lucy yanked me back. "Whoa," Nicholas said. "Hang on a minute."

"We don't have a minute," I pointed out.

"And you don't have the proper training yet," he shot back. "So just wait." He jerked his hand through his hair as Quinn let out another yell across the street. I hoped he didn't get Connor killed. "Lucy, Christabel, and I can head for the house," Nicholas suggested to Hunter. "Why don't you and Chloe see what you can do about the gasoline. Don't let anyone light it."

Hunter nodded. She and Chloe snuck out the back of the alley, where we'd come in. Nicholas threw a stake behind them, catching the *Hel-Blar* who'd caught their scent and darted after them. The *Hel-Blar* clutched his wounded arm, turning to snarl at us. Blood oozed between his fingers. Lucy's crossbow bolt hit him right in the heart. His blood was still dripping, caught in midair as he turned to ashes.

Nicholas crept out slowly, checking rooftops. When he waved us out, we followed quickly. Lucy had our backs with her surprisingly deadly miniature crossbow. The light glinted off all her silver jewelry. Down the street, the silhouettes of Hunter and Chloe grappled with a hugely muscled hunter. Even from a hundred yards away, I could see he was built like a bull, all neck and shoulders.

We couldn't help them right now, though, not with three *Hel-Blar* suddenly on us. Nicholas staked one right away but the other two were quicker and more savage. They were chomping at the air, trying to get to Lucy. I kicked out but, since I wasn't used to my recently developed speed and strength, I just ended up spinning myself around. Everything blurred as if I were on a merry-go-round. I spun back, trying not to be dizzy. Nicholas jumped in front of

Lucy so quickly she stumbled back. She tripped, landing in the dirt. Her crossbow flew out of her hands.

A *Hel-Blar* grabbed my hair, saliva dripping onto my shoulder. I jabbed back with my elbow and heard his ribs snap. Whoa. Super-strength. I jabbed again, using the stake. The stench of mushrooms and blood was palpable. Nicholas threw his own stake, dispatching the *Hel-Blar* before his jaws could clamp down on my throat. He crumbled to ash.

The other one took advantage of Nicholas's momentary distraction and punched him so hard in the stomach, Nicholas flew backward, sailed over Lucy, and landed half in an empty horse trough. He groaned, trying to get to his feet.

A *Hel-Blar* licked his lips at Lucy, teeth gleaming. She scrabbled wildly but her crossbow was out of reach. He shuffled closer, eyes so red even his pupils gleamed bloodily. Nicholas was too far away. My aim was nowhere nearly good enough. I threw a stake anyway, just to break his concentration on my cousin as his next meal. He batted the stake away.

Still, it was just long enough for me to kick the crossbow.

"Lucy!"

She grabbed it and struggled to reload it. I threw another stake, with the same relatively useless effect as the first one. The *Hel-Blar* ignored it and leaped on Lucy.

She lifted the bow and released the bolt just as he fell on her. She choked on ashes and dust, wiping them off her face. "That's disgusting," she panted, sweat fogging her glasses.

Nicholas skidded to a halt beside her. "Did he get you? Are you okay?"

"I'm fine," she said, scrambling to her feet. She rubbed her knee. "Ow."

He ran his hand over her head and her arms, eyes flaring silver. His touch was tender, but his voice wasn't. "Stay behind me, damn it," he said, as if there were rocks and whiskey in his throat.

"I *was* behind you," she grumbled.

I bent to pick up a strap of silver stakes. Ashes dusted my hands. "Oh no," I said. "This was Emma."

Someone screamed inside Saga's house.

We ran toward it. Connor and Quinn jumped down from the roof and landed right in front of us before Lucy reached the door. Lucy whirled and nearly shot them. They were already tumbling out of the way.

Quinn's smirk slipped. "Careful with that thing!"

Connor glanced at me. "You okay?"

I nodded, relieved to see that, although his hair was standing on end and his jeans were ripped, he looked unharmed. His fangs were out and his eyes looked like blue glass beads from Greece. "You?"

"Fine." He looked at the house. "We'll go around back."

"Where's Hunter?" Quinn asked sharply.

"She and Chloe are making sure we don't all explode," Nicholas said.

As he reached for the doorknob, a hunter came around the side of the house. Lucy leaped between him and the rest of us, even though he was holding a throwing axe and a crossbow of his own.

"I'm Helios-Ra!" Lucy shouted. When he relaxed slightly, seeing as she was all of sixteen, she darted forward and punched him right in the nose. "Sort of," she amended as he reeled back, hit his head on the porch, and fell over. The stake in his hand clattered to the ground.

"Don't you have Hypnos?" Nicholas asked, amused.

"Oh yeah. I forgot." She shook out her fingers, knuckles already going red. "He had a hard nose, too. I might bruise."

We heard another shout from the second floor and the recognizable sounds of a fight. A musket fired above us, showering splinters. I shoved past the others and burst into the house. The table was overturned and one of the jugs was on its side, spilling rum. I took the stairs two at a time.

"Shit, Christa, wait for me," Connor called out, hard on my heels.

Chaos.

There were huge bullet holes in the walls; the window was hanging off its hinges. A human hunter lay in a heap by the door, her leg clearly broken. Connor bent long enough to relieve her of all her weapons.

Saga was standing on a bench, barefoot and waving her cutlass. She slashed at another hunter and sent him tumbling out the window, down the overhanging roof, and to the street below. She was as blue as the center of a flame, blue as spilled gasoline. Her teeth were sharper than her daggers. The smell of rot and mildew clung to everything. Two *Hel-Blar* circled her in the cramped room. She refused to move, even though there was blood on her legs. Her whistle, usually hanging by a braided cord at her belt, was gone. She was protecting Aidan.

"We got *Hel-Blar* down here!" Quinn yelled.

"So do we!" Connor yelled back.

"Well, you're about to get more!"

Connor swore and rushed to the landing to stop the incoming *Hel-Blar* that got past the others.

Aidan was pinned to the wall behind the bed with a stake through his shoulder. He was bleeding profusely, but at least it hadn't pierced his heart. He was trapped, though, and weak. He hadn't fed. Even I could see that. I had to get him free.

"Christa, stay back," he choked.

Too late.

One of the *Hel-Blar* slammed into me. My forehead bounced off the wall. Pain clouded my vision for a moment. He forced my head to the side. I struggled but I couldn't get loose. Aidan clawed at the stake, opening his wound. I smelled his blood in the air. The *Hel-Blar* laughed and then licked me. Thank God all my scratches had healed already. There was shouting behind me but all I really heard were those snapping jaws and clacking teeth. I tried to kick back but the angle was all wrong. He bent my neck farther, nails like claws.

I had a stake, and even though I couldn't reach his heart, I could reach something. I jabbed blindly, as hard as I could. He snarled but didn't let go. I jabbed again. I got him in the eye that time and he howled, jerking back. The stake was still stuck in his eye socket. I kicked him and he hit the floorboards. One of them broke under his weight. He stayed where he was, still howling.

"Get him free," Saga ordered me, leaping over the ashes at her feet and the *Hel-Blar* I'd blinded. "I'll help the others."

I rushed to Aidan, pausing just as I reached for the stake. I gulped.

"Um, how do I do this?"

He grimaced, pale under the blue. "Just pull it out. Fast."

"Oh God," I said, curling my fingers around the stake and yanking. "Oh God. Oh God."

There was resistance, a faint sucking sound, then it released suddenly. I stumbled back a few steps. Aidan grunted with pain, shoving the end of the blanket over the hole in his shoulder. His eyes veined red. "Goddamn it, that hurts." He pushed away from the wall. "I woke up as that hunter was stabbing me. I managed to kick her off enough to change her aim." He winced. "But not her training."

His steps were deliberate, as if they hurt. He kept his shirt fisted over the gash as he moved away from the bed, abandoning the blanket. He stood over the hunter, his lips lifting off impressive fangs.

"Hey, guys?" Lucy yelled up to us. "We kind of need to get the hell out of here! Like, right now would be good!"

"What now?"

"The town's about to burn to the ground," she answered, as if that were normal. "There might be dynamite, too. We're not sure."

Aidan stepped over the hunter and staggered out to the landing and down the steps. "Christabel, come on."

"We can't just leave her here!"

"She tried to kill me."

"We still can't . . . oh, never mind." I knew it was a lost cause, especially when he still had a huge hole through his shoulder. I reached down to help the sweating hunter up. She screamed when her leg moved. At least she'd managed to splint it with one of Saga's swords while the rest of us were fighting for our lives. She was hard to maneuver, like a huge bag of wet sand. She kept shifting, her eyes darting around frantically. She struggled as if I were going to bite her.

"Quit doing that," I muttered when she accidentally kneed me.

"I've got her." Connor was on her other side, holding her up. He looked straight into her eyes, leaned close enough that even I could smell the warm licorice and soap smell of him, and said, "Stop struggling."

She stopped.

"Okay, now that's a trick I need to learn," I said as we dragged her down the stairs. Quinn was waiting for us in the doorway.

"Move it—I can smell the diesel," he said tightly. He looked at the woman, disgusted. "Hunter's going to want to save her, too," he muttered. He grabbed the hunter from us, hoisted her over his shoulder, and started to run.

The wind was as soft as water when I ran so fast the world was just a blur of colors and scents: mushrooms, dirt, smoke, blood, sweat, the tang of gasoline, and something else I couldn't recognize. The others were waiting for us at the edge of the forest, bruised and exhausted. Hunter had a black eye. Quinn dumped the wounded hunter at her feet and then wrapped his arms around her.

There was a loud rumble, almost like a sharp inhale and then a loud exhale. A cloud of fire and smoke and debris fountained out of the ghost town. It rained embers and dust. Buildings fell in on themselves. A tree caught fire on the edge of town. The ground trembled under our feet. Pinecones and acorns rained down.

Saga watched, her pale face furious.

"What the hell are you doing here, anyway?" Aidan asked, leaning against a tree for support while the violent light touched us all. His chest was covered in blood and ashes.

"*She's* saving you," Lucy replied, pointing at me. "The rest of us are averting a vampire civil war. You know, the usual."

Nicholas gave her his lopsided grin, turning away from watching the destruction of the town. "I hope that damn hunter plane blows up, too—"

"Behind you!" Lucy yelled. A *Hel-Blar* ran at him, maddened by the fire and the blood.

Nicholas dodged but he was slow, taken by surprise.

His brothers tried to get to him, but they were too far away.

"Down!" Lucy added, fumbling with her crossbow.

Nicholas dropped.

Lucy fired.

There was a moment of stunned silence as we wondered what would be faster, gravity or the momentum of that sharpened bolt.

And then Nicholas straightened, shaking ashes out of his hair.

"Damn," Quinn said. "Nice shot."

Lucy grinned at him, then at Nicholas, who kissed her

passionately and with enough tongue to make us look away. Lucy's blouse was ripped and dirt matted her hair, but she looked as smug as only a girl surrounded by appreciative Drake brothers could.

"The fact is," she said, "you Drakes would be lost without me."

EPILOGUE

♦

Lucy

I'd barely made it through the front door of the dorm when my phone vibrated. Hunter and Chloe shuffled off to their room. The wounded hunter was at the hospital. Aidan and Saga had taken off somewhere. Christabel went back with the Drakes, and for the first time I didn't envy her. Helena and Liam would be infuriated, even more than when Solange and I took off one night when we were twelve to explore the underground tunnels leading out of the farmhouse.

Speaking of Solange.

Oak tree. Now. Please.

I stared at the screen. I hurt all over. I was covered in ashes and dirt and I kind of smelled like old mushrooms. I just wanted a shower. And I was still mad at her.

But the oak tree call trumped all.

Muttering to myself, I turned around and stomped back outside. At this rate I was going to get kicked out of the academy before my very first class. Good thing Hunter had already shown me the best way to sneak off campus and where the contraband keys for the school van parked in the bushes were hidden.

I parked at the edge of the field so I wouldn't get the van stuck in the mud. Solange was standing under the tree, pale as a winter cloud even through the branches. I hurried toward her.

"This better be good, Sol," I muttered. "I need chocolate, soap, and sleep. In that order."

She stepped out of the concealing leaves. Her eyes were haunted, wild.

And she was covered in blood.

"Oh God, Sol," I said. "Are you hurt?"

She shook her head. "It's not my blood."

"Okay, that's good."

She shook her head, sobbing.

"That's *not* good?" I corrected. "Whose blood is it?"

Her mouth trembled, her voice as tiny as mouseprints in the snow.

"Kieran's."

LOST GIRLS

◆

ALYXANDRA HARVEY

1983

Elisabet rattled the cage, pursing her mouth in distaste. "Is that all?" The three girls behind the bars huddled together. One wept and one was silent, eyes wide and wary. She was covered in bloody bites at her throat, elbow, and wrist. The third girl spat on the iron bars.

"She'll do," Elisabet approved, waving at one of the raven-feathered guards. "Bring her. Lady Natasha's in a mood."

◆

Violet Hill was a dangerous place.

It hadn't taken long for Helena to scratch beneath the veneer of laid-back hippie to the jagged underbelly, where each step was more treacherous than the last. All towns had a unique personality, one she could have drawn like a storybook character, and Violet Hill was a cranky old woman who could as easily offer you gingerbread as stuff you in the oven and cook you for the main course.

Helena happened to like that in a town.

And she liked the mountains eating up the sky and casting long shadows over everything. She might climb up to the top and live in one of the abandoned hunter camps once she figured out how not to get eaten by a bear. Tripped-out junkies and drunken frat boys she could handle, but she was pretty sure kicking a bear in the balls wouldn't be nearly as effective. But it might have been good practice.

If she'd thought of it earlier.

Before a fist to the face knocked her back and had her nearly biting off her tongue.

Cursing and spitting blood, she held up her gloves to protect her face while the spots cleared out of her vision. She knew better than to get distracted. It was sloppy and could get you killed: at home, in back alleys, and in underground clubs like this one.

Sofia grinned at her, blood smeared on her teeth. Her hair was teased into spikes, like needles. Helena's own long and straight dark hair was currently tied back so it wouldn't interfere with the fight. She wore tight shredded jeans and her faded Clash T-shirt. It wasn't much of a costume, like the spectators preferred, but it was her first fight. If she won she'd have money to get proper sparring gear, which would offer more protection than the tulle and leather *Mad Max* outfit Sofia was currently wearing. Helena wasn't into dressing up like a superhero. Blood was a bitch to wash out of spandex.

She'd started coming to The Vortex because the manager didn't look too closely at who was buying drinks or washing up at the bathroom sink. And in the back room, affectionately nicknamed the Thunderdome, girls fought in a makeshift ring for a 20 percent cut of the gambling profits.

Girls without any other options, angry girls, poor girls, lost girls.

Girls like her.

Helena waited until Sofia got closer before retaliating with an uppercut. Her jaws clacked together with a vicious snap and she reeled back. Helena would pay for that later.

The audience clapped and shouted, the hum of violent sound shaking Helena's bones until she felt disoriented. She stayed light on her toes, always evaluating her exit strategies. It was both instinct and a long habit that had served her well at thirteen and still served her well now at sixteen. People always underestimated you when you were young, even when they knew you. Being underestimated was as effective a weapon as a knife or a fist. And Sofia really ought to know better.

Helena pretended to be more tired than she was, slumping weakly as if dizzy. She tried to look like the scared sixteen-year-old girl they expected to see, and waited. Sofia preened, tossing her head back with a smug grin at the crowd. She wasn't much older but she was used to this, knew how to play them, knew how to get them stomping their feet and shouting her name.

Besides, she and Helena were always butting heads. When Helena had first arrived in town, Sofia had offered her a place in the lost-girls tribe. Helena had only joined them when girls started disappearing, when having a gang at your back was no longer a luxury. Leadership gradually shifted from Sofia to Helena, even though she didn't want it. Now they made sure the back alleys were safe for the others. Two girls went missing in the last month alone and though the newspapers claimed fatal drug overdoses, Helena knew the truth.

Vampires.

So she patrolled with the lost girls. They watched one another's backs. Helena could turn almost anything into a weapon. Billie was brilliant with a blade, Sofia was naturally vicious, and Portia could run faster than anyone. Iphigenia was too frail to fight, but she was smart and she saw everything.

Like the vampire circling the ring right now.

Helena followed Iphigenia's telling gaze, and swore. "Vamp at two o'clock," she muttered at Sofia.

Sofia didn't look. "Let the others handle it."

Ordinarily, Helena would have done just that. She was kind of busy, after all.

But then she saw the familiar face.

He was different from the others. There was a stillness inside him that made her think of the girls outside the yoga studio down the street or a cat waiting for a pigeon to land. Money passed hands, men whistled, girls laughed. And he just slipped between them, so softly they barely saw him.

But she saw him.

Liam Drake.

The rat bastard.

He was pale, not the kind of pale of her underfed brethren who huddled under bridges for warmth, but the kind of pale that reminded her of moonlight or winter fog. He looked to be in his twenties, with dark hair and wicked cheekbones. He circled the fight, glancing at her again when he got close. She could have sworn she could smell him, even through the fumes of smoke and the deep fryer in the kitchen. He was cool night air, rain, and copper. She felt light-headed and couldn't help but stare at him as if he was pulling her right out of her body.

She almost forgot to react when Sofia suddenly ran at her.

Her eye was nearly poked out by hair spray–stiffened hair. She straight-armed Sofia, ramming the heel of her hand into her chest. She let the momentum of the hit pull her forward and swept her leg behind the other girl's knees. Breathless, Sofia fell backward, landing hard. Her head struck the floor. She blinked dizzily and didn't even try to sit up.

The crowd hesitated, then erupted into cheers and insults. Sofia cursed her viciously and the girls waiting to fight on the other side of the ropes glared at her, but Helena didn't care. No rules. Grady, the ref, was clear about that before they'd climbed into the ring. She wanted to lean on her knees to catch her breath and steady her shaking arms, but she wouldn't give anyone the satisfaction of seeing even a moment of weakness. Billie caught her eye and grinned. Behind her, Liam paused in the audience. He winked at her before melting into the shadows toward the exit. Warmth flooded Helena's belly and made her cheeks red and she wasn't entirely sure why.

"Good job, kid." Grady held her arm up for a victory lap. She barely heard him. She didn't want drunken accolades or threats, she just wanted to follow Liam Drake.

And kick his ass.

She yanked her arm free and jumped the ropes, shoving through the grumbling until she was able to push through the back door and dart up the grimy concrete steps to the alley behind the club. A group of guys smoked in a huddle. A girl was throwing up behind a Dumpster, and an older man gave her an oily smile. She considered kneecapping him on principle but she didn't want to lose Liam. He was already down the alley and turning the corner. She knew from experience that he moved faster than lightning when he wanted to.

There was something between them, a recognition she hadn't felt since before her brother died in that car crash. It was annoying. Even back then her mother hadn't cared what happened to Helena, but Sebastian had cared. He had always been there to play peacemaker, to see that Helena got enough to eat and new clothes for school. And then he drank too much beer and drove his car into a tree. She didn't let the memory slow her down; she never did. It didn't do any good.

And it would let her quarry get away.

She hurried down the alley, mice dodging under the Dumpsters and the wind pushing litter against her ankles. The music from The Vortex thrummed faintly through the cool night air. Her cheek throbbed, a bruise already forming. There'd be another bruise on her left elbow, and her right wrist would hurt for the rest of the week. Sofia was stronger than she looked.

She popped around the corner, stopping at a dead end, full of pop cans and cigarette butts. There were brick walls and a startled cat.

But no gray-eyed Liam.

"Bloody coward," she muttered. He thought he could ditch her. While she hadn't thought they'd get married and have lots of fat babies together, they'd fought feral *Hel-Blar* together near one of the abandoned factories. Before that he'd been kind, watching her with a glint in his eye that made her toes curl. Afterward, a scorching kiss in the darkness.

And now nothing.

She raised her voice. "I know you're out there, Liam Drake."

No response. The alley stretched back to The Vortex, and went off to the right into a rabbit warren of narrow, unlit passageways. Inexplicable disappointment made her mouth taste like lemons.

"Stupid," she muttered at herself. There was no one waiting for her, no moment with a devastatingly handsome young man. And she didn't want that kind of thing from Liam anyway. She knew better. Girls like her didn't hear poetry and compliments.

Girls like her heard screams in the dark.

Typically their own.

◆

Cass was so grounded even her grandchildren would be grounded.

She and her grandmother went into the rougher parts of Violet Hill, which was really only a single downtown block near the warehouses, and handed out coffee and sandwiches to the homeless.

Everyone knew Posy Macalister. She clomped around in denim overalls and construction boots and terrified everyone but the street kids. They understood she was the one to go to when they were too wary to try the shelters or Children's Aid. Posy believed in people taking care of one another, even though she claimed that people in general were dumb as dirt.

Cass believed in it too; she loved helping her cantankerous grandmother, even on those bitter winter nights when she thought her nose might actually fall off her face. It felt good to help. Even though she technically knew better than to stray alone in any part of Violet Hill at night. It probably served her right that she was lying on the ground, feeling her own blood seeping into her hair.

Screaming seemed like a really good idea about now.

If only she could remember how.

She felt funny, foggy. Fear rocketed through her but she just couldn't seem to make herself move. The woman who lifted her off the ground looked too slender to be able to support her weight but Cass hung bonelessly off one arm, as if made of feathers. Blood dripped from the ends of her hair. The woman licked her lips.

Inside her head, Cass screamed but her throat would only make a small mewing sound. Her grandmother taught her better than this. She had Wolfgang train Cass to defend herself. He'd tell her stories, family secrets, and rhymes to help her remember how to keep vampires at bay. But the rhymes fell right out of her head the minute she met a real vampire. She was embarrassed. It was one thing to believe in nonviolence and quite another to die horribly drained of blood because you couldn't even muster enough will to protect yourself.

She flopped like a dead fish, her arm dangling uncomfortably. She felt the tip of those teeth sink into her neck, felt the sharp jab of skin breaking, the uncomfortable pull of blood being sucked out of her veins. Her neck burned, then tingled. It didn't hurt after a moment; pain was too simple a feeling for the complicated sensations rolling her about like a paper boat on a stormy sea.

The woman pulled back slightly, sighing with disappointment. "This one's a vegetarian," she said distastefully. "I thought the hippies were finally extinct. They never taste as good."

"Then give her to me, Elisabet." A man, equally slender and pale and with Elisabet's same curious amber-colored eyes and blond hair, stepped out of the shadows. "You're too picky."

She sniffed. "I have standards, Lyle."

"And I have an appetite." The man smiled hungrily at Cass. "So pass her over."

"No." Elisabet tightened her hold petulantly, her long blond hair swinging to curtain Cass's face. "She's mine. Get your own."

"Technically she belongs to Lady Natasha."

Elisabet's eyes glittered. "Are you threatening me, little brother?"

"Just hurry up."

She wiped blood off her lower lip with her thumb. "I hate Violet Hill. I wish Lady Natasha didn't insist on visiting this backwoods village. Everyone tastes . . . green. Like spinach." She grimaced. "I miss Texas."

Cass continued to hang limply, feeling smug triumph mix with the fear and confusion. Her grandmother rolled her eyes when Cass picked the bacon off her breakfast plate or refused to eat the turkey at Thanksgiving. The slight reprieve gave her time to fill her lungs with air. She gathered every last bit of energy inside her and then opened her mouth.

If Elisabet had been human, Cass's scream would have shattered her eyeballs.

Instead, Cass's grandmother would have to finish the job.

"Get the hell away from my granddaughter!"

◆

Helena reached the alley just in time to see Posy Macalister swing a heavy flashlight across the back of a vampire's head. Posy's granddaughter, Cass, the one who was always handing out baked-tofu sandwiches no one wanted to eat but took anyway because they didn't want to hurt her feelings, tumbled to the ground. There was blood in her hair and on her shirt but she pushed to her feet. The blond vampire girl staggered against the wall. A guy who could only be her brother swore viciously and attacked.

Helena didn't think. She didn't have to. Leaping into fights was what she did best.

She'd been busted for fighting at school more times than she could remember. She didn't get busted anymore, because she'd dropped out. She'd been on her own since the day she turned thirteen and her mom shoved her down the front steps and changed the locks. She learned how to poach stale bread from behind bakeries and barely wilted vegetables from behind the grocers, how to slip past bouncers at the clubs, how to make a passable fake ID, and how to find clean public bathrooms.

But she still hadn't learned how to avoid a fight.

To be fair, it wasn't exactly a skill she was eager to learn.

"Hey! Back off the old lady," she shouted, swinging her already bruised and bloody fist at the blond vampire who was snarling. She reached for the stake tucked into her left boot. Billie had whittled the stakes to killing points from branches they gathered in the park near their bridge. Hers was plain but sturdy. The weight of it was a comfort in her hand.

"Who are you calling an old lady?" Posy muttered, throwing the flashlight with the force of the old farm wife she was. It caught the guy under the eye, snapping his head back.

"Oh, Elisabet, now we're going to have some fun," he promised silkily. Helena couldn't believe he was still standing after that blow. Something about the two of them made her shiver, and she hadn't been afraid of a fight since before her brother died.

Elisabet backhanded Posy into the wall. She hit it hard and slid into a pile, groaning. Cass didn't waste time with more screaming. She leaped to stand protectively over Posy. Helena grabbed a handful of Elisabet's long hair and yanked savagely, spinning her away. Elisabet screeched and before she'd finished twirling, her brother was on Helena.

"Lyle, I want first blood," she spat.

Helena punched Lyle in the face. He punched her back. She flew backward, dropping her stake, her shoulder slamming hard into a Dumpster. The bin creaked in protest. Elisabet and Lyle closed in, smiling. Helena scrabbled back, searching for anything else she could use as a weapon. She kicked out with her boots to give her some time. Elisabet reached down and grabbed her arm, hauling Helena to her feet. Her wristbones crunched. Elisabet bent her head and licked the blood off Helena's battered knuckles. Disgusted and infuriated, Helena struggled.

Posy blew a high-pitched whistle as her granddaughter helped her to her feet.

Lyle was reaching out to grab her other arm when a hand closed over his shoulder and spun him away. He crashed into the metal fire escape. It rattled like iron rain, the sound shivering through everyone's teeth.

Liam Drake suddenly appeared and flicked Helena an inscrutable glance before blocking Lyle's counterattack. He moved like water, water deep enough to drown in.

Helena tried not to let herself get distracted by his lean, charming face or his wicked right hook. Instead, she concentrated on keeping Elisabet away from her neck. She smashed her elbow into the vampire's face. Her nose cracked, spurting blood. Being this close to Elisabet was making her feel fuzzy and tired. She was way off her game. But if there was one thing she knew, it was fighting despite insurmountable odds. She didn't recognize defeat as an option.

Still, it certainly helped when Liam knocked Lyle into Elisabet with such force they both tumbled away from Helena. When Lyle leaped to his feet, hissing, Elisabet yanked on his arm. "Wait," she said. "We don't have time." All three of them tensed, as if they heard something Helena didn't, under the sound of Posy's ear-searing whistle. She blew three short bursts that sounded like a code. "We have to go," Elisabet insisted.

They vanished into the darkness. Liam closed in on Posy and her granddaughter, nostrils flaring.

"Cass, behind me." Posy put a protective arm across her granddaughter. Cass was pale, but her jaw was set.

"I'm not going to hurt you," he murmured. His voice was like brandy cream. Helena wasn't actually sure what brandy cream was, but she'd read about it once and imagined it was like his voice, dark and sweet, and laced with fire.

He touched his fingertips to Cass's chin to tilt her head back and look at her wound. His back teeth clenched but his hold stayed gentle. "You'll be all right," he said. "You won't need stitches and you're not infected." He looked straight at Posy. "So don't worry. And don't let your guard down."

She snorted. "Like I ever would, boy."

He turned back to leave, passing so close to Helena that she could see the peculiar pale glint of his gray eyes. He paused beside her. The way he looked at her, when he finally deigned to acknowledge her presence was as if she were a rose where everyone else, including herself, saw only thorns.

"What?" she asked belligerently.

The sound of motorcycles roaring down the alleys from all directions interrupted whatever reply he might have made. Instead, he vanished up the nearest fire escape.

Posy limped over, supported by Cass's arm. "Are you hurt, girl?"

Helena shook her head, buzzing with adrenaline that suddenly had no place to go. It flooded her bloodstream, making her feel jittery and angry. "I really hate vampires."

"We have to get out of here," Posy said as the motorcycles rode into view. Three tattooed, leather-and-jean-clad men looked grimly at them.

"How many?" one of them demanded.

"Already gone." Posy waved her hand. "Cass needs some bandages and I need some gin. Get us home, boys."

Helena gaped as the old woman swung her leg over the bike, climbing on behind a grizzled man who looked like he might eat kittens for breakfast. Even Cass perched on the seat as comfortably as if she was sitting cross-legged and meditating, or whatever it was flower children did in their spare time.

Posy pointed at Helena. "She saved Cass's life. She comes home with me."

They sped away, leaving Helena blinking at the last biker. He grinned. "Get on. No one argues with Posy."

Helena crossed her arms, eyes narrowed. "I'm not going anywhere with you. Do you think I'm stupid?"

"No, I think you're a smart lass." He had a Scottish accent and bruises on his knuckles. "And maybe a little scared."

Helena sputtered, "I am not!"

"Posy won't hurt you. Unless you eat her chili. I'd steer clear of that if I were you. Name's Bruno," he added. His hair was long under his bandanna, and tattoos poked out from under his collar and cuffs. "Are you coming or what, little girl?"

He was barely twenty, despite his attitude and the crinkles at the corner of his eyes. And she wasn't scared. She didn't do scared.

"Fine," she said, sliding onto the bike behind him.

"Atta girl," he approved, taking off the minute her fingers hooked into the back of his belt. Like hell she was going to wrap her arms around him. "Mind the exhaust there, it gets hot."

She rolled her eyes even though he couldn't see her. "I've been on a bike before."

"You haven't been on a bike until you've been on mine," he said as they came out of the narrow alleys and onto the deserted road. "What's your name, sweetheart?" he shouted over the rush of the wind.

"Helena," she shouted back. "And if you call me sweetheart again, I'll knife your tires."

His laugh trailed behind them.

◆

"You like her," Geoffrey said quietly as they watched Helena take off on the back of a motorcycle. They stood at the corner of the highest roof in the Warren, with a view of the lights and the humans scurrying below.

Liam stared at the taillight of the bike until it winked out of sight. "You know the rules."

"Yes, but she's not like Deirdre."

Liam clenched his back teeth. "I know that."

"This one's strong."

He sighed. "Does it matter?"

Geoffrey looked thoughtful, sad. "Yes," he replied finally. "I think it does."

"Even if Natasha's noticed?"

"Especially then."

◆

"I thought I was clear about staying, young lady."

They were in Posy's kitchen: a wounded girl, a street girl, and three tough-looking bikers—Bruno, Mason, and Wolfgang— gathered around a scarred harvest table. Between the blood, the bruises, and the tattoos of laughing skulls, everyone knew the old lady was the scary one.

Cass winced. She was holding a striped dishtowel to the now-clean wound on her neck as Posy rifled through a worn first-aid kit for bandages. "Sorry, Nana. She was all huddled in the corner. I thought she was hungry."

Bruno snorted. "She was, lass."

After assessing all the exits (sliding glass door, two windows, front door, and a mud room), Helena sniffed at the herbal tea Cass had given her, longing for the black coffee everyone else was drinking. Who wanted to drink boiled flowers? But Cass was so earnest that she kept the cup, feeling like the street kids who ate baked tofu just to see her smile. Bruno caught her eye and winked, sliding his coffee to her and taking her tea. There was something sweet about someone so tough-looking drinking mint and rose petals.

"Jan, sit down before you bleed on my floor."

"Nana, I told you, it's Cass now."

Posy rolled her eyes. "Last week it was Star. I can't keep up."

"Cassiopeia is a star constellation, Nana."

"I'm calling you Beth from now on."

Cass sat in a chair. "That's not even my name."

"No, but it's easy to remember." Posy might be acting calm and composed, but her hands trembled when she pulled the towel away from her granddaughter's throat. She let out a shaky breath. "It's not so bad. But don't tell your mother what happened."

They exchanged knowing, slightly ironic glances. Mason stood up and went to have a closer look. He smelled like smoke and beer.

He grunted. "No stitches, she'll be fine." Then he left without another word. The grizzled old biker Wolfgang sat back, relieved.

Posy gently taped a white bandage to Cass's throat. "He was right," she said thoughtfully. "The man in the alley."

"Liam Drake," Helena spat.

Posy raised her eyebrows. "Know him, do you? The Drakes don't share their names with just anyone."

Aside from being someone she'd considered kissing a lot, Liam was also the first vampire Helena had ever met. At first, she'd thought she was talking to a cute boy in the park. When she found out otherwise, she'd tripped over her own foot and fallen in the river. "Yeah," she sneered. "I'm so lucky."

"And now you've really annoyed them."

Helena smiled, showing a lot of teeth. "Good. Too many damn vampires in Violet Hill lately."

"Don't forget the witches," Cass interjected pleasantly. "And maybe werewolves, but I can't seem to get an eyewitness confirmation of them. And someone at school claims his uncle's girlfriend's cousin saw a Sasquatch last year."

Helena crossed her arms. "I know all this."

"You know about the Sasquatch?"

"Okay, maybe not that part."

"Definitely a spike in disappearances," Wolfgang agreed. "And there's new activity at an old school outside of town I think might be mixed up in all of this, but I'm not sure how. No one can get close enough to find out, not even Posy, and she's been here the longest."

"I grew up here," she confirmed to Helena. "I was born in the mountains, at the start of the Depression. We didn't even have running water up in our cabin. We ate fish and trapped rabbits." Posy pulled food out of the fridge. "Anyone who grows up in those mountains can tell you strange creatures are there." She slapped meat onto fresh bread, then added cheese. "After my brother got bit, we learned not to go too far alone at night, and to always carry a knife or a sharp stake. A girl died not too long after but then it all seemed to go away, like a bad dream. Until about four years ago when they found a girl drained of blood outside of town. She was the first."

"My sister was the second," Bruno added quietly. "I only came here because they found her body in the lake after she ran away. I'd never even heard of this place before then." Bruno's jaw clenched and there was a glint of something dark in his eyes. Something Helena recognized. "Posy had me pegged practically the second my boots hit the sidewalk at the bus station. I was going to kill them all, you see." His accent was even thicker now, and bitter. Helena sat down without really realizing it. She knew what he felt. She'd have done the same thing if Sebastian had died that way. As it was, she'd broken into the junkyard and set the wreck of his car on fire the night of the funeral.

"Not that it would have brought her back," Bruno said, sounding tired. Cass reached over to hug him. He patted her arm awkwardly. "Fell in with a rough crowd, and when I got out of juvie, Posy took me in for a week until I got my bearings again. I was one of her first strays."

"And still my favorite." Posy smiled at him affectionately. "The whistle was Bruno's idea," she explained to Helena. It was a good idea, Helena thought, one she'd mention to the lost girls. "He's always looking out for us."

"Someone has to." Wolfgang snorted. "Especially now that the disappearances have started again."

"I know," Helena said grimly. "My friends and I are doing our best to stop them. But it's not working as well as we'd like."

Cass shivered, touching her bandage. "I, for one, think your best is pretty damn good."

"The thing about vampires," Wolfgang said, looking at Helena, "is that they tend to be creatures of habit. And vengeance. You need to be careful."

"I can take care of myself," she said. "I should go." The others would be looking for her. And if she stayed away too long Grady would keep her cut of the profits from the fight.

"Sit down," Posy ordered, interrupting. "You won't be sleeping behind a Dumpster tonight."

Helena could have pointed out that she never slept near the

Dumpsters. They stank. And the lost girls had rules: no handouts, no social workers, no shelters. "I'm not going to one of those shelters," she stated. "So save your breath."

"At least eat something." Posy slid a plate piled high with sandwiches onto the table.

Helena was hungry enough to stay for a meal. She reached for a sandwich and took a huge bite, even though her leg muscles twitched with the urge to take off. "So, what, you guys just go around killing vampires? I thought you fed the homeless." Crumbs landed on her shirt.

"I do," Posy said. "And I do what needs doing."

"Not all vampires are evil," Cass said firmly. "Some of them are good."

Helena honestly didn't know which category Liam fell into. Even after he'd kissed her that one time.

Maybe especially because of that kiss.

"One of them saved Wolf once," Cass added.

Liam had saved her too, damn it.

Wolfgang nodded. "Back in my drinking days," he said crisply. "Drank myself stupid and nearly got bit for the pleasure. Some woman wearing the strangest dress, like Queen Victoria herself, saved me. Never saw her again."

"You saved Cass's life tonight. I can't ever repay that," Posy said softly.

Helena squirmed, embarrassed. "It's fine." If the old woman offered her money she'd walk out. She wouldn't take pity or charity. Even though her stomach grumbled just seeing the bowl of fruit on the counter, and that was after she had eaten two-and-a-half sandwiches. She wondered if she could steal a few for the girls and sneak out before dawn. Iphigenia loved oranges.

"What do you know about Liam Drake?" she asked. She may as well get information while she was here.

"Not much," Posy admitted. "He keeps to himself. Haven't seen him since I was a girl, and that was only because I snuck out to meet a boy. Your granddad," she added as an aside to Cass. "I saw Liam first. Looks exactly the same, even now." She looked at her wrinkled hands. "Hell of a thing."

"Wait, so he's really old?" Helena asked. Posy speared her with a look. Cass giggled. "I mean . . ."

"I know what you meant, young lady," she said, disgruntled. "But yes, he's older than I am."

It was totally wrong that someone so old could be that hot. He should have dentures and a comb-over. It made her head hurt.

"Drakes keep to themselves," Wolfgang confirmed. "Probably for the best."

"I hope you'll stay the night," Posy offered, even though Helena still had a hundred questions about Liam. "I still have the bunk beds from when my granddaughters were little. It's just Cass now that Lucinda's away at university. Or you can take the couch." She ran a hand over Cass's hair, as if checking to make sure she was still okay. "Those vampires saw your face, Helena, and they have long memories. They might come back. I hope you'll let us help you."

"I'll take the couch," she said reluctantly, mentally kissing her prize money good-bye. "But just for tonight."

Besides, she knew in the primal, hidden corners of herself—the parts that recognized the electric smell of an approaching storm—that someone was out there in the darkness.

Watching her.

◆

The girl was going to be a problem.

◆

Helena snuck out of Posy's house as dawn turned the sky the color of tangerines. She took some food but left the handful of dollar bills crumpled on the coffee table. It took her twenty minutes to walk to their squat under the bridge. The wild tiger lilies masked most of her movements, though no one was likely to be about that early. Even the crazy joggers with their sweatbands and matching leg warmers waited until there was a little more light.

She found the others sleeping under their sleeping bags, except for Iphigenia, who was huddled with her knees to her chest. Her lower lip trembled when she saw Helena crawl under the ivy they'd pulled down as a screen. Only one of the candles stuck into the craggy wall was lit. The light made her look even younger and thinner. "You're back!" she exclaimed. "We thought you'd be taken."

"I'm fine," she said, tossing Iphigenia one of the stolen oranges.

Portia sat up, her hair tilting dramatically to the left. Her eyes were red and worried but the kick she aimed at Helena's ankle was vicious. "Where the hell have you been?"

Helena jerked back, ankle throbbing. "I ran into some trouble."

"Good." Sofia scowled, opening one eye. Billie kept on snoring, oblivious. "You punched me in the face, you bitch."

Helena wasn't remotely sorry. "You punched me first."

"Grady wants you to fight again tonight. Wear something pretty."

"Kiss my ass."

Helena grabbed a few hours' sleep, ignoring the girls as they devoured the fruit she'd left for them. When she woke up there was only a banana left, on which Sofia had written rude things with a marker. Helena ate it anyway, then rinsed her mouth out with the mouthwash they hoarded like candy. It was their single prized possession and the first thing they bought with any scrounged money, before hot dogs, before coffee when they were able to find a decent cup, even before chocolate.

Iphigenia watched her rinse the dried blood from her hair in the river. The water was getting cold as summer faded. "What happened to you?"

"Nothing," Helena assured her. Iphigenia was such a worrier, she didn't need to know. "Just don't go anywhere alone at night," she said. "You still have that knife?"

She nodded. "Yes, I put it in my bag. Portia said someone was following her last night."

And Helena had been sure she was being watched. She slipped her own hunting knife into the side of her boot and started to climb out from under the bridge.

Iphigenia scrambled after her. "Where are you going?"

"To get my money off Grady before Sofia sweet-talks my share off him."

"I'm coming too."

They'd found Sofia, predictably batting her eyelashes at Grady. He was sprawled at a table near the empty ring, smoking and drinking bottled water. He claimed it kept him pretty. There was glitter in his hair. "My favorite girls," he said. "All together."

Helena's smile was brittle. "Hi, Sofia."

Sofia narrowed her eyes. "What?"

Helena ignored her, looking at Grady. She didn't smile or flirt. "Where's my money?"

Grady looked wounded. "Would I cheat you, darling? You ran off so fast I thought you were leaving it for me to reinvest in the Thunderdome."

Helena held out her hand. "Like hell."

He shook his head, blowing smoke rings. "You could be a little nicer, like your friend here."

Sofia smirked. Helena just raised an eyebrow. "I don't do nice," she said. "That's why I won the fight."

Grady laughed and passed her a stack of folded dollar bills. He knew the lost girls preferred small bills that attracted less attention. His gaze roamed appreciatively over Iphigenia's thin body, her huge blue eyes, and translucent skin. "When are you going to join the fun, beautiful?"

Helena stepped in front of her. "Try never."

His eyes went hard. "All the girls fight for me eventually, Helena. Even your precious lost girls."

"Yeah, about that. You said you wouldn't pit us against each other."

He grinned. "I lied." He leered at Iphigenia. "You're kind of skinny, but put you in a short skirt and no one will care if you punch like a girl."

Helena slammed her boot on the chair, right between his legs. He froze, gulping. If she pressed any harder he'd walk with a limp for the rest of his life. "Leave her out of this."

He swallowed audibly. "Sure."

Sofia walked lazily around Helena, sighing. "You're such a drama queen."

Helena pressed down a little harder just to prove her point. When Grady went cross-eyed, she backed off. "Let's go," she told the others.

Sofia followed more out of a show of solidarity than any real desire to go anywhere with Helena. Iphigenia followed them quietly.

"You have to stop being such a bitch," Sofia muttered.

"Why?" Helena asked. "He's sleazy."

"He also pays the bills, such as they are."

"Whatever." She shrugged the bills off. "I have things to do. Look after Iphi."

"Yeah, yeah."

"Sof?"

"What?"

"Do you think vampires can be the good guys?"

"Are you high?" Sofia asked. "Vampires are picking us off, remember? They're not our friends."

She'd have thought the same thing before Liam found her in the alley last night.

"Never mind." She waited until they'd wandered off before heading deeper into the Warren. The alleys were deceptively welcoming at this time of the day, even with the afternoon sun cooking the garbage under clouds of flies. The sounds from the back doors of restaurants were cheerfully boisterous, and someone was blaring Billy Idol out of a fire escape window. Everything here made sense. Survive. Don't be a victim. Avoid Scrawny Johnny at all costs, if you wanted to get out of the Warren with all your limbs intact. He was the meanest drunk Helena had ever seen and she'd heard the other street girls whisper about him.

What happened last night didn't make sense.

Starting with the fact that she'd let her head be turned by a pretty set of cheekbones.

Glowering, she stopped at the spot where Elisabet and Lyle had attacked her. It looked like any other alley: Dumpster, skids, litter in the groove of the pavement by the sewer. Cheerful light glinted off the peeling fire escapes, the broken windows at the top of the building on her right. Most of the storefronts were abandoned on this corner.

She stood over a dark stain on the ground, where Cass's blood had fallen. They'd intended her to be the next missing girl. The gash under her hairline would leave a scar. Helena intended to leave a few scars of her own.

She investigated the entire area, even the broken skids that she'd knocked over. She didn't find anything that might help her track down Elisabet and Lyle. If they were the ones taking all the girls, she wanted them. She wanted them dusting the end of her stake. She spent several pleasant moments envisioning her revenge.

Until there was the soft scuff of a boot behind her.

She'd stayed too long. The sun had set behind the buildings, casting long violet shadows. It was too dark now. Not the kind of darkness in which she could hide but the kind that hid things from her. She whirled, using her elbow like a mace. She hit a hard chest and kicked a little lower. A hand blocked the strike, held her immobile. She spun out, kicking.

And then she was pressed against a brick wall, fingers over her mouth, gray eyes staring a warning into hers.

"We're not alone," Liam mouthed. "Don't move."

His hand dropped away and she drew in a shallow breath. He was even more beautiful up close. His gray irises were flecked with black and silver, his mouth inches from hers. His teeth were sharp, faintly pointed but not particularly vampiric. His body touched her from shoulder to ankle, shielding her. She didn't know what to think. She wasn't used to being shielded and she wasn't entirely certain she liked it.

But she liked it better than being caught by Elisabet and her psychotic brother.

"I can smell her," Elisabet murmured. "I want payback, Lyle."

"I know," he replied. "Haven't you said so a dozen times since we left the caves? She's a street rat, she could be anywhere."

"No, she's close. Can't you smell her?" she asked again, sounding as if Helena was a pastry fresh from the oven.

Liam eased away from her and she felt inexplicably cold. He motioned to the Dumpster beside them. Helena blinked at him. He pointed. She shook her head. He shoved her gently toward it. She dug in her heels. She was not going to hide in a pile of garbage. She had her pride. Not to mention her sense of smell.

When she refused to move, he just picked her up and tossed her into it. She landed on old Chinese food and rotten cabbage and watched as the lid closed down over her head.

Vampire or not, she was going to kill him.

Twice.

It felt like forever until the lid lifted again, letting in blessedly fresh air. His pale face came into view. "They've gone," he said. He had a faint accent, almost British but not quite. She couldn't place it. "You can come out now."

"That," Helena stated, leaping over the side of the bin, "was disgusting."

"But necessary."

"Easy for you to say."

"Elisabet caught your scent, love, and she knows the taste of you now. She'd have tracked you to your bed and killed you there."

Helena shuddered, both from the wet noodles clinging to her arm and the thought of Elisabet finding the lost girls. "Don't call me love," she said, just because she thought she should.

"Come with me," he said gently.

"Where? Your place?" she asked acerbically.

"The dojo at the end of the edge of the Warren has showers. I can get us inside," he said, amused. "No offense, but you smell horrid."

Of course he wasn't hitting on her. She had moldy lettuce in her hair. Feeling like an idiot, she scowled. "Fine."

They didn't speak as he led her there, using the side alley next to the dojo to pick the side door lock. She watched him curiously. He flashed her a brief smile, but it was enough to make her breath catch in her throat. "I know the owner."

She wasn't sure she believed him, but she didn't care. She didn't want to smell like garbage. And she didn't want him to smell her like this either. She slipped past him and headed across the studio to the back. She went through the door marked "Ladies" and took the fastest shower she could, watching the door the entire time. Helena washed her clothes too and slipped into a white dojo T-shirt she found in one of the lockers, along with black *gi* pants. She stepped back out into the studio feeling strangely vulnerable.

Liam was silhouetted against the window, hands in his pockets. He turned to look at her. When he took a step toward her, she moved back, grabbing one of the practice staffs from the wall and holding it horizontally in front of her. "Bar's closed, pal."

"I didn't bring you here to feed on you."

"Then why did you?"

"To keep you safe."

She snorted. "Yeah, right."

He studied her for a quiet charged moment before moving. He was so fast he bled colors and light. He tossed the staff aside. It may as well have been a matchstick for all the good it did her. He spun her around, his arm around her neck. His voice was raw, lips brushing her ear. "If I wanted to hurt you, I could," he said. "You're safe with me."

"You have a hell of a way of proving that." She kicked back, clipping his knee with her boot. Then she slammed her head back into his face. He stumbled, loosening his hold. She swung a fist at his pretty face but he dodged it easily. She went for a kidney punch and he caught her hand. It was like punching a wall. "Ouch."

Liam let her go so quickly her shoulder muscles twanged. "I'm sorry. I've been away from people too long. I forget how fragile they are."

"I'm not fragile," she said, insulted. "I can look after myself." She was tired of having to remind everybody of that. None of the lost girls had been captured, had they? She thought they were doing pretty well, all things considered.

Eyes narrowing, she kicked out, leaning until she was parallel to the floor. He bent sideways, defying gravity and basic physics.

"I really hate vampires," she muttered again. She kicked at his knee and he sprawled on the ground. "Ha!" She probably shouldn't gloat. Hell with that, she was totally going to gloat. She deserved it. Especially since one of the cuts on her arm from her sparring match with Sofia yesterday had opened up. Blood trickled hot and slow down her bare arm. "Think you can—"

His face changed, eyes silver, teeth sharpening. She felt like she had that day when she'd watched him through a veil of freezing river water. She tingled and shivered. Helena lifted both her fists protectively, turned sideways. She'd barely pivoted when he was on her. He should have looked silly in his dark pin-striped suit; instead he just looked elegant, deadly. He closed in like a panther, all sleek muscles and intensity.

There was clearly something twisted inside her that she could find that kind of animal stealth so hot.

Helena reached for the discarded staff but it was barely in her hand when he twisted her wrist and it clattered to the floor. She backed up. He followed.

"Don't run." He sounded like he was pleading. She froze, inches away from the wall. "Too late," he said, desperately.

She should be afraid.

She wasn't.

It was the weirdest thing. She felt free, powerful. As if this deadly dance was as romantic as holding hands at the drive-in. He sparked something in her, or they sparked it off each other. It didn't matter. He was leashing his hunger, struggling to stay human. It was noble, difficult.

Liam wasn't like the others.

Neither was she.

She flashed him a crooked grin, catching him utterly off guard. Then she hooked her leg behind his knee and shoved him. When he fell, she followed him. He landed on the cold hardwood floor and she landed on him, still grinning.

"I'm not afraid of you," she whispered. "I wonder why that is."

"Because you're a fool." His voice was harsh but his fingers were gentle as they slid through her hair. He traced the line of her jaw with his thumb. His other hand flattened against her lower back, brushing her skin where the edge of the T-shirt rode up. He looked at her mouth. She almost forgot how much she wanted to punch him. Her lips tingled and he hadn't even touched her. He drew her head down to his, paused just before his mouth could claim hers.

He let her go abruptly. "This is a bad idea." He shoved her away and got to his feet slowly, painfully, as if he didn't trust himself. His fists were clenched, knuckles white. "I'm sorry. I came to warn you," he continued hoarsely. "Those two from the alley are reapers."

It took her a minute to get her brain off the feel of his cool muscled body under hers. Damn him for making her feel that way. Damn him for pulling away.

And damn her for not wanting him to.

"What the hell's a reaper?" she asked as a cover for the question she was embarrassed to admit she wanted to ask: Why didn't you kiss me?

"The Domokos siblings—the blonds from last night. They're the reason all those girls are disappearing, the reason that girl was bitten."

"Cass? Do they know her?"

"No, but now they know you. And you're interfering in their games, Helena," he said. "Lady Natasha doesn't take kindly to that."

"Lady Natasha can kiss my ass." She paused. "Who's Lady Natasha?"

He smiled briefly. "Natasha fancies herself the queen of the vampires."

Helena rolled her eyes. "Lame."

"Perhaps. But she enjoys her little harvests."

She paused for a heartbeat, feeling sick. "Harvest? As in . . ."

He nodded. "As in she likes to feed on them, yes."

"How do we stop her?"

"You don't."

She gathered her wet clothes, the staff. "I do too."

"Helena, this is my problem. I'll deal with it."

"Because I'm a girl?" She threw a wet sock at his head.

"No," he replied softly. "Because it's my fault."

◆

The moment shattered when they left the dojo. She stepped out into the alley and was once again a hungry street girl with damp hair and a suspicious nature. He was a vampire, cloaked in mystery and solitude, and as moody as a fourteen-year-old girl with PMS.

But she couldn't forget the glimpses she'd seen.

She shoved her hands in her pockets. It was later than she'd thought. "I guess I'll see you around."

His profile was chiseled, flawless. It kind of made her want to mess him up. "I'm not leaving your side," he said quietly.

She frowned. "What?"

"I have to keep you safe."

"This again." She rolled her eyes. "I'm fine. Go away."

"You're sixteen."

She went cold. He thought of her as a little girl. She'd imagined everything in the dojo. He'd been acting as a vampire, not as a man. It shouldn't matter.

It mattered.

"Liam," she said as calmly as she could. "I'm not your responsibility."

He put a hand on her arm, stopping just outside the glow of

a streetlight. His expression was stark as he drew her behind the concealing bulk of a parked van. "Do you know why my family is so reclusive?"

She shook her head mutely. When wild animals ventured out of the forest you didn't speak to them, you didn't move. You just waited.

"Because five hundred years ago a woman spoke a riddle and named a Drake daughter not even born yet as the next vampire queen."

"Is that even possible? Having a child? Aren't you undead?"

"It's possible in our family."

If there was one thing Helena knew about, it was girl fights. "Let me guess, this Natasha chick isn't too happy about that."

"Not happy and slightly insane."

"I know a lot of girls like that." She offered him a small smile. "Maybe you shouldn't hide," she said. "You should fight. You have friends." She was startled to realize she'd fight with him if he asked her. When exactly had she lost her mind?

"I thought so too, once," he said.

"What happened?"

"I fell for a girl."

Helena decided she wasn't the least bit jealous. Really. "So?"

"So Lady Natasha killed her." He glanced up to make sure they weren't being watched. The shadows were busy lately. "Do you know why Cass was bitten?" Helena shook her head. "Because I talked to her grandmother once. Her pregnancy probably saved her."

"That was like fifty years ago." She paused. "How old are you anyway?"

"Old enough."

"You look twenty-six, twenty-seven, max." And that was because of the eyes, not because of any lines on his face. He would have looked younger without all the sorrow and guilt.

"I'm not. My brother and I have seen a lot of innocent girls destroyed by Lady Natasha. The last girl who disappeared? She ran out in front of my car when she was drunk. I took her to the hospital. She was gone the next night."

She stared, horrified. "So Lady Natasha is targeting us on purpose. Killing street girls because there's no one to protect them."

He didn't smile but his eyes crinkled with dry amusement. "Until you."

"That's why you took off after I fell in the river and drew a crowd," she realized slowly. "And why you wouldn't talk to me anymore, even after we killed that *Hel-Blar* vampire."

"Now, you understand." He touched her arm, a quick moth-soft touch. "So, please. Please let me stay and make sure you're safe."

◆

He followed her to the club, staying in the shadows where no one would see him. She had to force herself not to look over her shoulder. It felt strange to know there were friendly eyes in the dark. The bouncer at the side door of the club nodded at her when she skirted the lineup.

"You're late. Grady's mad."

"Grady's always mad." Helena pushed past him into the smoky darkness of The Vortex. She felt Liam behind her but he didn't say a word, just broke away and lost himself in the crowd and strobe lights. Helena went down the hall to the cramped changing room with the tiny attached washroom. Sofia lounged on the only chair, Portia leaned against the wall eating Pixy Stix, and Billie crouched in the corner whittling stakes.

"Nice of you to finally show up," Sofia drawled. "Give the girl one win and she thinks she's a rock star."

"Oh, shut up," Helena muttered. "I've got fifteen minutes until the fight."

"And that's what you're wearing?" Sofia asked dubiously.

Helena glanced down. She'd forgotten she was wearing the clothes she'd taken from the dojo. Hers were in a sodden mess in her backpack. "Shit."

Sofia sighed theatrically. "I've got something you can wear."

"Hell no. I'm not wearing a tutu."

Portia wiped sugar off her shirt. "You can wear this tank top," she offered, pulling it off from under her fishnet top. She contorted impressively. Grady would have put her in the ring on the spot if he'd seen her.

"Thanks." Helena caught the black top and switched her T-shirt out. Her baggy black pants were hardly inspiring. She didn't really care. She couldn't stop thinking of Liam's mouth so near to hers. *Focus, Helena.*

"Trade me these pants for your skirt?" she asked Billie. "Just for the fight." Her denim miniskirt was shorter than anything Helena would ordinarily have worn but at least she could move freely in it.

"Still needs something," Portia said.

"Are you going to help?" Billie kicked Sofia's swinging foot.

Sofia snapped her gum loudly. "I already offered a tutu."

"Never mind, I have an idea." Portia reached for the can of spray paint she always carried in her knapsack. Half the art on the alley walls was hers. She shook the can with a grin. "To the lost girls."

Helena closed her eyes so she wouldn't get paint splattered into them. The chemical scent floated in the cramped space. Sofia coughed. Portia chewed on her lip, the way she always did when she drew. It didn't take her long. "There."

Billie chuckled. "Awesome."

Helena looked down. Portia had spray painted, in pink no less, a circle with a stylized face, elongated fangs, and a slash across it.

NO VAMPIRES ALLOWED.

For the first time, the thought made Helena uncomfortable. She wondered what Liam would think when he saw it. Never mind that he wore elegant suits and she wore spray paint; he'd saved her life.

"You don't like it." Portia sounded disappointed.

"Of course I do," Helena rushed to assure her. "I need some makeup, don't you think?" She hurried into the bathroom where she could be alone to wonder why she was suddenly concerned about delicate vampire sensibilities. The whole thing was ridiculous.

"Get your head in the game," she snapped at herself. She grabbed one of the black eyeliners in the plastic cup on the back of the sink. She was lining her eyes like an Egyptian queen when she saw it.

Iphigenia's favorite striped scarf.

Stuck to the wall on the tip of a knife.

She turned slowly, her stomach dropping. There was a piece of paper stuck between the blade and the scarf. It was a charcoal sketch of Helena. Calligraphy curved around the edges:

*Your presence is required by
Lady Natasha in Crofter's Woods.*

She stumbled out of the bathroom. Sofia and Portia were bickering as usual. Their voices sounded thin, distant. The floor shook from the crowds shouting and stomping their feet in the Thunderdome. Billie frowned at her. It took a moment to realize the other girl had spoken to her. "Helena, what's wrong?"

Reality slammed into her like a wave breaking over the shore. She fought the undertow, lifted her chin. "Iphi's missing."

Sofia waved that away. "She's probably in one of her hiding spots."

Helena shook her head, lifting the scarf. "It's got blood on it." Silence fell like an icicle, cold and deadly. She flung the paper out at them. It floated like delicate pollen, before landing faceup on the dirty glitter-strewn floor. "Let's go."

They darted down the hall. Grady stopped them before they reached the back door, motioning to Angelo, one of the bouncers. He was built like a bull and took his job very seriously.

"Where do you think you're going?" Grady asked silkily. The blue eye shadow he wore didn't make him look any less threatening.

"We have to go," Helena said. "Iphi's in trouble."

"You owe me a fight."

"Later." She shoved past him. He caught her by the hair even as Angelo pushed her down the step, away from the door. Helena hissed.

"You can go after the fight," Grady said. "Not before."

Portia and Billie bristled. Sofia was the only one who didn't look particularly concerned, but Helena read the tension in her brittle hair flip.

"Grady," she purred. "Can't you cut us a break? This is important."

"No."

She ran a hand up his arm, the one still clutching Helena's hair. "What if I fight for you?"

"You're not on tonight's list, sweetheart."

"I'll fight for free," she offered. "Just tonight."

He considered it. Sofia pouted invitingly. Helena reached for the pocket knife she knew was in Billie's skirt pocket. She always had a knife.

"Deal," Grady finally said. "Because I'm feeling generous." Helena snorted. He pulled savagely on her hair. "What was that, sweetheart?"

Sofia glared at her warningly. For Iphigenia, Helena didn't punch him in the crotch. "Nothing."

"That's what I thought." He waited another heartbeat before releasing her. He nodded to Angelo. Helena, Portia, and Billie were through the door before it was even halfway open.

She could have called for Liam. God knew they could use the backup. But Lady Natasha hated him, was targeting him. She wouldn't add to his troubles. And the lost girls were her responsibility anyway, not his.

She had enough blood on her hands.

◆

Something was wrong.

Liam felt it, smelled it in the thick club air. He searched the crowd for a threat. He was about to head to the back to find Helena when Grady stepped out to the microphone hanging from the ceiling. A girl in a sequined bikini pranced behind him, smiling the smile of a thousand toothpaste ads.

"Ladies and gents," Grady boomed. "Welcome to the Thunderdome!"

The audience reacted so loudly Liam wondered if there was blood in his ears. Sensitive hearing wasn't always an asset. He kept his gaze moving quickly, checking the entrances. He still felt it, some secret pull of danger.

"Tonight for your entertainment we have the feral and very fine Finnegan, battling the delectable and sexy Sofia!"

Liam had to fight to keep his fangs retracted.

Helena was gone.

◆

Portia hotwired a car parked on the edge of the Warren. It took them half an hour, at top speed, to race to the edge of the forest that led to Crofter's Woods. They left the car under a canopy of branches and went on foot the rest of the way. Billie handed out stakes. Portia bit her nails. Helena wanted to scream.

As the path narrowed to a trail, a branch cracked. Helena whirled just as a shadow broke away from the trees. She threw a stake before she fully registered who she was throwing it at. A girl squeaked as a second shadow knocked her to the ground. The stake slammed into an elm tree. Cass pushed Bruno's long hair off her face. "Ow."

"Easy, killer," Bruno said to Helena, helping Cass to her feet.

"What the hell are you doing here?" Helena demanded as they stood. "I nearly staked you!"

"We saw you heading out of town," Cass replied. Blood spotted the bandage on her throat. "And we heard another girl went missing."

"So?" Helena asked.

"So, I'm not an idiot...," Cass pointed out. "You're about to do something stupid. No one heads into the mountains at this time of night without a monumentally stupid plan."

Bruno grinned, flipping his pocket knife between his fingers. "And we want in."

"No way," Helena said automatically, even though they could probably use Bruno. "You can't 'om' your way through this, Cass. What are you two doing out this late anyway?"

Cass blushed. "Don't change the subject." She crossed her arms, crystal necklaces catching the very faint moonlight. "I'm coming with you. Or you can leave me behind and I'll follow alone. By myself. All vulnerable and shit."

"Nice threat." Helena looked impressed despite herself.

"Thank you. Now what's the plan?"

"Iphigenia's down there somewhere," Helena explained darkly. "We get her out. If Lady Natasha's around, I get to shove a stake in her chest." For Iphi. For all the missing girls. For Liam. "They're waiting for us in Crofter's Woods."

"I know that place," Bruno said, all teasing gone from his voice. His accent was suddenly so thick Helena had to concentrate to understand him. "They'll have guards posted. I have a better spot."

They followed him around the bend to a rocky ledge. They crawled on their bellies to the edge, peering through the leaves. The clearing was ringed with torches. In the center, Iphigenia was tied to a red pine. The wind tossed needles over her. She was pale, her short cap of blond hair glinting like gold. She must be terrified.

But she was also alone.

"There," Helena said, rage making her feel hot all over. "We might be able to get her out before they know we're here."

Bruno pulled the shotgun she hadn't seen strapped to his back. "And if not, I'm a really good shot."

"We're dealing with vampires," Helena reminded him.

"Might not kill them but it'll sure as hell slow them down."

"Um, guys?" Cass asked.

"What?"

"Hello? Big fat trap down there?"

Helena scrubbed her face. "I know. But it doesn't matter. Billie, you should stay up here," she suggested, mind racing. "You're better with knives. Find a tree to climb and you'll see them before they see any of us. I'll go in alone." She ignored the requisite protests. "I mean it. They asked for me, they'll get me. Anyway, they won't take me seriously, a single raggedy girl. So we'll use it. It might be the only advantage we have."

"I don't like it," Bruno muttered.

Helena shrugged. "It doesn't matter. It's all we've got."

Cass took a lighter out of her purse. "Maybe not." She smiled softly, looking more like her grandmother than a New Age freak. "If we burn them out, they might not notice you freeing Iphigenia. Vampires like to be stealthy and there's nothing stealthy about a forest fire."

Portia whistled. "Nice, Tofu Girl. There's hope for you yet."

Bruno winced. "You're going to double back and siphon the gas out of my bike, aren't you?" She nodded. "Well, shit." He got up to help her. "Don't move until we're back," he ordered Helena.

"Watch out for the reapers," she told them.

"The reapers? That doesn't sound good," Cass remarked.

"They're the ones that bit you."

"Definitely not good."

Helena smiled at her, sharp and deadly as a fox in a henhouse. "Payback's a bitch."

Cass smiled back.

◆

The forest was on fire.

That could only mean one thing, Liam thought.

Helena.

◆

Helena's heartbeat felt so loud she was sure any vampire within a ten-mile radius could hear it. She breathed slowly, making sure her stakes were secure. She'd already checked them six different times on the climb down to the meadow. There was one in each boot, one in her skirt pocket next to Billie's knife, and one tucked into the small of her back. She was as ready as she was ever going to be.

She crept through the forest, wincing every time a twig snapped underfoot. She could drift through the Warren and never be seen, but put her in the middle of the woods and she was hopeless. She circled a tree and then passed through a bush she sincerely hoped wasn't poison ivy. The wind shivered through the leaves. She crouched at the edge of the trees. It felt like forever before she caught the scent of fire. Smoke curled between the trunks, obscuring even the sharpest of vampire vision.

Now or never.

Helena went low and raced across the open field, her neck prickling nervously. She had a stake in one hand, a knife in the other. She heard a shout in the distance but couldn't be sure if it was vampiric or human. She kept running.

"Hurry," Iphigenia sobbed, pulling against her ropes. "I'm scared."

"It's okay." Helena slid the last few feet toward her. "Are you hurt? Did they bite you?" Iphigenia shook her head. There was dirt on her face and across her shirt and her jeans were ripped, but Helena couldn't see any blood. "I'm going to get you out of here. Just hold on."

She sawed through the thick ropes with the knife until her skin chafed and blistered. Her blood smeared the twine, made her grip slippery.

Iphigenia struggled. "Hurry!"

"Almost got it," Helena assured her. The certainty that the trap was about to close around them made Helena short of breath. Every nerve ending felt jagged. The knife slipped, cutting into her palm. She wiped the cut on her shirt and went back to sawing. The ropes finally frayed apart. Iphigenia stepped out of the pile coiled around her like pale snakes.

And then she screamed as loud as she could.

Helena recoiled, then tried to slap her hand over her mouth. "Iphi," she said, thinking her friend hysterical. "Don't be afraid. I'm here to get you out."

"I'm not afraid," Iphigenia assured her, drawing another breath and jerking free. Her next scream was more specific. "She's here!"

"Iphi?" Helena goggled. "I don't understand."

"They wanted you, Helena. Not me." She shrugged one shoulder. Her waifish pixie face hardened. "It's always you."

"But . . . why?" She could not wrap her head around the betrayal.

"They promised to turn me." Iphigenia looked enthralled, fascinated. It made Helena want to throw up. "So I can be strong, strong like you."

Helena shook her head, as if it could change the truth. She took a step back. "This can't be happening."

Iphigenia's scream called her vampire allies out of hiding. They raced between the trees, pale and deadly. They moved so fast, as if Helena was in slow motion. A knife flew past her head, but it missed its vampire target and landed in the ferns. Billie's knife. Bruno's shotgun went off from the ridge but Helena couldn't see where the bullet had struck. She was too busy fighting off Iphigenia. She finally let go with a right hook, sending the tiny blond girl sprawling in the mud.

"You were a lost girl," she spat.

"And now I'll be immortal," Iphigenia spat back. "No one will ever be able to hurt me again. Not Grady, not my brother, no one."

"Iphi."

Iphigenia folded her arms. "You pissed them off, saving all those girls."

"I thought you were saving them too."

"We both know I was holding you guys back, that I'd be next." She shrugged. "So I had to save myself first."

Helena stayed low in the concealing smoke, kicking out when a vampire woman streaked past her. She rolled through the long grass and jabbed down with her stake. Ash clung to the wild-flowers. She crawled away, hoping the fire and the smoke would conceal her.

No such luck.

"Got her!" Three more vampires sprinted in her direction. Bruno shot again but with the fire eating through the leaves and belching thick smoke, he was shooting blind. Helena threw a stake but she missed too. Heat from the encroaching flames hissed at her. Sweat stung as it dripped into her eyes.

She couldn't hide here any longer. Her escapes were being cut off by fire and vampires. She jumped to her feet and ran, flinging stakes behind her. Bruno's shotgun blasted again, and another, closer. She slammed right into a guy with black hair and nose plugs. "Who the hell are you?"

He looked military, in cargo pants with a walkie-talkie strapped to his shoulder. He even had night-vision goggles on his head. But he didn't look that much older than she was. "Roarke Black. Stand down."

"Bite me."

"We have it covered," he insisted. "This is no place for a civilian." He relented enough to incline his head. "We've been keeping an eye on your gang. Good work."

"You were the ones trailing Portia!"

"Yes. Now get out of here. Don't run until you're sure they're chasing us!"

He and three others, also armed to the teeth, launched themselves into the melee. Crossbow bolts whipped through the air. They burst through the clearing and spread out in all directions. The vampires followed, unable to resist. Iphigenia had already gone to ground. One of Billie's knives shot past Helena, nearly slicing the tip off her nose. She jerked back, swearing.

There were a lot of the commandos.

But there were a lot more vampires.

She let out an ear-piercing whistle. Three of the other vampires snapped around to look her way. She waved her fingers teasingly. "Hello, boys."

Then she ran.

She pushed her legs until they felt like they'd crumble, ran until her chest tightened and her breath was like hot sandpaper at the back of her throat. She could hear them behind her, closing in. She tried to stay out of the shelter of the ridge, hoping Billie and Bruno could see her pursuers. One of them fell back, knife in his eye. Helena leaped over a log and kept running. Bruno's gun took out a second, so Helena had just enough time to turn and stake her through her rib cage, as the vampire clutched her leg. There was only one vampire left and he halted. "Screw this," he muttered, taking off.

Helena leaned against a tree, panting. The light from the fire pierced the smoke, dancing cheerfully. It was surreal. She forced herself to stumble back toward the clearing.

"I told you these backwoods hicks would make a mess of it."

Helena froze, recognizing the musical sing-songy voice.

Elisabet.

"Lady Natasha won't be pleased," Lyle agreed. "But she can hardly blame us."

"We're her reapers, idiot. Of course she can blame us. We're meant to be reaping. Now even that blond twit of a girl is gone."

Helena didn't dare move, didn't dare even exhale. Somewhere, very faintly, fire-truck sirens sounded. The only reason the Domokoses hadn't seen her or caught her scent yet was because of the smoke and the general mayhem. Shadows shifted, veiled in curtains of gray fog and ash.

"There are two girls left in the cage," Lyle reminded his sister.

"Leftovers." Elisabet sighed. "She won't be impressed with that."

"Better than nothing. Let's bring them to her as a peace offering."

There were two girls left. Helena held onto that thought, punched on it like a hungry cat. Two girls who weren't dead. Yet.

She followed the reapers, hoping the sounds of the fire and the fighting would cover her footsteps. Portia and Cass intercepted her.

"I can't believe Iphi's a traitor," Portia said, disgusted. Blood ran down her leg from a deep gash. "That little weasel."

"Helena?" Cass frowned at her. "You're going the wrong way. That way's full of fire and fangs."

"There are more girls that way," she said, straining to see where Elisabet and Lyle had gone. If she waited much longer, she'd lose them altogether.

"We're coming too," Portia said, gritting her teeth against the pain of her leg.

Helena shook her head. "You're wounded. Cass, take her back to Bruno and Billie. I have to go."

"It's like you do it on purpose," Portia muttered. She leaned on Cass, shooting a glare at Helena. "If you die you're really going to piss me off."

◆

Finding two vampires in the dark smoky woods wasn't easy.

If it wasn't for a pair of sleepy doves startled into the sky at their passing, Helena might have wandered for hours. She followed the commotion, staying well back when she caught a glimpse of moonlight on pale skin and gold hair. The Domokoses moved quickly, eyes glowing even from a distance. They were scared.

Good.

They crossed a valley to a small cave nestled among rocks and roots. It was really more of a weed-choked hollow created by a long-ago avalanche. Inside, Helena caught a glint of iron.

The cage.

Lyle pulled out two bony girls in tattered clothing, wearing necklaces of dried blood. They were alive, though, and able to walk. She stayed far back enough that she couldn't hear what they were saying. One of the girls was trembling so violently she looked like an aspen leaf falling from a tree. Helena scurried after them, picking her way around twigs and branches, praying she wouldn't get caught.

She paused on a crest of rocks, staying hidden in a scraggly bush. Elisabet and Lyle were coming around the crest, toward another set of caves ringed with torchlight and guarded by fierce vampires. A woman came to the opening and looked out impatiently. Helena fell back, holding her breath. She had straight white-blond hair in a perfect waterfall down her back. She wore an old-fashioned dress and a ransom in diamonds. She glittered and preened, deadly as ice breaking on a winter lake.

Helena knew she had to head them off at the pass, had to get the girls free before they reached the caves and reinforcements. It had to be now.

She had no weapons left except a single stake. She scrounged on the ground for rocks, scrambling back around to the other side of the hill. She aimed the first rock at Elisabet's head. She nearly took out one of the girls instead. The second rock caught Elisabet's ear. The third was snatched out of midair.

It wasn't enough.

Helena crouched down, jamming her back against a boulder. She dug with her feet, kicking and shoving dirt, pebbles, rocks, anything she could reach. The rockslide wasn't enough to bury Lyle and Elisabet, but it was enough to distract them. The girls scurried like rats to safety. Helena kept kicking rocks. When there was nothing left but dry dirt she hurried to the ledge, helping them up.

"Run," she gasped, not caring that running was generally a bad idea around vampires. There were no choices left. They had to get out of there.

Fear outweighed starvation and fatigue and pushed them down the rocky hill and through the trees. Helena whistled around her thumb and forefinger, three short blasts, hoping Bruno was close enough to hear. She looked over her shoulder, saw fangs and furious eyes.

She cut right, away from the girls running on bleeding bare feet. The Domokoses followed her. She knew she couldn't keep up this pace much longer. And it didn't matter. Vampires were faster, always. She tried to stay within view of the glow of the fire, but she was getting turned around. She was lost and exhausted.

She stopped running when she was gagging on her own breath. She turned warily, not saying a word. Elisabet and Lyle smiled at each other.

Helena raised her chin. If she was going to die here, she'd die with curses on her lips and their blood under her fingernails.

She only just barely saw someone standing behind them.

Liam.

He paced them like a sleek vengeful panther, dark hair blending into the night. Only his eyes gave him away—and the flash of his fangs.

Shock made Helena laugh. Elisabet turned her head.

Liam attacked.

Helena leaped at Lyle, last stake in her hand.

He deflected, sending her crashing into a tree. She slumped, using the same tactic she'd used in the Thunderdome: look more wounded than you are. She waited, gasping. Lyle approached her slowly, even as his sister blocked Liam's stake.

"Liam Drake." Elisabet laughed. "Protecting this one, are you? Won't Lady Natasha be interested to hear that." She smirked. "She so enjoyed Deirdre."

Helena was the one who hissed at that.

Lyle grabbed her by her tank top and hauled her up. Her feet dangled. She let herself go boneless. His fangs lengthened. She staked him. Unfortunately, she wasn't strong enough at that angle to pierce his heart. The stake ricocheted off his ribs. He snarled. She tried to gouge his eyes out but he had her pinned. His fangs brushed her neck.

And then she was falling, ash drifting around her.

Liam's stake finished the job, piercing Lyle's heart, ripping her tank top, and landing in a maple tree. Elisabet whirled, too shocked to scream for a moment, before rage made her insane. She howled like a rabid animal, pupils ringed with red. She went for Liam's throat with her teeth, her nails, every part of her a weapon. Liam fought back but there was already a gash on his upper arm. His shirt was ripped. Elisabet slammed a stake into his chest, just under his collarbone, missing his heart. He pulled it out, blood dripping into the grass.

Elisabet continued to howl. She was strong, snapping Liam's shoulder out of its socket with a single blow. He snapped it back, blocking the tip of her boot as it jabbed at his kneecap. It wasn't enough.

Helena yanked at Liam's stake embedded in the tree, trying to work it free. Sweat made her hands slick.

Liam went down, blood on his face.

Elisabet grinned savagely. She retrieved her stake in the grass and pierced Liam's shirt, skin, flesh.

Helena finally got the stake out, tears of frustration stinging her eyes. The end was broken. She didn't care.

She leaped on Elisabet's back, jamming it toward her heart as hard as she could. Elisabet screeched, releasing her own stake as she flung Helena off. Helena managed to turn over, hands and knees bloodied from her landing, just in time to see Liam pluck the stake from his own chest and drive it into Elisabet.

She turned to ash, drifting like gray snow between the trees.

Helena sat up, wincing in pain. Three short whistles sounded from the woods near the fire. Bruno. Everyone was okay. Helena whistled back as Liam crawled to her, gathering her up in his arms. "You just took years off my life."

She smiled. "Good thing you're immortal."

◆

Liam took her to the lake. It was cold but Helena didn't care. She stripped down to her bra and underwear and jumped into the water, rinsing the blood and mud and ashes off. Liam followed, pale and perfect.

"Anyone ever tell you you're insane?" he asked.

She pushed her wet hair off her face. "Once or twice." Maybe it was shock, but she felt good. Happy. The girls were safe, she was safe. Liam was at her side. There were a million stars above them and the blood was out of her hair. She drew her fingertips around the gash the stake had left under his collarbone and over his shoulder. "Does it hurt?"

He shook his head, drawing her close. "I don't feel anything but you."

His mouth took hers or hers took his, she wasn't sure. She only knew that his claim on her seared through her and burned all the way to her toes. He tasted her, his tongue touching hers, his hands stroking her bare spine. She wrapped her legs around him. The cold water held them up as they finally gave into the longing and the need between them.

"We have to stop," he murmured against her lips.

She looked at him as if he'd proposed tea with Lady Natasha. "Why?"

He groaned. "Because I'm way too old for you."

She rolled her eyes. "You're undead and you're worried about a little thing like age?" Her tongue touched his lower lip.

He swallowed and pulled back, jaw clenched. "You're turning me into a dirty old man."

She tilted her head. "How old are you, really?"

"Eighty-one."

She blinked. "Oh." She ran her hands up his muscular arms. "You look good for a decrepit old perv."

He laughed despite himself. "I've never known anyone like you." He kissed her again, quickly, too quickly. "I'll wait for you."

"Where am I going?"

"Not you. Me. I'm leaving Violet Hill."

"Forever?" The water was suddenly cold, freezing her to the bone. She swam to shore. "Then why bother with all this? You should have let Lady Natasha kill you, since you're letting her win anyway." She pulled her clothes on angrily, teeth chattering.

Liam was suddenly behind her, arms around her waist. "I'm not leaving you," he murmured in her ear. "Never. But you're sixteen. I'll come back for you in two years. After I've had some time to draw Lady Natasha away from this town. She doesn't know to fear you yet, not with Elisabet and Lyle gone."

"Are two years really going to make that big of a difference? You'll be eighty-three instead of eighty-one. Big deal."

"But you'll be legal. And you'll have a chance to find a sense of yourself, a sense of who you could be. You might not want this life."

"I want you," she said softly. Admitting it took as much courage as facing down a vampire queen and all of her minions. "And I'm going to take those two years to learn how to really kick your sorry undead ass."

He turned her around, kissing her tenderly. "Promise?"

She nodded solemnly. "I promise."

"Good." He kissed her again and it flared so hot and so desperate it was physically painful to pull away. "I have to go," he said. "But I'll find you."

She dug her fingers into his hair and pulled his mouth back to hers. "If you don't find me, Liam Drake," she vowed, "I'll find you."

ALYXANDRA HARVEY is the author of the Drake Chronicles—*Hearts at Stake, Blood Feud, Out for Blood* (also available in one bind-up edition, *Ruling Passion*), and *Bleeding Hearts*—as well as two stand-alone novels, *Haunting Violet* and *Stolen Away*. Alyx likes medieval dresses and tattoos and has been accused of being born in the wrong century—except that she really likes running water, women's rights, and ice cream. She lives in an old Victorian farmhouse in Ontario, Canada, with her husband, dogs, and a few resident ghosts.

www.alyxandraharvey.com
www.thedrakechronicles.com
www.facebook.com/thedrakechronicles

Read the Drake Chronicles

from the beginning . . .

Ruling Passion—includes *Hearts at Stake*,
Blood Feud, and *Out for Blood*

And the passion continues
with Blood Moon, coming soon

Don't miss
Alyxandra Harvey's darkly romantic,
spine-chilling ghost story

Walker & Company
www.bloomsburyteens.com

Love the Drakes?

Prepare to have your heart stolen, as Alyxandra Harvey's enchanting new novel transports you to Faery, where nothing is as it seems . . .

Walker & Company
www.bloomsburyteens.com